# Praise for Relentless Aaron

"Fascinating. He's made the best out of a stretch of unpleasant time and adversity. . . . He was able to turn what was a lemon into lemonade. That's a commendable effort."
—Wayne Gilman, WBLS news director

"It's very real. He's an excellent writer, with good stories and good suspense."
—"Week in Review," KISS FM

"With his initial release, *Push*, Relentless redefines the art of story-telling. Weaving a riveting tale of big money, incredible sex, and gut-wrenching violence, while seamlessly capturing the truth and hard-core reality of Harlem's desperation and struggle, Relentless isn't just writing books, he's landscaping terrain that will be experienced by generations to come."
—Troy Johnson, founder of the African American Literature Book Club

# Extra Marital Affairs

## Relentless Aaron™

ST. MARTIN'S GRIFFIN ❦ NEW YORK

This is a work of fiction. All of the characters, organizations, and events portrayed in this novel are either products of the author's imagination or are used fictitiously.

www.stmartins.com

Library of Congress Cataloging-in-Publication Data

Relentless Aaron.
    Extra marital affairs / Relentless Aaron.—1st ed.
     p.  cm.
    ISBN-13: 978-0-312-35935-5 (pbk.)
    ISBN-10: 0-312-35935-7 (pbk.)
    1. African Americans—Fiction.   I. Title.

PS3618.E57277E98   2006
813'.6—dc22      2006044511

First Edition: September 2006

P1

To all the brothers and sisters on lockdown: This book, those that precede it, and those to follow are solid evidence that once you set your mind to something, you can and will achieve it; but you must first decide (for good) in your mind, *This is it! This is what I will do!* And from that point on, never turn back. No matter where you are, make life rich and rewarding.

To Makeda at Jazzmyne Public Relations: I picture you in a hammock, about to blast off (again) as you read this! Be clear . . . I'm a fan of yours, too! Thank you so much for helping me spin this golden thread. To Gloria Dulan Wilson: I'm so glad I found you again! To Lorna and the women at ARC Bookclub, as well as other clubs throughout the nation who chose to hear my voice, a million thanks! To Naiim, Mr. Perkins, Mr. Reeves, Rick, Ruth, Tiffany, Courtney Carreras, you rock! To Mike Woods and the whole *Good Day New York* TV crew, to the folks at ABC News, and especially you, Cory, at *The New York Times, thank you* all for helping me over some difficult bumps in the road! To the many bookstores around the world who carry Relentless Content: Thank you for affording me space on your shelves. I intend to cause a major increase to your bottom line as the bestselling author of this era. And that's no lie! Big big big bold shameless thank-you to: Joanie Smith, Lisa Jackson (a.k.a. Bonnie). You are the greatest! You, too, Shetalia. Thanks for helping me hold it down! Can't forget the people who most helped me in the streets: Alexis, Alisha, Venetria, Danica, Shereen, Keisha, Sabrina, Jen, The Don, Michelle (from the buses), T, AJ, Ashley, Dejone', and to all those supporters from the salons to the streets; from the housing authority to the transit authority; and especially to all my folks at the Beacon Theatre. Last, but certainly not least: infinite love to my family, Paulette, DeWitt, and Fortune. You all keep my energy on *high*! Thank you all. Now . . . let's rock this town!

# acknowledgments

To my friends and mentors: By now you're all tired of seeing your names in print, so I'll just say you know who you are. To Julie and family, to Emory and Tekia Jones: Thank you all for your faith in me. To Tiny Wood (my close friend and confidant who likes to hear me say "This is *bananas!*"), thank you for your support and focus. To Michael Shapiro, thanks for everything. Larry, Kevon, and Gail at Culture Plus, keep the faith: Life is about a cycle of good and bad; just be ready for both at all times. Thanks to Karen and Eric at A&B Books; to Nati at African World Books; to Carol and Brenda (C&B Books), Curt Southerland, Darryl Stith, Adianna, Sadia, DTG, Joanie, Kevin, Lance, Lou, Mechel, G. H. Soho . . . and especially you, Renee McRea. Thank you for adopting me! To trust: Much respect to you for helping me put this whole puzzle into proper perspective. To Tru (Conn), your phone calls helped get me hype in the early stages of this. Thanks to Earl Cox, Pete Oakley, and Troy Johnson. Thanks also to you who understand my struggle more than most others. Peace.

# one

For Mason and Adena Fickle, enough was never enough. More and more, they went on looking for that next big thrill. The problem for them—one they never had too much trouble solving—was not necessarily "who" or "what" would contribute to their thrill seeking so much as it was "how" they'd keep their thrills fresh and challenging. And they didn't experience simple thrills like clubbing with other swingers, swimming nude in a forbidden lake, or having sex in broad daylight out on the shoulder of I-80. These things the Fickles now considered boring.

The Fickles' quest now was to be creative. And yet, it was one thing to be creative; it was another to be freaks, and it was quite another to be *creative* freaks.

The most exciting ingredient that the Fickles realized during their extramarital affairs was how they were able to keep it all secret in a township where everyone knew everything about everybody. Sure, the couple had friends who were neighbors, like Barbara and Bill Clemons down the block. And they even considered the Clemonses to be their best friends. But some things weren't shared with even your best friends. After all, who would think of Mason as any more than a bespectacled accountant who worked for a Fortune 2000 company? A big deal in East Stroudsburg, Pennsylvania.

And who would think of Adena as any more than a housekeeper, a maid really, who cleaned guest rooms at the local Days Inn? Both of their occupations were less than exciting, and saw these two scurrying home at the end of a hard workday to indulge in some much-needed sleep, a deep sleep wherein they could go on dreaming about "someday" and that lucky lottery ticket.

But it was all smoke and mirrors. In fact, the Fickles were a lively couple, fulfilling those fantasies that *were* possible, like the night they lured an absolute stranger home—a bartender from the neighboring township. Brenda was her name; and, among other things, they all took turns sucking each other's toes.

Or, there was that other absolutely possible fantasy, where the Fickles snuck onto the local high school grounds and did it on the fifty-yard line of the football field at midnight. Not to mention that these two even climbed up on their own roof time and again—at least a half-dozen times so far—to claim ownership of each other. Sometimes Mason was the "master," other times Adena was in charge. For certain, these two were just the opposite of everything you'd envision, putting sex right up there next to oxygen on that must-have shelf in their minds.

And now it was springtime, when pollen mixed with hope in that fresh breeze. It was a time and a climate for new beginnings, young love, and colorful landscapes. It was a time when animal species appeared (as if from thin air) on the lawns, in the sky, and in the water. It was also a cue, frankly, for Mason to get out there and cut the grass like a good husband should.

"Hurry up, Mase. I don't want dinner to get cold!" Adena called out to her laborer/lover, trying to be heard over the manual lawn mower. But maybe she didn't notice the earbuds he had in place, or that he was pumping his favorite old-school slow jam, and singing like he had no sense—like it was himself, and not Lenny Williams, who was supposed to be the lead on the song. Mason was even a slight bit off-key. But he couldn't have cared less. *"I love you! I neeeeeeded you!*

The song might've been Mason's fuel as he pushed that machine so easily back and forth along their front lawn, trying to get the place in shipshape condition before the block-watch people made another complaint to the BMCB (Blue Mountain Community Board). Another issue altogether, that was.

"It's bad enough they get a budget to operate their flimflam group of rednecks," Mason later blurted out before chewing what he had forked into his mouth.

"Honey, take your time and enjoy your food. Don't just wolf it down like that. You worked hard out there, the least you could do is relax while you eat."

"I wouldn't be wolfin' shit down if I didn't have to keep grass two inches high. I mean, who came up with that absurd rule? *Grass should be less than two inches high.* What if I don't *want* my grass below two inches! It's *my* goddamned grass!"

Adena lowered her head and concentrated on her next bite rather than look her husband in the eyes. Not just that she would agree with him, but that he looked so sexy when he was mad. It would bring on her untimely smile.

"And then they got the nerve to get uniforms. *Uniforms!* Navy shirts with bright white letters advertising BMCB like they the police or sumpthin'. Shit—"

"Baby . . ." Adena tried to chill the flames.

"Fuck."

*"Baby,"* Adena almost begged.

"This township ain't but yae big—ain't hardly no crime goin' on here, 'cuz you *know* they'd have a lynchin', as easy as they get away with shit around here. Not just up here on Blue Mountain, but down on Main Street, too." Adena squeezed her eyes closed and hoped he wouldn't. "Look at how they treated you for a damned parking ticket."

He *did* go there. *Jesus. Here we go again.*

"That fat-fuck sheriff. I shoulda—"

"Baby, please."

"And her three fat deputies all stuffed in their cruiser—can't even afford to fix the other one they usually stroll around town in." Mason was so right. Calling a spade a spade, even in his heated tirade. One sheriff and her henchmen keeping total peace in and around East Stroudsburg, where everybody was already dependent on one another for resources, even if it was the need for somewhere or something to bitch about. The town had it all, plus a shitload of forestry.

Only because of terrorism, and those violent events that show up on the tube so frequently, had East Stroudsburg gone nuts with the preventive measures. They voted for additional manpower, and a budget for the trailer-size mobile unit that sat in the center of town.

"They don't even have anybody to sit in that whale. It's a ridiculous expenditure, with video surveillance, satellite dishes, and strobe lights. . . ."

The whale was indeed overdone for this small community, which had virtually no crime (not physical, anyway) and nobody to operate the vehicle—nobody but one sheriff and a few tagalongs. However, the whale did have another purpose, since it recently got hit with eggs and tomatoes, probably from angry farmers (or their sons) who protested against the new mobile precinct. Somebody even keyed the whale, scratching THE WASTE onto its side.

"Why didn't BMCB catch *that* act?"

Adena had to admit that Mason even got *her* all worked up when he went into specifics like this. And now, she even felt like commenting as his *ride or die* partner for life.

"Maybe they even had something to do with it?" Adena proposed. "You know how BMCB hates BWP. And you know some of them in BWP got farmers for cousins, friends, and whatnot."

"You're right. Especially since SPD thinks me and . . ." Adena appreciated Mason, including (or allowing) her into his bashing moment. She could see him easily gravitating toward the street slang you wouldn't usually see or hear from Mason, the Fortune 2000 accountant.

"We should express our gratitude to BMCB on behalf of all the residents who don't give a fuck. We should get them some handcuffs," Adena suggested.

"Oh, hell no." Mason barked. "We got more use for handcuffs than they do."

"Since when?" Adena asked, amused at how the tone of this latest "town hall meeting" had taken a turn for the better.

Mason turned wide-eyed and serious. He put the chicken bone down and wiped his hands.

"What exactly is *that* supposed to mean, buttercup?" Mason flashed one of those phony smiles, the one where his lips were pursed and stretched back practically to his ears.

"Maybe it means you're *slippin'*," Adena said.

Mouth open, Mason stared at her in shock. And it seemed to be just the reply she expected. Anything to get off the BMCB subject.

"Wait a minute. Am I not satisfying you by not pulling out the toys? Or is this just something we both overlooked?"

"Well, you're the one who's always asking, 'Whose is it?' So . . . I leave it to you to call the shots."

Adena let a smile slip out and Mason just broke out laughing. It marked the end of his rant and the beginning of a long night. Before the two finished dinner Mason suggested, "How about we have some fun tonight?"

"You call the shots," Adena said again with the sparkle in her eyes. Little did the Fickles know, this was just one more step toward an experience that would change their lives.

# two

Adena had been very lucky to find a man like Mason, a hardworking, dedicated, faithful man who, like her, had left the big city for some peace, some quiet, and some comfort. They had stumbled upon each other at the local K mart in East Stroudsburg, where he had come for some fresh drawers and she for some emergency sanitary napkins. To say the least, Adena was in a hurry, and more or less cut Mason off en route to the cashier.

The store wasn't busy at all, so a cashier nearby announced, "I'm open over here."

Mason excused the rude woman, at least in his mind, and he sidestepped to register 4.

"How are you today?" asked the cashier in an extra cheerful tone.

"Hmmm," Mason replied, up in the air between a sour and a sweet response. "I guess I'll be all right," he finally answered, cutting an eye over toward register 3. He had to admit the woman was cute, despite her actions. *Maybe there's a reason for her rush,* he told himself. And that was the end of it. So blind toward drama was he that very little could flip his switch nowadays. Those days were gone now, part of his *out with the old (underwear), in with the new.* And since it had only been a day since he'd set foot in Pennsylvania, dramas and arguments were not his focus; to make a living and to live comfortably was. So much of that stuff was the past, now; his brother, Bobby, and the mob he ran with were all in jail now—long sentences—for nearly collapsing the financial well-being of Philadelphia. It was a place that middle-class blacks were calling home more and more, especially with all those ads that ran in the big-city newspapers in New York; all of them luring new residents into the rural way of life, promising them "peace and tranquility for no money down." Mason's mother, Mrs. Zanobia Fickle, was heartbroken about the arrest and conviction of Bobby. But it was the sentencing of her son and the judge's words—*natural life behind bars*—that sent Momma Fickle into massive heart failure. She was an intensive care patient for just three days before she finally passed on.

So, with no more family for love and laughter, and with a community of onlookers more or less ready to lay the entire Fickle tragedy on Mason's shoulders, he was left no other choice. He drove eastward until the atmosphere was rural enough to keep out that city mentality, but resourceful enough that he could hold a job and have access within the same twenty-four-hour day. And when he saw that the K mart, the Wal-Mart, and the Arby's brand names had invested here, it was evidence enough that he could be a worthwhile asset, a contribution to the community he lived in. After all, wasn't that life? To give and take? To work hard and to reap the rewards of your labors? So Mason made Blue Mountain, a community just outside of Marshalls Creek, his new home. Mason's accounting knowledge and background would be respected anywhere, he was certain, since he had invested eight years in the profession. He had references, a four-year college education, and that element of common sense to lean on.

And, just as he expected, Mason easily landed a job in nearby Allentown. His first position was at PNC Bank as a teller. However, he was quickly promoted to a top teller position, delegating responsibility and keeping watch over twelve other tellers. This, he did for almost twenty-four months, until the office job came along—account executive for East Stroudsburg Mutual, the Fortune 2000 company that maintained insurance for some forty thousand people throughout the country. It was at about this time (more than two years since that rude interlude at K mart) that Mason met Adena formally, the two of them sitting side by side at Brownie's, a restaurant in the heart of downtown East Stroudsburg, Pennsylvania.

Adena and Mason exchanged glances, but it was her glance that said, *I know you from somewhere*. Mason snickered to himself, as if he could read her mind, but even more when he recalled the exact play-by-play action and how this woman had nearly run him over once upon a time. Feeling successful and confident these days, Mason didn't mind speaking up first.

"It was at the K mart," he said.

"Excuse me?"

"We met before—or . . . we ran *into* each other, I should say."

"Oh?" Her response pushed him to take it a step further.

"Mmm-hmm. And, you almost ran me over. But I think you were in a rush."

"Oh . . . I . . . I'm sorry."

"Oh please. Don't mention it. I didn't know my ass from my toe, anyway. Especially in those days. My name is Mason."

"Adena," she said as they shook hands.

"Interesting name."

"Yeah. The type of name that'll get a girl a position at McDonald's or a supermarket, but not in any *real* paying job."

Mason hadn't evaluated things enough before now, but he quickly realized the woman was burying herself in a thick milk shake and a strawberry shortcake.

"I'm . . . I'm sorry to hear that. I don't see why you'd have a problem. Not if your looks mattered, anyway. What do you do best? What's your profession?"

"Hmmm, I could easily tell you what I do best. But since you asked, I don't have any particular profession. Never did college.

Spent my young life with a no-good asshole who got me pregnant and left town."

"Oh, you have a child. Okay, so you're a mother. That's a kind of pro—"

"No, I'm not a mother. I *lost* the baby, I got my tubes tied, and now I'm a mother*fucker.*"

Mason let her carry on, hearing beneath the noise, *I have low self-esteem. I expect little of myself. Blah, blah, blah. Blah. Blah.*

Once again, Mason tried to explain. "I'm sorry. I know life ain't easy. But I learned long ago that you have to get on your grind early in life to be prepared for anything."

"Oh, don't get it twisted, mista'. I'm on my grind. I know how to get paper. Plus, I got my own place, my little bank account, and I drive a Lexus. I've had men from here to Albuquerque bendin' over backwards for a piece of me, even if I *don't* spread my legs."

Mason swung around to see if anyone was in on their conversation, how raw it had gotten in so little time.

"I feel ya," was all he could say in response. By the time his chicken Caesar salad had half disappeared, Adena asked, "So what's a good-lookin' man like you doin' sittin' at a lunch counter in, of all places, East Stroudsburg?"

"Thanks for the compliment. You're not a bad catch yourself. Ahh . . . I was meeting with a client; the bank across the street. This just happened to be the nearest restaurant that's not Mexican or Irish or kosher."

" 'Or kosher' . . . you're funny."

Mason laughed along with Adena, suddenly appreciating how fast she caught on to things. And it was at that moment that he looked closer—the hair swept back into a neat ponytail that hooked to the side, a fragrance he couldn't be sure of, her full lips and a smile that emerged every so often. Her body could use a few cross-country runs, but it wasn't far from those lanky cheerleaders that Mason once gawked at during a Sixers game. Plus, the eyes told a story of a world outside his own. Sure, there was poor self-esteem, but there was also a desire for a better way of life. And he had once wanted the same thing.

"So, where do you work now?"

"At the Days Inn. It's been a year now. And, I know I was trippin' earlier, with the whole bit about my name . . . maybe I just needed to eat. I get edgy when I don't get my grub on."

"Oh, you *definitely* did that," Mason said, indicating the missing shake and empty plate.

Again, Adena laughed, a hearty one this time. "And you? Where do you work, Mr. Brooks Brothers?" She reached over and plucked the collar of Mason's blazer.

"Mister . . ." She leaned closer to sniff a few times before she guessed at his cologne. "Oh . . . nice choice with the Calvin Klein."

Mason's jerked his head back some, surprised at how sharp this woman was.

"And don't think I haven't also been checkin' your wheels outside. Nice truck."

Mason laughed aloud. "For someone with low self-esteem, you sure do analyze like a conditioned player."

"Are *you* a player?" she asked

"Not at all. I just work damned hard."

"Well then, I'm just like you. My only thing is, I been around the block enough to know a fraud when I see one." Adena paused, picked up her check, and left a tip. Mason nearly choked on the silence.

"A *what?*"

Adena strutted to the cashier, paid exact change, and left through the front of the restaurant. But Mason was fast in pursuit.

"Now wait a goddamned minute!" Mason nearly hit the glass door against the wall as fast as he flew out after her. Plus, he had to navigate past a couple of businessmen strolling the sidewalk, both of them teetering between fearing for their lives and jumping in to help the woman he was after. "How'd you come to that conclusion?"

Adena had stopped close to the curb to casually light up a cigarette. Meanwhile, her actions cast a notion that there was not a care in the world, least of all her assailant. The businessmen stayed their ground. "Slow down, playboy. Nobody said you were a fake."

"But you just said—"

"I just said that I know a fraud when I see one. But, Mr. Fickle, I was basically trying to get your attention. A lot of times when you call a spade a spade, a person is gonna shut up and take a punch, 'cuz they know the truth." Adena exhaled a stream of smoke before she went on. "But you, Mr. Fickle . . . you're no phony. And that tells me, a girl who's interested"—she stroked Mason's arm with her forefinger—"that you are very real."

Wait a minute. How you know my last name? I didn't tell you my last name in there. Who sent you, Adena? Who's trying to set me up?" Mason held Adena's arms as though he'd captured a crook. "When I left Philly I told them to leave me alone! I'm out! Finished! Through!"

"Ouch!" Adena peeled Mason's hands from her arms "You're hurting me, Mason!"

"Well, who sent you? Tell me!"

"You wanna know? You *really* wanna know?"

Hands on his hips, Mason said, "Yeah."

Having already dropped her cigarette when he had shaken her, Adena regained her cool. She cast her gaze on the cigarette, mashed it with the tip of her shoe, and then she stepped closer to Mason.

"Relax. I'm gonna tell you," she said. Her body was brushing his, until her lips were near his ear. "The reason I know your last name is because of your license plate, sir. And besides, you even have a baggage claim check still hanging on your briefcase. So I got roughed up because I'm sharp."

Mason looked over at his truck and then he realized he'd left his briefcase inside. "Oh shit," he blurted, and he started back into Brownie's to retrieve it. "Hold on."

When Mason returned to the sidewalk, complete with his ticketed briefcase, Adena was gone. Mason could only search the eyes of those onlookers—the waitress in the window, the businessmen nearby. Calculating, Mason guessed that Adena had gone for her car.

*Don't get it twisted . . . on my grind . . . bank account . . . a Lexus!* The clues she'd dropped were still fresh on the chalkboard of his mind. And like an epileptic with a fit, Mason searched the parking spaces to and fro. He did not want Adena to get away. She was fine. She was sharp. She was witty as hell. But more important, she deserved an apology.

He wanted to shout her name, but this wasn't life or death, it was simply a loose end. And besides, now that he'd faced that first alluring female in a long, long time, it made him want her in every way imaginable. She was something and somebody that he had to have.

Finally spotting an all-white Lexus, Mason picked his steps up a couple of notches so as not to let her get away. But there was no need to fret. Adena was already lowering her window. He let out an appreciative sigh.

"Hey, I . . . Why'd you run off?"

Adena made a face.

"Yeah, right. Stupid question. I'm surprised you didn't smack me. Listen . . . I'm really, really, really sorry for what happened back there."

"*Really* sorry?" Adena asked, lighting up her second cigarette.

"No, *really, really* sorry. You have no idea the things going through my mind. The past is—"

"No, you're right. I don't have any idea. And I don't think I *wanna* have any idea."

"How can we forget this happened? Can I make it up to you? Dinner maybe?"

"Right. So you can talk me into a romp in the sack, a one-night fling? Is that what you think I am?"

"No, please, we could do breakfast—"

Adena's eyes widened in response.

"I mean lunch . . . happy hour. *Whatever.* Just let me spend some time with you . . . treating you like a lady, and not—"

"How you treated me back there?"

"Er . . . right. I'm so sorry. Now, can I make it up to you?"

# three

And so began their physical relationship. Even back then, Mason had her *twisted*. Adena never imagined that her body could stretch like this—on her back, with her knees folded all the way to her ears, and her ankles locked behind her head. This might be damned near impossible to do by herself, or even painful for her muscles to bear, if it weren't for Mason down there, licking her, sucking her, and eating her as though it were his last meal. And even today, Adena could remember those moments when she stuttered, and others when she thought she'd black out; but it felt so good! It was all so *amazing*. And, not to play down the action here, but Mason was burying his face, his tongue and nose all up in her chocolate pudding as if it were the end of the world. And yet, this was only the *beginning*!

From one opening to the next, he licked and kissed and licked and probed, making Adena think this was the last time she'd ever see him. And, as if that might indeed be the case, Adena gripped his head with two hands, pulling him more intensely, wanting him deeper inside of her. If he was gonna love and leave, she was gonna get hers!

*Doesn't he know my tubes are tied? Doesn't he know that he can bang me sixteen ways till next May and I won't get pregnant?*

The thought occurred to Adena to remind Mason that it was okay to take it all the way with that average, customary, missionary sex. But she lost that thought the second another spasm pushed through her body, and all she cared about then was getting her shit off and filling his mouth with as much of her as physically possible. She grabbed his head again, then she got daring and grabbed his ears. Something from somewhere forbidden and untapped flowed up through her.

"*G-G-G-God!*" She hyperventilated, fighting, gasping for air. Crying out to gods and demons and singing angels that she'd never seen before.

"Take me! Take me, Mason!"

Adena grabbed him with more determination and no mercy. If Mason had plans of making this their first and last encounter, then she'd make sure he ate her so good that he'd be flossing tiny pubic hairs from his teeth come morning time. It's what he deserved for the tongue lashing he gave her that afternoon on the sidewalk. And now that she thought of it . . .

"Eat it, baby. Eat it! *Eat* that pussy!"

She was tugging at his ears again, then one ear and his head, then both hands behind his head.

Adena was beginning to feel like a master. She was thinking that he *wanted* her to feel that way. And if that was the case, so be it. A master she'd be. She encouraged Mason to stop, and she swung her body around so that she was sitting over the edge of the bed.

"Come 'ere, Daddy. Kneel before Adena."

And she was dammed if that didn't work! He was obeying like her puppy! Like her servant!

*God, this is great!* "Now eat your chow!" she said, and she lay back on the bed, watching the candle shadows on the ceiling. "Oh, yes, Daddy . . . eat! Eat! Eat some more!"

Adena even got the nerve to hook one of her ankles around the back of Mason's neck, pulling him ever closer. This was too good to be true, for her to be calling the shots like this, when anytime in the past, things had been just the opposite. *She'd* be the one on her knees. *She'd* be the one giving pleasure.

*I could lay here forever!* But Adena wasn't stupid. Sex and lust and love were also give and take, just as Mason preached about life and contribution. She knew well that a relationship would never last if there was only one-way satisfaction. And this wasn't gonna be one of those "hit it and quit it" rendezvous, not if she had anything to do with it. So, she eased Mason's head from between her legs.

*Damn, you made me feel special!* she thought, but didn't plan on saying this to him. She didn't want to show her hand and make this man feel comfortable enough to become a slacker later or to take advantage of her somehow. Lord knew she had had those types before.

"Now, let me show *you* a few tricks, Daddy."

Adena got up from her bed and gripped her partner's stiff tool, guiding him into her living room. A candle was still lit in there as well, and it lent enough of a glow to see Mason's face glisten. It was a sight to see, and it somehow made her feel proud and satisfied. She immediately wanted to return the favor with some good old-fashioned reciprocity. Without further ado, Adena climbed up on her couch and positioned herself so that she was kneeling doggie style. She looked back at Mason and also back at her ass, with one hand playing and stroking that still-wet launch pad of hers. The intention was to give a him a show, while prolonging their first (and maybe last) night in each other's company.

She stood up and danced so that her cheeks jiggled for him. She bent over to touch her toes, showing Mason how flexible she was. She made her body wind and stretch and bounce while he sat and writhed, his dick standing erect. She posed. She teased. All of this from a woman who at first didn't want to show her entire hand, but who now wanted to show it *all*!

Adena smacked her ass cheeks like a final hurrah, and she got down on the carpet, facing him.

"Come feed me, Daddy." And she readied herself, with her hoop earrings dangling with her every move.


**M**ason was beside himself with desire. He had no intention of moving this fast on a first encounter, but she was making it so damned *easy*! And to think he had gone without a woman's flesh for over two years! The grind, the relocation from Philly, and the issues left behind all took their toll on his social life. He had become a hermit. His sexual activity had been reduced to his five fingers and a *Blacktail* magazine on Saturday nights, On occasion he'd skip a Saturday to catch up on sleep. But all in all, he tried not to miss one date.

And now, here he was with a perfect stranger—perfect because she looked and felt like everything he needed. Just to think he'd practically cursed this woman out earlier that day. Then there was dinner, the race up I-80, and now this.

Adena had gone from putting on a mini stage show for Mason's eyes only, to now sucking the living daylights out of him while on her knees. What more could he want in life?

*Again with the slurpie noises . . . god damn her!*

Adena looked up at Mason as she went on her mission of fulfillment. Her face began to perspire, and at times she overindulged with the sound effects. But for Mason, this was heaven on earth. He'd just about let himself up once, twice, three times as she pulled at his foreskin and skated her tongue up and down his swollen dick.

"Aw—shit!" Mason cried when Adena's hands grabbed his ass cheeks so that his dick reached the back of her throat. Sure, she gagged as if her life hung in the balance. But a few moments later she testified with her mouth full, "I love sucking dick." Mason could only twitch. There was not even a brief intermission. The sucking just continued like a marathon, up until Adena stopped to direct things some more.

"Fuck me. *Please*, fuck me." But this wasn't as much a plea as it was a demand, since she was already on hands and knees, back up on the couch.

Mason put aside his conscience and went for it. He wanted romance with Adena. God knows he needed that in his life. But the lust, the temptations, and her mouth called out for more.

*This is incredible!* his mind shouted, praising the nicotine-stained ceiling of her apartment. It had been an hour. From 11:30 to 12:45, in fact. And Mason had had all of the stopping and starting he could stand. Every time he felt himself ready to come, he withdrew. And every time she tempted him to explore her further, he went at it again. The protein in the calamari was working like magic!

But all good things—even this!—had to come to an end. He had no idea how, but this had to lead to a mutual climax. Plus, the sounds, the cries . . . the dirty mouth on this woman were driving him wild!

"Aw fuck! Uh-uh-uh-uh-uh . . . dick me, Daddy, dick me, Daddy! Don't stop."

Mason recalled her saying something about having her tubes tied, but everything they'd said earlier (*anything* they'd said!) was left with their clothes on the bedroom floor. All that mattered now was her fucking, then her sucking, then him fucking, then her sucking. Again and again they switched until Mason finally cried aloud, louder than Adena had all night. He grunted like a mule (mixed with a wild bear) before that great surge pushed through his body. He was on top of Adena at that moment, in her ass. But, as if she calculated his climax, she pulled herself from under him and whipped her head around, tongue out and ready, so she could catch his potentials in her mouth.

Meanwhile, Adena looked up at Mason with those innocent puppy-dog eyes, and it made him explode with no remorse.

What resulted was more of a mess than a goal achieved, that "mutual climax" he wanted. His creamy ejaculate wound up in her hair, on her forehead, and it partially coated her chin and that pearl piercing her lower lip. Whatever snuck into her mouth was history. And now *he* was the proud one, even if his body and mind could never be ready for what he was about to get himself into.

# four

The aftermath of their wild sex-capade felt awkward for both Mason and Adena. They'd be lying if they were to lie together and hold on to each other like lovers.

"Wanna drink?" Adena asked. It was a weak thing to ask, but it served to fill that dead space that kept them both wondering what in the world had just happened; or worse, what was next?

"Sure. Whatcha got?"

"Nothin' like you tasted," she answered, trying to keep the flicker on their flame.

Mason fed into it and responded, "You have something to cool us *both* down after than long, nasty session? A beer maybe? And I don't even drink beer."

The two laughed.

"No beer, but I can throw together a mixed drink."

"Sounds good. Not too strong, though. I wouldn't want you to take advantage of me."

Again with the laughter. The just-right antidote for this nervous back-and-forth interaction between them.

When the two finally did clean up and relax with their drinks, it was Adena who advocated the raw talk.

"Crazy, huh?"

"*Very.*"

"You do anything like that before?" Adena asked.

"Which part? So much, so soon . . . I can't lie and say I've never had a crazy first date before. It was a while ago. . . ."

"Okay."

"And . . . well . . . I swore it would never happen again. Except *you* came along."

"Of course I did," she said. *And more than once, lover man.* "Then, why me? Enlighten me. What's so special about a silly old maid from Days Inn?"

"You really gotta stop that, baby. For one, you're not silly or old. And two . . . a job is a job. People make the world go 'round, whatever it is they do."

"True."

"So cut out the bottom talk and keep it up."

"Oh . . . okay." Adena sighed.

"Now, as for *why you?* Woman, you *excite* me. Point-blank. You had me from the lunch counter at Brownie's."

"What? Get out."

"No. I'm serious, It was something about you that I wanted to have in my life. Something like a missing piece to a puzzle."

"Okay, Mr. Yukon XL. Now you're scaring me. Too deep for me."

"Well then . . . how 'bout you. Why me? And what made you open your floodgates to a man you just met? Have you ever done this before? Or maybe I should've asked that question a lot earlier." Mason, with the late rationale.

"Cool it, playa. Don't go talkin' to me like a whore, now. You ain't speak that way when you put your dick in my mouth, so don't do it now. And, *no* . . . I've never gone all this way, or this far as I have, with a man on the first date. And we didn't really have a date, which makes it *really* crazy."

"Yeah, it does," Mason said. "But I wanna believe that this is something else . . . like we're supposed to be this way with each other, freaky as we wanna be. Around you I feel free, where I can let loose my every inhibition."

"I kinda feel that way, too," Adena said.

"And," Mason continued, "there was a point tonight—or last night—when I would've given you my whole world if you'd asked for it. And that's supercrazy, because I went through hell to get all I have."

"Well, I'm worth all that, and then some," Adena argued. "And just as free as you felt, so did I. So now what? Where do we go from here, since you are the brains between the two of us?"

Mason wagged his head, realizing that she had just thrown the ball in his court.

"Okay." He suddenly snapped. "The first thing I suggest is we slow the hell down. For real. The last two hours was like the wildest drug, and I need to come down easy from that shit."

With a smile, Adena agreed.

"Maybe this drink'll do the trick. What is this anyway?"

"Hypnotic and pineapple. Smooth, right?"

"Real smooth. Smooth, like a massage on the inside of my body."

"Hey! That's something I can do. Lemme massage you—show you one of my *other* talents," she offered with a crooked smile.

T he next day, Adena went nuts. It was two o'clock in the afternoon and she couldn't get in touch with Mason. She was afraid this would happen, that she'd given all of her body and its wealth of pleasure to a ghost.

No calls, no knock on the door, and no flowers?

*Well,* she figured, *I might be pushin' it with the flowers. Since when in the world did any black man get that romantic after the freak fest like we had? Shit.* Not in *her* world, anyway.

There was a number that Mason left with her, and she called it enough to memorize his voicemail recording; enough to lose sight of how many messages she'd left and how much more desperate they were becoming.

The first message was sweet: "Last night was so incredible, lover. I wanna just take it there over and over again, for as long as you say. *Forever* would be fine with me."

The tenth message was warming up to grief.

"I hope everything is okay with us. Remember *us*, Mason Fickle? Hello? Is this the number you give to your weekend jump-offs? Am I interrupting something?"

Eventually, Adena turned downright hostile: "You muthafuckas are all the same! You talk that shit, you wild-out in the bed, and use us like we're a piece of meat, then you vanish like we don't have feelings. Well, mista know-it-all, for *your* information, the fuck wasn't all that *anyway*. And if I kept a journal, I'd put you down as *the bitch who ate my asshole for a half hour*, ya fuckin' pig! And, oh—if I see your ass in the K mart, next time I'll probly *spit* on you." Adena hung up, but still wasn't satisfied. She felt used, and she wanted Mason to tell her face-to-face that he wasn't interested; that last night was a lie, and that her sex wasn't a fireworks show.

From one extreme to another, Adena went about her mission. It was Friday afternoon now, and she was already a no-show at work. She already called in to lie about her headache.

*Fuck it*, she thought as she threw things around her apartment, her awful attempt at cleaning up after her adventure. And in that haste, there was an instant when she froze. An idea hit her: Allentown Mutual. *Of course! I'll just have to go and visit him on his job!* Adena, the fatal attraction.

I'm sorry, ma'am. It's our policy not to share our employee information over the phone. Privacy, ya' know."

"Well, you admit he works there, so why can't you tell me which office he's at?"

"I'm sorry, ma'am. I can't—"

"I know—I know, Well, I'll just have to go office to office, now *won't* I." By 4:00 P.M. Adena was drained, asking herself why she put herself through this. *It's his loss,* she resolved. And yet, she continued her mission.

There was a clue. The license plate, of course. How could she be so stupid?

L enny, I'm sorry to lie about the emergency but I need your help." Adena had made a second call, to the police station. Her ex-boyfriend was an officer in Scranton and had access to vital records. It was just a matter of putting on a good performance, and he'd be putty in her hands, she was sure.

"See, I was in need of an address. See, a client of mine bounced a check, and—"

"A client? I thought you still worked over at the Days Inn."

"I do, I do. But, Lenny, you wouldn't know about the business I got on the side. I started it up after you . . . after we . . . well, you know. When our thing ended."

"Right, okay, I don't need to know any more. But how can I help?"

"I have a plate number."

"Okay."

"Don't play, Lenny. I need the address of the driver. It's a small thing, really. I just misplaced his information and I need to have him cover this bounced check right away."

"There's not gonna be any trouble over this, is there? Something that would bounce back to me?"

"No, no, no, Lenny. Nothin' like that. Promise. How you been, anyway?"

"All right."

"Good, good. So, can you help an old friend?"

"Already checking. Okay . . . says here the name is Mason Fickle. Address is 290, on Cubaugh."

"Thanks, Lenny. And if it means anything to you, I wish things worked out between us."

"Little late for that now, doll. You be good. And careful drivin' in this rain."

"No problem."

The minute Adena hung up she was on the road, doing sixty in a forty-five zone. She figured on facing Mr. Fickle within the next fifteen minutes.

Mason didn't have to fabricate a reason why he couldn't come to work because his hard-work ethic was the kind that was irreplaceable. If he said he wasn't coming into the office, his immediate supervisor understood.

Besides, he couldn't think straight after the roller-coaster ride the night before. And it wasn't just the sex that took him for a spin, but the drink Adena fixed. *Jesus!* How could he eat a light meal and expect that a strong mixer wouldn't lay him out? He must've been side tracked, he realized.

It was close to 4:00 P.M. when the banging began to irritate him, and then it woke him. He threw on a robe and marched to the front entrance to his house.

"Who the—"

It was Adena, with her fist balled up for the next bang on his door. Only now his face was there.

"Who's in here?" Adena wedged her way past Mason and his doorjamb until she was searching his home.

"What the hell?" Mason was beside himself, but still took the time to close his front door and pursue Adena.

"Adena. A-dee-na!"

"Just tell me who I gotta compete with, Mason. Whose ass I gotta kick." Adena was now removing her hoop earrings, bracelets, and the rings on her fingers. Then, as if she had gone through this same mess before, her hands were busy whipping her hair into a tight bun at the upper rear portion of her head. It was like magic, how her hair seemed to quickly disappear.

"What are you talkin' about? God, my head. Why all the banging? What's the craziness about?" Mason checked his watch. Where did the time go?

"I'm talkin' about you ditching me. I'm talking about you ignorin' my calls. I'm talkin' about—"

"Wait a minute! Stop! You are straight trippin', boo. For real. I been in that bed ever since early this morning when I left you. I been knocked out cold thanks to that drink you made! You ain't got no competition, 'cuz I ain't got no girlfriend, no wife . . . nobody. So cut the psycho shit."

"Really? You mean . . . last night *wasn't* a lie? You really meant the things you said? You're not leavin' me hangin'?"

"No, no, and no, Adena." Mason approached Adena and wiped the wetness from her face. It was the first that he realized she was all wet. "You're drenched," he said.

"Standin' out in front of your door, bangin' like a psycho. Oh, Mason." Adena cried instant tears and all of the rain and distress soaked into his terry bathrobe. "Don't quit on me, Mason. Please, don't quit on me. Last night was so wonderful. And in my sleep I couldn't stop thinking about you. You might be the best thing that ever happened to me. A real man, with real drive and ambition." Adena turned her eyes up to his and a kiss connected the two.

"I never thought I'd feel this way either, Adena. But you might be the one to complete me."

Yes, Mason said these things; but deep down he needed someone who would appreciate him, even if she was bordering on "stalker." He had been alone, in exile for too long, without someone to love for too long. Whatever the consequences, Adena was energy that he needed in his life.

# five

Those sweet memories seemed like so many moons away from the realities these days. The relationship that started off with a bang that night at Adena's apartment evolved into an explosion just weeks later, when the two exchanged wedding vows before a chaplain—also a friend of Adena's—in Mason's living room.

Yes, the marriage may as well have been final on the night these two engaged in that session of marathon sex, but there were the formalities to consider. A little backward, for sure; however, this all made perfect sense to two lovers who were crazy for each other.

And now, five years later, it seemed that their hunches about "the best thing that ever happened" and "you might be the one to complete me" were right on target. Even if they had bitch-slapping, ghetto arguments, even if they had a day here and a day there of angry separation, the Fickles were finally living up to the title "unbreakable."

But besides the brick and mortar of their husband/wife union, there was something extra.

For their entire time together, Mason and Adena were still living out their ultimate sexual fantasies. It was, Mason suggested, one of the big reasons why they were able to withstand their storms, since there would be no children to keep them from running away from the relationship. Moreover, neither of them had close family to make things more sticky and hard to deny. It was family that so often meddled and stuck their noses in kin folks' business. Such as with the Clemons couple down the block with their friendly, well-meant questions.

So, the only so-called family bond that the Fickles knew was their own: their work schedules that complemented each other; the bank account that they were building together; and, of course, the "sessions" that they engaged in, these two loving each other so hard once, twice, and even (sometimes) three times a week.

For their individual energy levels, they kept up their vitamin intake—Adena with the pill popping and Mason with the noni juice. They maintained high-protein diets as well as their respective workout schedules.

Adena was three years into the Billy Banks kickboxing program, always kicking Mason out of their bedroom so that she could focus. Meanwhile, Mason had his own routine, sticking with classic stuff like push-ups, jogging, and stretching. There were no other hobbies or indoor/outdoor activities for these two. No joining community organizations, no bowling nights, although they had been asked over and over again. And no movies at the local theater. Not even church. None of those things had anything to do with that one Fickle ritual, that one Fickle passion. Cut and dry, the Fickles liked to fuck, and fuck often. They might need candles and incense and silk sheets to accommodate them, but come Saturday night, the shades were pulled, the doors were locked, and those two attacked each other like hungry beasts. It was only during their fourth year of marriage that a certain conversation led Adena to want to explore *other* sexual thrills. She was with a group of other workers at the Days Inn, all of them women, discussing the growing trend of accepting third parties in the bedroom.

"I don't care if the world was coming to an end and the threesome was the last thing to save it. If my man even so much as *suggests* that he wants a third person, I'll wring his neck!"

Laughter broke out among the half-dozen women in the Days Inn dining hall. The hotel manager had called for a 6:00 A.M. meeting, but, as usual, he was the late one. Good management was hard to find.

"Momma, you don't know what you missin'," Lilly said. Lilly was the short one with two ponytails and green eyes. "It's something special when three consenting adults get together to give each other pleasure!" The word *pleasure* sounded more like "ple-jar," thanks to that Latino flavor in her accent.

One of the other women mumbled, "Oh dayum."

"*Pleasure?* What do you know about pleasure, young woman? I got almost twenty years on you, and I done had all the pleasure a woman can 'xperience. How much more can a human being have?"

"I'm not as young as you think, Momma. And just 'cuz you been there, done that doesn't mean I can't have mine, too. So what if I wanna experience things. That's my choice."

Again, the mumbles.

Again with the "Oh dayum."

"Better watch it, little lady. Your choice might be AIDS. And ain't no pleasure worth havin' that monster up in you."

"So, people just gotta be careful," Loween added. "'Cuz, even if you don't agree, Momma, people gonna do what they gonna do, irregardless."

Lilly and Loween shared a high-five.

The mumbles again, plus somebody uttered, "Aw Jesus need to help the children, for sure."

"And," Loween continued, "all a ya'll might not admit it, but I know at least nine outa ten of us had the experience, or at least *thought* about it—don't lie. Even you, Momma."

Momma chucked her head back and sucked her teeth. There'd be no holding back now.

"Chil', me no wan' no threesome. Me no hunger for no three-some. And ain't no book, or movie, or tee-*vee* show gon' change Momma's mind." Now it was Momma with the high-five, shared with a fellow Jamaican housekeeper.

Adena rolled her eyes while the chorus went on yakkin'. As far as she was concerned, none of the women, young or old, was on her level of thinking. For ten minutes she listened to the good, the bad, and the ugly positions among the universally popular ménage à trois, until the quarrel sounded more like an episode of *Jerry Springer*. Yet all she really absorbed from the haggling was that this became every girl for herself, each of them wanting to have her say—wanting to tell on themselves, whether for or against. Everybody always had their two cents.

"What about you, Adena? How you feel about it?"

That was the question that suggested to her that everybody was at least curious, especially since all the housekeepers got all quiet awaiting the words before they left her lips.

Choking back a laugh, Adena said, "Y'all just as crazy as hell. I ain't gettin' dragged into this, no way."

A few expressed that Adena was a party pooper, even if they didn't voice that opinion. But she cared not. What she had at home could satisfy a stadium full of women, even if the audience was merely permitted to watch from the bleachers. And Adena, even if in her mind alone, deserved a high-five for that reality.

D inner that night was pancakes and turkey sausage, the Fickle tradition of being as backward as they wanted to be. But nothing could have prepared Mason for what Adena had to say: "You wanna have a threesome this Saturday?"

Mason immediately choked on the food in his mouth and had to gulp down some milk just to clear his throat.

"You all right, baby?"

The hell if he was all right; eyes tearing, hunched over his plate, and at loss for his next breath.

"Where . . . where did *that* come from?"

"I guess I—it probably crossed my mind once or twice. There're always doin' that mess in the porno videos we watch. Plus, they can't get enough of the idea in rap music."

"Ah-hah! It's you and that rap music again. I knew that nonsense was gonna be the death of us." The way Mason said that sounded so funny, how he changed the values of his voice to sound like a white person. Plus, Adena knew he was kidding, since Mason listened to rap (probably) more than she did.

"Stop playin', Mason. I'm serious about this. How would you feel if I brought someone home this Saturday?"

"Wow. You *are* serious."

"Well, I gave it some thought. I spoke on it with a friend—"

"A friend? A friend knows about our sex life?"

Adena sucked her teeth. "It's not like that, Mason. I had to speak to someone since a threesome does mean *three people? Hello?* Plus, I had to clear things with you anyway. So, how 'bout it? You game?"

"Game. Am I *game?* Adena. What's gotten into you? Are you flipping sides on me? Is this thing you wanna do just a way of getting the—"

Mason took off his glasses and laid them on the dinner table. It was a time to be serious.

"Have you been cheating on me, Adena?"

"What the hell? Baby, you are straight trippin'. I'm doin' this for *you and me.* Just for the fun of it. Just to quench our sexual appetites."

"Sexual appetites. Is that what we have?"

Mason lightened up enough for another bite. With his mouth full, he found it easier to segue in with the next question. "I get to be selfish here, okay. Since you brought it up, I hope you don't get offended by what I'm thinking—maybe this is just the 'man thing' to ask. You know I'm not a chauvinist or anything—"

"Could you stop beating around the bush and get to the point?"

"The point. Right. Um . . . this, uh, third party? It's a woman?" The question escaped Mason's lips with all of its guilty innuendos.

Adena sucked her teeth. "Of course not. It's a man, silly."

Again, Mason started choking, almost gagging.

Adena sprang up from her seat and thumped him on the back, laughing at his shock.

Only Mason's face suggested, *This is not funny.*

"You are silly, Mase. Of course it's a woman. It's Lilly, the Dominican cutie from my job."

Tearing eyes and all, Mason calmed himself. He could get so deep right now about the presumptions in his wife's mind and what might have planted them there. He could've challenged her wit and argued about how obviously fanatic her latter answer was—*of course it's a woman.* But the curiosity in his veins coupled with his (more than likely) getting the best of this proposition was all that was necessary to keep his lips sealed.

His answer: "Sure. Why not?"

Lilly had it "goin' on" for a short girl. She wasn't the too-short type, just shorter than both Adena and Mason. She was also one of the sharper knives in the drawer of Days Inn housekeepers, so Adena assessed, having worked by her side many a busy morning. The two could wrap the planet earth two times over with the amount of bedsheets they had changed together. And that was the one thing they respected about each other, the teamwork factor. They didn't have to babysit each other, and that made each morning a sort of mathematical bliss.

Like synchronized swimmers Adena and Lilly breezed through their workday, changing beds, towels, and garbage liners, vacuuming, dusting, wiping surfaces and vents from sunup to nearly sundown. It was a simple but monotonous job that (more or less) required a good working partner just to maintain one's sanity.

"I heard you the other day, talkin' about the threesome."

"I know you did, girl. I bet everybody feels some type a way about me now that I come out the closet."

"Are you?" Adena chuckled. "Something of a bisexual? Or just bicurious?"

"Well, dag, girl. Why don't you just come out and say exactly what you mean?"

Adena bellied up a laugh to agree with how Lilly always kept it real.

"That's the only way I know how to kick it, Lilly. I just speak my mind," Adena said, making sure that her fold was tight at the corner of the bed.

"I always liked that about you, Adena. Even though I never said it. I can respect a chick who don't hold back. Makes me feel I'm not alone."

"And your answer is?" Adena was still trying to get to Lilly's bottom line.

"I guess I'm more than curious, now. I ain't gonna lie—I been with men and women. I been with women alone and men alone. More with men than women."

"Damn, You got all variations goin' down."

"I'm just real sexual, I guess."

"How about real safe?"

Sucking her teeth, Lilly said, "Oh, trust. Safety first."

"How's that work? I mean, how do you know?"

"I only had, like, two, what you might call long relationships. Of course, those were exclusive boyfriends. But with everyone else I used protection."

"With the women, too?"

"At first," Lilly said, still busy dusting the dresser, then the lampshades and on top of the air conditioner, "I was scared to death. But the girl who turned me out used Reynolds Wrap."

"What?" Adena giggled at the testimony. "She put Reynolds Wrap over your stuff?"

"Girl, and I woulda never known the difference. She twisted my lil' ass somethin' wicked. I thought—correction, I swore that Dick was my best friend. But when homegirl put it on me that first time, I lost my muthafuckin' mind. Straight up. And this Philly chick ain't been the same since."

It cracked Adena up to hear a Latin girl get real hood with her dialogue. It seemed that every nationality was claiming the hood nowadays. But that also made Adena wonder if Lilly had grown any; if her sense of being *hood* was holding her back from things she could be doing, places she might be going or people she would otherwise meet. Certainly, Adena had seen her own weaknesses in that way, as well as she had experienced breaking out of that shell.

That was one thing that Adena could claim, if nothing else in this world. Growth. Everyone had to feel at home somewhere in the world. But that didn't mean you had to deny yourself the possibilities. The evolution of man was a subject she had to learn back when she was in Westlake Junior High, but those teachings didn't scratch the surface when it came to street fights, family tragedies, and financial woes. Those teachings didn't dig deep into why Adena had grown up without knowing who her real parents were, or how she had survived physical and mental abuse in this and that foster home, or why (for a time) she'd been homeless and had to live on the streets. That all amounted to a greater evolution, a relevant and meaningful part of her personal growth. She was a survivor who chose to progress. And she realized that living in the same "hood" didn't do much in the way of promising the future she wanted or expected for herself. Okay, so what that she couldn't bear children. At least she could please a man and keep him happy—or she intended to, anyhow. And indulging these "extra" thrills was part of her strategy, a plan that Lilly was about to play a role in.

"Let's just make him happy," was what Adena told Lilly.

**s i x**

**B**aby, did you finish making the salad?" Adena's voice traveled through the house to where Mason was finishing dinner preparations. How this threesome would play itself out was out of his hands since Lilly was Adena's coworker. So he stayed at home and got things ready—reservations for three! Meanwhile, Adena went to pick up the night's guest for the couple's first-ever threesome.

In the distance, Mason could hear his wife showing off the house, with all of the "touches" she'd put on it over the course of five years. He swore he overheard her say, "I turned this bachelor pad into a palace." No matter that she dissed Mason's housekeeping skills. *Whatever makes it work*, as far as he was concerned. The greater issue was his stomach bubbling inside, part of his uncertainty, his nerves, or even that he was hungrier than usual. In any case, Mason was eager to satisfy it all. He also couldn't wait to get a look at Lilly. Adena had described her to the letter, painting a picture of her as an "attractive, health-conscious" friend who was "clean from ass to mouth." And, in fact, Mason just missed meeting the young woman in person on a couple of occasions when he took Adena to or picked her up from work during the heavy Pennsylvania snowstorms. But now, finally, they were getting to the moment of truth.

A dena turned the corner before Lilly, both of them strutting through the dining room in stilettos. The boots, the fancy outfits, and the perfect beauty effects added a nice touch to an evening already steaming with anxiety.

"Here we are! Whassup, Daddy? Lilly, you finally get to meet the man of my dreams—"

"Heard so much about you," Lilly said on her approach.

"Baby, Lilly is our lover for the night. Your wish is her command," Adena said. Mason's eyes widened as he looked at Adena. He was amazed at how Adena was just so damned direct about this. It made him wonder when he might wake up from this dream. He looked at Lilly.

Lilly's grin caused Mason to smile. She was in agreement. And that provoked his own thought. *If they're willing then why should I hold back?*

Then, Lilly made things much easier when she came right up and kissed Mason with parted lips. Mason considered the kiss to be a directive of his demanding wife, the ringleader, and it forced all of those reservations from his mind. Those ideas of being a gentleman, and an unsuspecting husband who had no idea about this surprise visit were forgotten.

The feeling was unusual, how all three of them were on the very same page for their first encounter, but what else was new with Adena? For five years now, she seemed to know the score, and it comforted Mason to have her in control. His response to Adena's earlier question, "Are you game?" was a big yes. But never in his boldest dreams did he think that things would become so tangible so fast. And besides, Lilly was breathtaking and sexy. No excessive makeup, her green eyes were electric with promise, and her long hair had a wet-'n'-wild look, even under the Phillies baseball cap.

Mason put Lilly's shoulder bag aside and the three sat down to salad and chicken. Mason subtly interviewed their candidate, despite the fact that Adena had (so-called) prequalified her, discussing Lilly's past relationships, how she was living now, and whether or not she was a smoker or a drug user. And sure, the whole interview bit was reaching way past the surface, but wasn't that how deep diseases reached? Deeper, even?

Control freak or not, Mason's first priority, even before the sex and thrills, was to be the ultimate gatekeeper of what was and wasn't introduced into the Fickle world. It was a form of prevention that had to be done, just to keep up with the bottom line in the world they lived in. There was a lot to lose, so sex (even in the Fickle world) had to have rules.


There was no beating around the bush. While Mason cleaned up the kitchen, the girls giggled behind closed doors in the master bathroom. Even if he tried, he couldn't have stalled this anymore, since his dick was growing brick hard. Within minutes he was relaxed in the bedroom, waiting for his night of pleasure.

"I don't know what ya'll are laughing about in there, but you got one horny man out here."

The two giggled more and carried on behind the door as though satisfying Mason was *later* on the agenda. But Mason's sense of urgency was throbbing from head to toe. Just as he flipped the switch on the Bose sound system, the latch shifted on the bathroom door. Lilly came out alone. "And don't hurt my husband," Adena's muffled voice ordered.

A tad bit shy, Lilly said, "She wants me to warm you up."

"Oh, does she?" Mason said, already stroking his neglected, rock-hard dick. "Then, by all means . . . warm me up."

Lilly's hair was wrapped fashionably around her head now, with some of it sticking up like a tail, and some tendrils falling behind her ears. She was also naked, and now that he got a good look at her,

Mason began to feel lucky. A perfect stranger with all the qualifications, *plus* she had a tight-ass body. He could want for no more.

illy folded one leg underneath her as she sat on the bed. She smoothed her hand across Mason's leg, up and down his chest, and then back toward his engorged penis. She was becoming familiar while searching his eyes for agreement.

"What a hammer you got here. And I know just what it needs."

Mason mumbled, "A *sledge*hammer, if you look close enough."

It was her cue to ease closer. She began with the kissing, then the tongue flicks, then accepted him into her mouth. If this was anything close to an indication of things to come, then the Fickle home was about to facilitate the experience of a lifetime.

"Ooooh, and it's a good-lookin' one, too," sighed Lilly.

Mason chuckled in response.

"I never heard it called good-lookin' before, but I'm not gonna argue with you." He groaned with how good this felt inside her mouth. She toyed with him and worked him over like some starved woman's next meal. He was afraid that she'd stop, that the pleasure would stop, and that he would wake up from this dream.

As worked up as Mason was, he didn't realize Adena had emerged from the bathroom and was practically standing over them, lotioning her body. Then he opened his eyes and husband and wife exchanged a look, nothing more, as Lilly continued to work him over like the Energizer bunny. Eventually Adena crawled on the bed and went right to work. Caressing Lilly's breasts and nibbling at her nipples. Mason was surprised at how much Adena was into this "other person." And he couldn't help wondering if this was more about *Adena and Lilly* than *the Fickles and Lilly*. It was just a flash that breezed through his mind, picturing these two together without him, but one more flick of Lilly's tongue soon erased that thought. Mason simply went back to closing his eyes, tilting his head back, enjoying this latest fantasy fulfilled.

Adena joined in with Lilly, both of them giving exclusive attention to Mason's torpedo. He was throbbing inside Lilly's mouth, and
then between Adena's familiar lips. Lilly's kisses traveled up Mason's
body until she reached his lips, and they indulged in a passionate
bout of tongue wrestling. This went on for a short time, but long
enough for Adena to feel neglected.

"What cha'll doin'?" she asked. She was propped up on one elbow and had stopped sucking her husband's dick altogether.

Mason and Lilly pulled their faces back with confused expressions. Then Adena grabbed a handful of Lilly's hair and pulled her
head around so that they were face-to-face.

"Ain't nobody said to kiss my man, bitch. What the fuck is wrong
wit' cha?" Lilly's expression went from that electric seduction to
dumbstruck. But Adena wanted more than that.

"Well? Cat got your tongue, mami?" Adena took things to a whole
other level with the "mami" comment; how many Latino women
took offense at the phrase, as if they were being addressed as dogs. At
the same time, Adena pulled Lilly's hair tighter and it came loose. It
was clear to Lilly that Adena was upset and that she meant business.

"I'm sorry," Lilly said. "I thought—"

"You thought. You *thought*? I gave you specific instructions,
meeda. Suck his dick and get him warmed up. Ain't that what I said?
*Huh?*" Adena jerked Lilly's head to emphasize her seriousness.

"I'm sorry, I'm sorry!" Lilly squirmed.

"Adena, really."

"Shut up, Mason. Matter fact, you useless now." Adena was indicating how Mason's erection had softened. "So, sit over there." The
way Adena cocked her head meant business. "Now."

Lilly looked distressed, more than apologetic. Her eyes said it all,
how she couldn't believe what was going down. How her coworker
(and friend?) had flipped like this so suddenly. Lilly eased away from
Adena as though to raise herself up, only Adena still had her hair
clutched in her hand.

"Oh, no, meeda. Come over here." Adena positioned Lilly's face so closed to hers that their lips nearly touched. "Now, where you think you goin'?"

"Ma, I don't know how I messed this up," Lilly said, pleading. "But I'm not feelin' right about this. I think I should go."

"Go? Go? And leave me hangin'? Bitch, you must be crazy. Only place you gonna go is between my legs. Feel me?" Adena pulled tighter on Lilly's hair. "I said, you feel me?"

"Yes—yes—*yes*! You're hurting me, Deena."

"You ain't seen hurt, mami. Now get your face in the place. And don't come up for air till I tell you to."


This shit was at least amusing, and at most, as raunchy as Mason ever saw his wife. It was better than Jekyll and Hyde. Better than the psycho in the *Triple Threat* movie. It was even better than they had planned.

Mason restrained his urge to howl like Tarzan, but the instant Adena turned to Mason and winked, he lost it. He let out a strangled groan, a noise stuck somewhere between his throat and lips. *I can't believe this woman!* He couldn't believe how she had put on this act; how she had fooled both Lilly and him. And now, how she had Lilly still eating (so to speak) out of the palm of her hand. It was all just so overwhelming. And it not only excited him enough to get his erection back, but it took him to the brink of exploding. Then he watched a ten-minute master/servant episode between Lilly and Adena that ended with Adena writhing and having fits beneath Lilly. Both ladies' hair was wild, their bodies coated with perspiration. Adena's pussy was wet and sloppy with satisfaction. She looked over at Mason.

"You want some of this, boo?"

He thought she'd never ask and wasted no time walking over to their bed, while stroking his erection.

"You're a good girl, Lilly. Now—" Adena raised Lilly's head gently, and tongue kissed her. "We're not done with you." Without another word, Adena guided Lilly's head until her mouth was on Mason's dick. She took so much of him into her mouth that her nose mashed his pubic hair. She uttered gagging sounds that resembled some manic drowning victim's fright-filled fight for air.

Adena let up some to allow the girl to breathe, but the instant she appeared to collect herself, that face was mashed right back into Mason's lap.

This went on a few times, with Lilly obedient to the letter. And still, Adena pushed things a step further. She turned over onto her back, prepared for Mason's forced entry, leaving Lilly to be the spectator. And the missionary work turned into something more extreme as Mason pounded Adena again and again, evoking cries that turned to squeals, that turned to absence of breath. And when one opening had been pounded into submission, Mason worked his way into her ass.

Adena's cries, both the pleasure and the pain, as well as the scent of perfumes gone sour, filled the bedroom with the spoils of overindulgence. Meanwhile, Adena reached and grabbed and pulled at every shred of bedding she could until she got hold of Lilly's foot, leg, and then waist. Lilly was soon positioned so that her mouth joined in with Mason's labors, and so that her genitals were accessible to Adena's probing tongue. Adena, the puppet master.

Eventually, the sex became a triangle fueled by unending, selfless carnal sin, and those bodies were overcome, from the insides, by fountains, streams, and rivers surging though them in some simultaneous race to some infinite and unharnessed finale.

# seven

*Six months later*

The Fickles' first third-party encounter, when it was all said and done, turned out to be nothing more than another night of raunchy sex. It may have appeared to be exciting and even necessary for reasons of curiosity and adventure. However, it didn't really seem to enhance their love life. It just seemed to make them hungry for the next bigger sexual thrill, which worried Mason. It was as if his conscience was kicking in, telling him, *Mason, you never take time to think about how an empty encounter of lustful sex inevitably taxes you—not while the loins are bubbling, and definitely not during the act. You never think about how it tends to test your own self-worth and sense of decency—not while a powerful orgasm is begging to shoot out of your body! And it is usually so downright disgusting and evolves into acts that are so perverted and filthy that the level of excitement is hard to match. It's something like the high from a drug that you just can't seem to relive.*

I guess what I am trying to say, Adena, is I don't want us to become jaded," Mason said.

"Define *jaded*," Adena shot back. The two were lounging at

brother Damon's Club in East Stroudsburg, sitting at an intimate table for two, away from the bar and dance floor.

"Listen, I'm not tryin' to argue, I'm just makin' a point, baby. I don't want what we have to lose its power. We can't always do the sixty-nine. I don't always wanna get my dick sucked. And I don't always wanna eat your pussy. Remember me? The romantic one? Sometimes we gotta slip some lovemaking in here, boo. We gotta step up our game in other ways, not just the freak shit."

"What's on your mind?" Adena asked. "You flippin' on me all of a sudden? I thought you liked a woman who's in charge of her sexuality. I thought you wanted a slut in the bedroom and a—"

"I do love it when a woman is in charge. That goes without saying. Y'all got more on the ball than a lot of us men. But what I'm sayin' about *our* situation is being freaky and nasty *all the time* isn't my idea of growing together. That stuff we did last night? That girl didn't turn me on—"

"You didn't say that last night," Adena said with the whole head-wagging attitude.

"Okay, so my dick is the liar. But it's my mind that's the bigger thinker. I'm still a man at the end of the day, Adena. And I still enjoy raunchy once in a while. But we gotta use discretion. You *and* me. Like I was sayin' . . . the girl last night was fine, I gotta give you that. You brought a winner home. Except when she pulled that rubber out? And you had her suckin' my dick *with* the rubber? I could've got up out of the bed and gone to a movie, and you know I *never* go to the movies."

Adena chuckled. "You still came in her mouth. What's your answer for *that,* Mr. Worldly?"

"No, Adena. I came in the rubber. And again, you know a man's dick has a mind of its own. Of course I'm gonna come. That's a man thing! You know that."

"Then what're you tryin' to say? You didn't like her, but you came anyway?"

"You're confusing the conversation, Adena."

"No. You're confusing me. Mason. If you didn't like her you could've said it last night when I asked you if you liked her."

"But I *do* like her. She's cool."

"But you don't wanna wear a rubber."

"Exactly."

"Well, ain't *that* some shit. You . . . the one who's always kickin' that *let's be safe, one night is not worth a life* shit. You don't want the rubber now?"

Mason cocked his head back and looked up at the ceiling.

"Oh my God. Adena, Listen. I don't wear a rubber with you and I haven't for years. I don't wanna start now—wait a minute. Let me finish. I'm not saying I need to go raw dog in some stranger. I am sayin', I don't like to wear rubbers. It *sounds* strange, yes. But I like the sensation of skin—your skin against my skin. Anything else to me feels phony. Last night, even though I came? That felt *phony.* And I'm sayin', if I gotta wear a rubber, then we gotta space things out more. We can't have back-to-back freak shit so often. Crystal will be okay."

"You didn't like last week, either?"

"It was okay. No fireworks, but okay."

"You came then, too. Plus you were kissing all on her."

"I'm a stop discussin' this with you, Adena. 'Cuz you don't see it from my point of view. I'm basically sayin' this shit is gettin' played out, and nine times out of ten I need our bedroom to be *ours,* not the playpen to test out the freak skills of the maids at your job."

Adena got up, grabbed her purse, and left Mason with one last word: "This freaky maid from the Days Inn makes your bed, cooks your food, and licks your ass, nigga. Let's see if you can do that by yourself for a while." Adena was getting loud and didn't care that a busboy could hear her. Then she turned and strutted out of Damon's.

"That's exactly what I'm talking about," muttered Mason in the wake of Adena's scenic exit. "Sometimes a man don't wanna get his ass licked. Dammit."

Mason was already by himself with nobody to hear his side of the argument. As a reward for telling it like it is, he not only finished his drink, he finished hers, too.

A rguments are a pain in the ass, Mason. And they can have the worst timing. The man will somehow insult the woman, then she'll return another insult—basically, all kinds of hate-filled words and emotions are exchanged. Next thing you know, you got a real-life drama on your hands with both parties all ready to go their separate ways."

Bill Clemons was playing psychiatrist with Mason this morning, instead of being at work where he was a corrections officer with the B.O.P. It came naturally to give advice to anyone within his reach, since that was the kind of man he was: helpful, compassionate, with an air of "tough love" about him. Only, this was a first, to help one of his neighbors he considered a close friend.

"Oh, I know what you're goin' through, Mason. I gotta hear this kinda stuff all the time, except it's a lot more raw and violent in my profession."

"You gotta accept my apologies for layin' this on you this morning, Bill. I never meant to be a burden, honest."

"But, isn't that what friends are for, Mason? If you can't turn to a friend with these issues, then who can you turn to?"

"Not my wife. Not now, anyway. And she's supposed to be my closest friend."

"A damn shame," Bill said.

"But, I kinda think we need this room to breathe. We're in each other's faces whenever we're not at work, and—" Mason collected himself, ready to confide in Bill with a deeper, darker secret. "Bill, we got another problem that *nobody* knows about."

"Oh, Lawd. Okay, let's have it. You committed a crime? You

abuse her? Or she's pregnant. Gotta be one of the three—and I hope it's one of the second or third choices."

"Actually, it's none of the above, Bill."

Bill's face expressed both relief and curiosity.

"Adena and I, we have this, uh . . . this problem." Bill's expression alone told Mason, *I'm listening.*

"Promise me this won't go any further than you and me, Bill."

"No problem."

"Not even the Missus?"

"I promise. And my word is my bond. Now, can you spill the beans. You got me ready to piss my pants."

"We're sex addicts, Bill."

Bill's nose made a noise as though something had gotten caught up in there. He was evidently holding back a laugh, considering the way his lips pursed and the smart look in his eye.

"See, now you are clownin' me," Mason said. "This is *serious*, Bill. This is a real problem for us. If we're not at work, eating, sleeping, or on the toilet, we're fucking. But even those lines have been crossed."

"How so?" Bill asked, finally serious.

"At work, for instance. Adena sneaks in through the back door, she tells my secretary to keep a secret, and she somehow infiltrates all the security efforts to eventually lock my door behind her, and she puts on this strip show while I'm on an important business call. What's worse is I actually *liked* this, and to one-up her, I do the same for her. I go to her job, I get past virtually no security measures, and I then strip for her in one of the hotel rooms that she didn't clean yet. I come to find out that the sheets we got nasty on were *already* nasty, and . . . well, we were a mess, Bill."

"I bet you were."

"Oh, you ain't heard shit. At The Private Table Restaurant, over on two-o-seven, she pulls off her panties under the table during dinner and lays them out on the table, next to the candle. Some real freak shit, Bill. I argue about it, but it's too late when the waitress already sees it. The manager even came over and asked us to behave! Can you believe that? I'm a grown-assed man, Bill. And some twenty-something is telling me to behave."

"You're a grown-assed man, but still doin' teenage things, Mason."

"Wow. And, Bill . . ." Mason went on as though Bill hadn't said a word, "the woman has brought at *least* ten girls home in the past year. At *least* ten. I can't even remember some of their names. And I debate with her about these activities. I really do. But again and again *I can't help myself.* I turn into a sucker every single time. The last straw was last night. The girl she brings home is superfine, but this girl puts a rubber on me, she gets me off with a blow job—as if to get me out of the way—before she buries her face in Adena's crotch for like an hour. *An hour, Bill.* I can't help thinking that my woman is more into women than men."

"Men? As in multiple men?"

"No, men, as in me. She swears up and down that she doesn't do other men behind my back—only me, she promised. But, hell, what's the difference if she gives my stuff to another woman. It's still stuff that belongs to me."

"You two are crazy, Mason. A couple of freaks, for sure. But crazy. And I'm getting so many mixed messages from you right now. You do and you don't want the extreme sex. You do and you don't want the threesome. And I haven't once heard you say you love this woman. Plus . . . plus . . . *plus, you don't want a rubber on you?* Are you *stupid?* Have you finally flipped your lid? Do you know the shit that's goin' around today?"

"I—"

"No, nononononononono. Let me tell you what I've personally seen. I got guys who come in the system with bubbles on their assholes. *Bubbles!* And, Mason, they're *white* bubbles, almost as big as golf balls. The prison has so many of these dudes—both new and old convicts—that they had to build a separate wing just to house them. We, the correctional officers, even had to take additional training and seminars and lectures and shots just so we know how to coexist with these characters. So if we're getting dozens of these guys in the penal system, a controlled environment, can you imagine what's out there on the streets?"

Bill's words felt like the teeth on a pitch fork working their way into the hard dirt of Mason's world. All he could think of were those virtual strangers, whether they were pretty or not, who had shared his bed. Their faces flashed through his mind differently than they had before. Before, it was a turn-on to revisit those events, those images of his meat smacking some girl's smiling face, or drilling another woman's ass, or mouth. But now that Bill had his say, the images were different, the girl's were sexy Grim Reapers draped in their black robes, with too much makeup. These phantom vixens were suddenly hunting Mason, beckoning him to stop running, to stop avoiding them, and to stay still so they could suck his dick to the bloody bone. Mason shuddered and shook his head to rid himself of the thoughts.

"You all right, Mason?"

"I'm good. Just forgot to do something . . . I just remembered a call I had to make," Mason lied. "But I understand what you're getting at, Bill. You're telling me some good stuff to make me think. But, I'm careful. I am. I can't say that I'm a one hundred percent know-it-all, but one thing is for sure—I'm protectin' my dick."

"Yeah, I hear you loud and clear, champ. Let me leave you with this. And I promise not to preach to you anymore. When it gets down to the nuts and bolts of life, we're all nothing but two-legged creatures who, without the ability to speak and reason, or argue, would otherwise be the victims (or practitioners) of routine religions and cults with their individual idiosyncrasies. But a closer look will tell you that too much of anything, *even sex*, can kill you. At least, it can turn you into a burnout—a callous, jaded, boring robot that's simply headstrong and brainwashed about whatever it is you might think, act, or feel like. Even your beliefs become tunnel-vision themes that leave little room for adjustment or debate. And everybody who's conscious knows that life is not simple, cut and dry. So . . . I say all of that to say, Mason . . . get a life, man. Don't sink any deeper than you are. Take this situation as your wake-up call, whether you stay with Adena or not. Get a grip. You might need some church, a marriage counselor, or even a vacation, but do something and do it now, before it's too late."

A dena, too, had her dialogue with a friend, who coincidentally was Bill's wife, Barbara. Barbara ran a beauty salon in downtown East Stroudsburg called New York Style. It was Main Street's only black salon, which, despite the racism, the jealousy and harassment, still managed to maintain its ten-year run on the block. It was a busy Wednesday thanks to the "wash and set" special, and there was always information being shared about who was marrying whom, about who bought what house, and about the latest injustice from Main Street to Blue Mountain. Something was always going on in East Stroudsburg.

"Girl, are you kidding? What you two have is *good* problem. You're gonna end up kissing, making up, and your relationship will be stronger than it ever was. Me? I gotta deal with investigators coming in my salon tryin' to find violations to fine me for. And violations don't come cheap, chil'. The last one I got was for five hundred dollars, just because the lid was off the garbage can. That might be my profit for a whole week, girl. And you think *you* got problems? Try telling the phone company, or the automobile finance company, or the landlord that you can't pay them because your garbage can didn't have its lid on correctly. See if they give you leniency."

"I'm sorry to hear your issues, Barbara. I guess we all got our own crosses to bear. . . . I just know the ones I got are a little heavy right now. One minute I wanna pack my bags and leave; the next minute I want my man back, and I wanna squeeze him and never let go."

"It's easy to let go, Adena. Especially for you two, since you don't have kids. But it's harder to do what you gotta do to keep love alive. Sometimes sex can help, and other times it gets in the way."

"This time it might be getting in the way," Adena explained. "See, our argument came up *because* of sex. Actually, sex is at the *center* of our problems."

Babara had been scrubbing Adena's scalp, sudsing it up to a heavy lather, before she stopped to take a long look at her client and friend.

"Is there something you want to tell me, Adena?"

And now Barbara, too, was informed about the exact issues behind the Fickle argument. Only, Adena didn't see their problem as the obsession with sex. What she saw was her husband "falling off," changing who he was, after five years.

That's what she told you?" exclaimed Bill that night when he and Barbara were under the covers.

"Sure did."

"Well then, somebody's not tellin' the truth."

"What'd Mason say to you?"

"He wanted me to keep it a secret."

"Right. I'm listening."

"He wanted me to keep it a secret from you."

"*Annnd?*" Barbara snuggled up to Bill some more, ready for the gritty details.

"Annnd, I gave him my word."

Barbara started laughing. And her laugh was quickly interrupted as she said, "You *are* kidding, right?"

"Nope."

"Well, I'll be damned."

"Oh, now don't you start. I'm sure you got secrets you don't bring home. From what I hear, that salon has a ton of stories that you never tell me."

"And that means *what?*"

"Well, it's the same thing. I got stuff that I don't share with you—you got stuff that you don't share with me."

"Oh, but there's one big difference, Bill."

"Which is?"

Barbara immediately had her husband in a choose-or-lose position with her hand clutching his testicles.

"Which is my squeezing the life outta you. *Now* are you gonna tell me your dirty little secrets?"

Bill winced, and there was a deep squeal that crawled up from his throat.

"Or am I gonna have to force them out of you?"

Bill turned stiff as a board. "Oooh, honey, you're threatening the family jewels, there," he gasped.

"And you don't think I'm dead serious?"

"Curious? Yes. But dead serious? I don't think you have the balls."

Barbara squeezed harder and Bill tried to pry her hands away, but there was no use.

"I can't believe you're serious about this," Bill said with torment in his voice.

"Okay, I'll be nice," she responded, and she loosened her grip.

"How the hell does their relationship matter all of a sudden?"

"It really doesn't, boo." Barbara caressed Bill's aching valuables. "I'm just very, very curious."

Bill let out a deep, relieved breath. He looked toward the ceiling, perhaps imploring the lord who ruled over all nosy wives. He was ready to give in.

"They got problems, Barbara. I mean *real* problems like the drug addicts and alcoholics."

"They're doin' drugs and mixing it with sex? I don't understand."

"No, they're not doin' drugs or alcohol, Barbara. Not as far as I can tell. What they're addicted to is sex. They gotta have it often. Plus, it has to get strange, freaky, and twisted for them to keep reaching satisfaction."

"Wow," Barbara said. "That's like a lottery prize that keeps going up."

"Exactly, except, in the Fickles' case, they're never really satisfied. It's always more, more, more."

"If you ask me, that sounds like a manageable problem," said Barbara with a slight chuckle.

"Not in their case. These two are pushing the relationship to the limit. They're diminishing their own sense of self-worth with some of the most disgusting, filthy acts." A sour taste showed on Bill's face.

Barbara was about to speak, but Bill cut her off. "Don't ask, but, most importantly, the Fickles are threatening their very lives with these sex acts. Threesomes, indecent exposure. And have you ever heard the term *ass-to-mouth?*"

"Whoa," Barbara exclaimed, her eyes wide open.

"Exactly. On more than one occasion, Mason has stuck his wood in another woman's ass, then immediately into Adena's mouth."

"How do you— He *told* you this, honey?"

"He sure the hell did. And he's done it the other way around, too, from Adena's ass into a stranger's mouth. I'm tellin' you, their stuff is *waaay* over the top."

"Mmm-mmm-mmm. I never woulda thought those two rolled like that," said Barbara.

"You! Imagine *my* face when he told me these things. He's playing with fire."

"Well, I don't know about you, but all this sex talk is makin' me very hot."

"Jesus," Bill said. "Now *you're* goin' crazy."

Barbara was kissing her way down Bill's neck, then his chest and abdomen.

"Not crazy . . . just . . . crazy for you. Did you say I hurt these . . . two . . . jewels down . . . here?"

Bill's head fell back and his eyes closed.

*Damn those Fickles.*

**eight**

For just over a week, the Fickles went without saying so much as a word to each other. And each day that passed seemed to make things worse. To work and back is the way it used to be, before the big argument at Damon's. But nowadays, the two found every excuse imaginable to not be at home. Mason, with his late hours at work; Adena with her outings and renewed interest in old friends.

Mason took things a step further and rented a room at the area's only black-owned resort, The Hillside Inn. He felt this was the answer that Bill Clemons hinted; *that break* he needed for thinking and for considering his future (with or without Adena). And besides, it was a gentleman's gesture, he felt, to take a step aside and allow Adena her own space at their home. Fight or no fight, Mason would always be a gentleman. So, he left Adena a short and sweet note:

> I need to take some time away, to think about me and my choices in life. I left some emergency money in the dresser draw, if you happen to need it.
>
> MASON

Mason taped the note on the bathroom mirror where he knew Adena would see it. It was the last thing he did before showering and packing some necessities.

A dena took Mason's sudden absence like a slap across the face. It was always the man who took off, who showed how unattached he could be, and whose mobility was greater than the woman with whom he lay.

*Thank God we don't have children,* Adena thought. And she became stubborn about the whole mess, figuring if he wanted to act the fool, she could, too. The first thing she did was to throw the chain on the front door, just in case Mason got smart and changed his mind. *We'll have none of that.* Next, Adena went to her closet to pull out a few skimpy selections, such as a low-cut yellow blouse (for her breasts to play peek-a-boo in), and a black short skirt (for her hips to play hide-and-seek in), and fishnet stockings to give the illusion that she was a freak under all of this dressing. (*The illusion?*) And finally the thunder-black stiletto boots, just in case anyone didn't get that "fuck me" message from the fishnet stockings. She laid these things out on the bed, then of course had to make some calls to see who could easily go along with her agenda.

"Hey, Tawana. What cha' doin', girl!"

"Hey, Sade! We ain't got wild in a while."

"You still makin' the girls cry, Harry?"

"Lilly, you know I get that itch from time to time. I never could forget that night we had together."

Adena swore up and down that Lilly, of all people, would be down for some fun. But it was no-can-do. Lilly was committed now to some new man who had a big bank account and an even bigger dick for her to ride. Most of the others had this or that excuse and were unable to come out and play. In the back of her mind, Adena wondered if everyone wasn't just bitter since, for the past five years her life, love, and happiness were about nothing more than Mason Fickle's world. And everything else revolved around it. She recalled so many times when she let the answering machine get the call, thinking, *Why should I take the call when everything I need is right there at home?*

Friends, wannabe friends, and others may just as well have been door-to-door salesmen, because that's how they'd been dismissed when it came to time in Adena's world. And now that the shoe was on the other foot, Adena began to feel lonely, preparing to party but having nobody to party with. She began to feel desperate when some of her calls weren't returned, and she had to resort to her stack of business cards—the ones she kept in a rubber band for, maybe, this very occasion. She'd collected these from so many wannabe suitors over the years. And she ultimately found she was getting more attention on these calls since she'd never paid them any mind in the first place.

"I was just lookin' to have a little fun, Terry. What're you lookin' for?" Adena didn't even feel right soliciting like this. It had been a while since she had gone on a new date. But these were desperate times, and her pussy had its own mind. It was hungry, and beggars couldn't be choosers.

"Sure, I can meet you there. Seven o'clock it is," Adena said before she hung up. Now Adena was off to the shower. She was sure that Mason wouldn't be home soon since they'd had their share of arguments in the past. She knew this to be his way of escaping the fights and assumed that what her girlfriends always said was true: *It's so easy for the man to leave.*

Adena noticed a small paper lying on the sink. Its ink was smeared and unreadable except for Mason's name at the bottom. Maybe this was his list of things to pack, Adena decided before she tossed the wet paper into the trash.

The "rendevous" was set for 7:00 P.M. at the Trolley Stop Restaurant inside the Fernwood Resort on Route 207. Adena was all too familiar with the resort, its dozens of amenities and the various restaurants, since she and Mason had spent their wedding night and honeymoon there. But this evening's visit was altogether different. Actually, one might call it a sinful occasion, as naughty as Adena was feeling. This was nothing more than a blind date. One that might very well lead up to a one-night stand. In the restaurant, all of the furnishings and decor were designed with a polished wood that made the establishment feel like a modern-day saloon. But that rustic essence was offset by carpeting, mirrors, wide-screen monitors, and an elaborate bar. Within seconds, any customer was swallowed by the warm atmosphere and the cheer on the faces of the staff.

"Good evening. Will you be having dinner, ma'am?"

Adena had been waiting to be seated for no more than a minute before the maître d' approached her in that earnest welcome.

"Yes, I'm waiting for someone, so there'll be two of us," Adena said. The images were still firing at her—the wedding night, the head-over-heels sex in their villa, in their Jacuzzi, and for most every day of their two-week honeymoon. She had to shake loose the past just to walk straight, but she managed.

"You okay, ma'am?"

"Huh? Oh—yeah. I'm good," Adena said, trying to be brazen about this. She accepted two menus from the waitress and took a seat. "Will your guest be coming right away? Can I get you a drink while you're waiting?"

"He shouldn't be long, but I'll have an Apple Martini while I'm waiting."

The waitress nodded and hurried to get the drink, leaving Adena in a fog, her mind working on staying in the present. She didn't even have the desire to curse out her late date, or to call him on her cell, as caught up as she was with the past and how little things had changed at their honeymoon retreat.

"Hello, looove," Terry cooed when he came to the table. He had flowers in hand, but Adena hardly cared.

"You're laaate," she responded with more than an edge of sarcasm.

"I apologize, baby. There was extra traffic on two-o-seven, right there at Marshalls Creek—never fails. Can't wait till they go through with the bypass project. Plus, there were two people before me at the florist, and . . . well, would you forgive me, Adena?" Terry looked like one big fat oaf of a man right about now, all smuckered up and pleading before her. She took the flowers.

"Would you sit down?" she demanded, hoping he wouldn't keep being apologetic. *What's done is done,* she determined. And now it was time for him to be the man she needed; that camaraderie and supportive soul she wanted by her side. Hell, she just needed a nice-size dick to sit on, who was she kidding?

This felt so foreign to Adena, sitting with another man after so long. She had the worms crawling around in her stomach, her special symptom when she felt nervous.

"So, what did you feel in the mood for? I'm speaking about the menu, of course."

Adena caught the sly inference in his query but she rolled right over that with her answer.

"I think I'll have the grilled salmon, and a salad to start."

Terry was about to ask a question, but he quickly caught himself.

"Oh . . . you already have the drink. Maybe I'll have what you're having."

"For dinner?"

"The drink. For dinner. After dinner—as in dessert. Whatever you're havin', I'm ridin' with you," Terry said with that proud way about him. Already, this guy was making Adena nauseated. She could see that he was going to be agreeable the whole night since he was trying to get into her pants. But Adena knew all too well that underneath the mask—the one everyone wears—there would more than likely be an entirely different person. It made her compare this man to her husband. Was Terry a confident man who knew what he wanted in life, like Mason was when she first met him? Was he secure with himself, his accomplishments, and his well-being, like Mason was, or was Terry likely to be a phony, whose true colors would show themselves with every passing minute?

Adena thought about these things, looked at Terry, and thought about the good man she had in Mason. On second thought, she might not want to give him up so quickly.

*Because, after all,* Barbara Clemons had said to her, *if you get a new man, that doesn't necessarily mean* brand new. *That just means he's recycling what you don't see. Same old problems in a different flavor.*

A dena decided to have dinner and then head home.

The truth was that she couldn't wait to get home. Home. She'd never thought about her safe, comfortable home as much as she did now. And thank God they'd driven to the resort in separate cars!

When they finished their meal Terry asked, "Want me to follow you home? Make sure you get home safe?"

*Been driving home alone for years, fool. Tonight ain't no different.* But what she actually said was, "I'm good, Terry. You're a sweetheart. Thanks for dinner." Adena walked over to Terry, bounced up on her toes to peck him on the cheek, and that was that.

Paying for dinner was never so easy. Not until she accelerated far ahead of Terry onto 207, with two cars to separate them, was Adena relieved enough to know she didn't have a stalker on her hands. This was just dinner between friends. Nothing more, nothing less. And that was an okay image in her mind as she considered getting her marriage working again. Her concern now was Mason: *How far did he go? Who has he been with?* And, *Is he serious about this breakup?* These were questions that she could only worry about. She could only weigh and measure what their relationship meant, both the good and the bad. She could only wonder how Mason was feeling or if he was asking himself the same questions about her. She could only hope things hadn't gone beyond the point of no return.

Y ou DOG!" she growled in his ear. Then she let go of a raspy moan, and she panted again before she hollered, "Deeper, Daddy. *Deeper!*"

And that's just what he did. He gave it to her deeper and harder and more thoroughly than he had for the entire thirty minutes they'd been fucking. The action had graduated from the blow job she performed so lovely on his hungry meat, to her hands-and-knees position on the cheap motel-room floor, and his pounding her from behind, then back to the blow job, after which he grabbed her face with both hands and held her there so that her open mouth could catch his ejaculate.

"Now gargle," he instructed.

She did.

"Now swallow," he told her, still holding her face.

The vixen closed her mouth and swallowed. Complete with the lip smacking, and the *aaahhh!* to go with it. There was a smile in her eyes and a satisfaction across her face.

"You like that nasty shit, don't you?"

"Yes, Daddy. Give me more," the vixen said.

And Mason continued stroking himself as the number-two man (two of five studs waiting in line) went through the same motions with the kneeling servant. But Mason didn't need to see any more of the DVD to make himself come. He was already twitching and shaking and furiously pulling at his hard dick until his bare body was messy with semen. After he came so hard, he simply fell back onto the bed, where a towel had been spread out just for this very explosive ending. He didn't care to see any more of the DVD and wished the remote hadn't fallen off the bed, because he would've shut the TV off by now instead of having to listen to more of the gagging, the skin slapping, the slurping—all of which had been important before the big finale. And what a finale it was!

And he lay there, regretting things. He regretted having left his and Adena's home earlier in the week. He regretted the things he'd said to her at Damon's and how he had sort of started this whole drama with his dumb argument. He regretted the man he had become, a hardworking man with a warped and maybe unhealthy view of sex. He regretted that he hadn't tried to stop their spiraling descent. He regretted the romance that he had allowed to slip away from sexy and erotic to disgusting and sometimes humiliating.

All of these thoughts he was having now that his body felt balanced. And for his body to be balanced, he asked himself, *I had to go right back to the porn movies?*

It felt like he was taking two steps backward, slipping into that same black hole of lust that he longed to climb out of. And what he wanted now, what he felt he so desperately needed, was to get back home, back to his wife, back to the way things used to be, especially if he had hope of fixing his marraige. The thing was, how in the world would they get back to normal? How could they put this all behind them in order to be *in love* again? In love enough so that they could have that healthy, fairy-tale affair that most women longed for and that made most men feel empowered, confident, and ready for the world? This was a job for a powerful marriage counselor. Or a sex therapist, at least.

# nine

For four days, the latch and chain had been fixed on the front door so that Mason was locked out when Adena was home. But now, Adena could see that she had been acting silly and extreme. So what if Mason wanted to slow down on the freak sessions? Couldn't she handle that? Were things so bad that she'd had to go off on him during that romantic night at Damon's? And more important, wasn't being with Mason so much more comfortable and enjoyable regardless of the sex? Did it have to come the point of separation?

Even if her hot head was in denial of the love they had for each other, Adena couldn't wait for Mason to walk back through that door. It was a hunger for a man that she'd never felt before. Where she wasn't so worldly, Mason filled that void. Where she didn't have as much wisdom, Mason was her teacher and mentor. And sometimes, while Adena lacked that right-minded common sense, Mason filled in her blanks.

However, above and beyond all of that, she felt comfortable with Mason by her side. She felt complete when they lay together, and even when they were apart. That was a sense of compatibility that Adena was banking on now as she hoped for her husband's return. *We've come too far for us to part now.*

---

A t one o'clock the next morning, Mason came through the front door. Adena had been restless, falling in and out of sleep after her dinner with Iron Mike Tyson, or more specifically with the video of Mike back at the restaurant. She lay still and tried to wake up some more before Mason entered the bedroom. And despite the many convictions and promises that she'd made about what she would say and do once he came home, Adena's pride kept her right there in bed. Maybe she was somewhat nervous, and maybe even feeling guilty about this nonsense and how it had come so far. Or maybe she needed Mason's confident words and actions to straighten her out; for him to be the man, the conqueror who was mentally strong, able, and worthy of his prize.

M ason had had enough of this. The distance, the separation, and the lack of affection; the DVDs, the jacking off, and the false sense of satisfaction as a result. This had all gone far enough for sure, but he still didn't quite know where to begin. He didn't know what she wanted to hear or if his position should change from what it was. So instead of all the deliberating, Mason got undressed and headed to the shower. When he came out with just a towel wrapped around his waist, he wasn't surprised to see Adena lying there the same as before, asleep. Determined, Mason slid under the covers. He eased up to Adena's back, kissed the nape of her neck, and slowly wrapped his arms around her until her body was flush against his.

"I'm sorry, baby," Mason whispered into Adena's ear. "I'm sorry. It's all my fault, and I'll never do it again." Sure, Mason knew that his words were not 100 percent truthful. But, he was following the best advice he had: Bill's suggestion to help smooth things along. Some words to get started with the healing. *Tell her you're sorry, you were wrong, and that you'll never do it again. It works every time,* Bill had told him.

———

Adena pulled Mason to her, which felt normal and familiar. Soon his hands began to wander and to fondle and caress her again. The healing had begun.

"I hate breaking up, Adena, But *oh my God*, making up feels like heaven!"

Adena was still glowing from their long night of healing, repairing, and (in Mason's words) *liberation*.

"It is . . . liberation, Adena. The best kind. See . . . last night, being inside of you took me to the moon, so in a way I was flying. But I also felt freedom. Where I didn't need to lie about me. I could express me to you in my most unmasked, most unconditional state of mind. I could say or do or be me, just as I hope you could. And we don't get to do all of that in public, because the public can't handle it—"

"I know they can't handle *me* right now," Adena added while she bit into her English muffin. Butter had made it down her lip and chin, but Mason caught it before it went farther, reaching across the table with his napkin. "'Cuz I look a wreck right now, how you nearly pulled my hair out."

Mason released a hearty laugh.

"But see, that's *exactly* what I'm talking 'bout. You go outside lookin' like a train hit you, people are just naturally gonna judge you. I guess that's just human nature, really, for people to size each other up based on looks. But in our home we can be as train wrecked as we wanna be and not have to worry about bein' judged."

"Right, right, you're onto somethin', Mason. Keep goin'."

"I—I guess that includes sex, too. I'm not gonna lie. What we do in our home is for us—"

"No matter how nasty?"

"Yes, Adena." Mason figured she was gonna try to corner him. "No matter how nasty. See, now you gotta go to extremes. I was speaking on liberation, and you take it right back to the smut."

"But, baby, haven't you ever heard of sexual liberation? Like, how we are sexual beings. Created by sex, longing for sex, letting go, and, as you say, being who we wanna be? Isn't that what liberation and freedom is all about? Why do we need to have rules, Mason? Why do we have to place limitations on what, how, where, or *who* we do?"

Mason placed his hand over Adena's.

"I'm serious, Mason. Sometimes, you have to realize when I wanna get fucked, I wanna get fucked—*how'd you put it?—unconditionally?* Yeah, that's it. A girl has gotta have it, Mason. I love dick, and I live for dick, so, can't you give me what I need?"

Mason was mesmerized. "You never stop being amazing, Adena. You got a habit—not necessarily a bad habit, but a habit nonetheless. And I don't mean to put that in a negative way, 'cuz, hey, that's what turned me on about you after the feistiness . . . after the sexy looks . . . there was your hunger for sex."

"It wasn't just a hunger for sex, babe, I hungered for you," Adena purred. And she got up to circle the table until she was sitting on Mason's lap.

"I gotcha now. I see your point. And yes, I'm here whenever you need me to satisfy your hunger, as long as it doesn't interfere with work . . . or our good health. But first . . . we gotta talk, Adena."

"About?"

"Just . . . I know you don't wanna hear this, but we *do* need to have some rules."

Adena sighed.

"But listen. It's just simple stuff, like, if we're gonna get nasty, then it should be a *clean* nasty."

"I'll agree. But be specific. What's on your mind?"

Mason huffed. "We can talk about anything, so here goes. . . ." Mason smoothed a hand along Adena's arm and felt her goose pimples. "When we do ass fuckin' . . . whether it's your ass or another woman's ass, those cavities need to be washed, douched, soap, water, the whole nine yards."

Adena'a eyes were smiling, as though she was proud of Mason for being frank and earnest.

"Agreed."

"*Whew.* 'Cuz you know once we're in the act, everything is goin' down all at once, and there's really no room for lectures. Plus, talkin' about shit like this can ruin the whole foreplay bit. How we look talkin' about this stuff while we're tryin' to get our rocks off?"

"It's not like we ever have foreplay, Mason."

"Well, you know what I mean. Next subject. And I said this before. . . ." Mason caressed Adena's cheek with the back of his hand. He was to glad this was going smoothly.

"Baby, Lord knows I love it when you lick my ass, but not all the time. Plus, sometimes I feel some type a way about that. Like, do you feel it's a demeaning thing to do? Or . . . well, what do you get out of it? That would be something to ease my mind. Because, if you don't mind me saying this—"

"Yes?"

"You are the ultimate slut when you're in my ass like you do. You eat that part of me like it's Thanksgiving every time."

"Okay?"

"And I can't help thinkin'—"

"Do you want my answer, or what?"

"Yes, yes. Go ahead."

"I lick your ass because I know that, one, it belongs to me. I'm the first and, if I have my way, the *last* woman to ever go there."

Mason swallowed and his eyes searched hers.

"And number two . . . Mason, I know that turns you on. Yes, I'm your slut when I wanna be. Yes, I can get ghetto and perform like a crack head. But when it comes down to the X-Y-Z, I get lost in giving you pleasure. Every time we're naked, all I wanna do is suck and eat and fuck the livin' daylights outta you."

Mason was too overwhelmed to respond. His reflex was to do

just what he did, grabbed her, hugged and kissed her, and then he lifted her down onto the dining-room floor.

"You're such a fucking crazy nympho, Adena."

"Yeah, but I'm a fucking crazy nympho for you, Mason."

The two kissed, and kissed, and kissed some more until their robes were open once again. His boxers were about the only thing getting in the way, until Adena stripped them off.

"Now that you made your speech, I wanna make mine."

Mason chuckled. "This I gotta hear."

"Last night? That was only part one of our comeback. This morning? This . . . morning . . . is . . . part . . . two." Adena had Mason's hard dick in her mouth once again. But then she suddenly stopped to ask Mason, "You were saying something about sucking your dick too much . . . you . . . want me . . . to stop . . . before it . . . goes too far?"

Adena hardly waited for a reply and her eyes (more or less) told Mason to lie back and enjoy the pleasure. And that's just what he did.

"I love you, Adena. And I'm down with anything you wanna do, even if it *does* border on feeding your addiction."

"You're just saying that because your dick is in my mouth," Adena said, so talented that she could talk and suck all at once. "Now, lay there and shut up, nigga. Momma needs some milk for her coffee."

"I knew there was a reason I loved you," Mason said.


Three months had passed since the Fickles' reuniting. And since their "talk" over breakfast (and thereafter), the two had become more in control of their activities. Yes, they played by the new rules, and yes, Adena used more variety in her impulsive attacks on Mason's body. But Mason also had to give a little, even if he was too tired to perform and had to lie there while Adena took what she wanted. Sure, he might've been out of it, or at a loss for sexual energy.

However, that didn't stop the show. If ever there was a doubt about a man's dick having a mind of its own, Mason's dick was all the proof needed to erase that doubt. There were too many occasions when Mason would be out of it, or even when he was asleep, so Adena would hop on and get what she needed. As long as it was stiff and throbbing, she could reach her climax quota. Adena's hunger was never satisfied.

It was when Mason went to Chicago for a weekend convention for his job that Adena went into withdrawal.

"Mason, do you have to stay until Sunday? Can't you, like, sneak out Saturday afternoon?" asked Adena, from their cozy home back on the mountain.

"You know I gotta be there for the brunch on Sunday. It's the closing ceremonies. Plus, they're giving out awards," Mason explained.

"What if I got you another pussy? Both of us could be waiting for you . . . legs open wide!"

Adena was acting silly on the phone, taking the whole "unlimited nights and weekends" cell-phone offer as far as it would go.

"It don't matter if you got ten pussies and yours was at the head of the list, Adena. I can't come home till Sunday night."

"Okay. That's the right answer," she said. "All right." She sighed. "I guess I'll just have to play with myself till you get home. I'll use my finger."

"Why don't you use the vibrator? It's in the drawer," Mason suggested. "You can leave it in your pussy for the whole night and it'll never get soft."

"I'll— Just get your ass home Sunday, 'cuz I got a surprise for you," Adena warned.

# ten

That entire weekend kept Mason and Adena busy. Mason was, of course, attending seminars regarding mortgages, amortizations, appraisals, and other resources that had already helped him become a star financier in Pennsylvania's blooming real estate market. Meanwhile, Adena had that surprise up her sleeve. And Loween was that surprise.

Loween Brewster came to work at the Days Inn on a summer internship program that evolved into a much longer stay. "An extended stay" is what was printed on the paperwork. But everyone and their mother know the real deal, how Loween was displaced by the devastating Hurricane Katrina and how it cleared the Gulf Coast of most of its residential housing, including where Loween lived.

Loween had been a resident of New Orleans until the so-sudden chain of events. Of course, there was Katrina, but there was also the frightening situation at the Superdome, where emergency housing was set up. Some might say that the scene at the Superdome was worse than the hurricane itself.

A few days of that tragedy was followed by a sort of "damned if you do, damned if you don't" choice offered to people who were left homeless, humiliated by the media with the new little "refugees," and threatened by violence, disease, and loss of hope. That is, these thousands of displaced residents had to find somewhere to go, or they had to hop on one of the buses that were taking folks to sur- rounding states where help was organized. Either way, authorities were warning, "Y'all gotta get the hell outta here." Loween was lucky enough to get an earlier bus to Houston, where the As- trodome was turned into a supershelter. But she then took advan- tage of a job offer from the Days Inn Corporation, promising food, clothing, and housing for those who were willing and able.

"Call me willing 'n' able," Loween said. She didn't even have to think twice when she heard the offer. She just jumped up, grabbed her little plastic bag of Salvation Army handouts, and got a seat on the bus to Pennsylvania. She also realized that she was one of the fortunate ones who had no children. And besides, if she didn't do something soon, her inhaler would run out of gas. It was the last she had to keep her asthma in check. Anything less than this could've left her panting and desperate for air with nowhere to turn. At least now, with a major hotel chain to support her, she could start anew. It didn't matter if it was in Pennsylvania or Timbuktu. So long as she could get a fresh inhaler.

The last asthma attack was preventable, if only because she had kept that backup inhaler on her person. And thank God she'd stuck with that, since Hurricane Katrina had swept away *everything* she owned.

For months, Adena had heard about Loween and how she was getting support from so many. But she never got to meet her in person un- til their schedules changed and they were working the same day shift.

"So, you're the famous Loween? Heard so much about you. Con- gratulations on the quick adjustment and getting back up on your feet. I'm not sure that I coulda got it together as fast as you."

Loween let out a much-deserved sigh.

"You can't exactly shrivel up and call it quits," she said. "Life must go on."

"I know that's right. I'm Adena Fickle. Nice to meet you."

"Loween Brewster. Likewise."

"So, I guess we're gonna be workin' together for a while."

"Guess so," said Loween, "'cuz I'm not goin' anywhere soon."

Adena showed some pride for Loween's presence with a compassionate smile in her eyes.

"So, you mind if I show you my system? It worked real good with my last partner, Lilly. We always got rooms done in record time."

"Uhhh  sure," Loween replied with some hesitation.

"And also, if you don't mind, I'd like to treat you to lunch. Nothin' major—the diner next door."

"Hey, would it be disrespectful for me to turn food down, girl? Sure. And next time I'll treat."

By lunchtime, Adena was praising Loween for *her* system of cleaning rooms.

"Dag, girl. And I thought I had the bomb system."

"You do. But I didn't tell you I used to do this down in N'awlins, ya know." Some of Loween's hometown drawl showed itself when she revisited those days. "Down at the Days Inn down on Canal Street."

"Okay, now it's comin' together. A sista was straight up *ignant* for thinking you was a beginner."

Loween chuckled at Adena's intentional mispronunciation of the word *ignorant*.

"Naw, you aiight. Just know that a storm didn't automatically make me no spring chicken."

"I hear that."

"And that's not the only job I had. I worked at the mall, the convention center, I was a bartender down on Bourbon Street."

"Oh Lawd."

"You said it."

"And the last job I had was at Two Sistas, a little soul food restaurant in the quarters. I sometimes think about them, wonderin' if they made it out."

"They got a place made of quarters?"

Loween let out a big laugh, almost losing some of the turkey melt sandwich she had just bitten into.

"You're so silly."

"No, really," Adena said, in the dark as usual.

"When I say the *quarters*, I mean the *French* Quarters; it's just another section of N'awlins. Just like ya'll got Marshalls Creek and New York City got Times Square, and Los Angeles got Hollywood. It's just a nickname for what people want to be that *special* part of town. Lemme find out you ain't been nowhere, Adena."

Adena turned bashful. "I guess I ain't."

"You real cool, Adena. A girl could use a friend like you just to smooth out the rough edges."

"Well, Loween," Adena reached out and shook her new friend's hand, "just call me Adena—the iron. I do wrinkles, rough edges and creases, but I *don't* do folds."

Both women laughed their hearts out. And then Adena dug deep.

"I hope your family made it outta that Katrina mess safe."

"I really don't have no family, Adena. Neva knew who the sperm donor was who my momma got nasty with. And Momma's locked up somewhere in Colorado."

Adena's eyes could've popped out of their sockets, as much as they opened up.

"Yup. Momma was what they known as the Beast of the South. She ran a ring of bank robbers—all women, from what I saw on TV. And they went bank to bank for somethin' like six years."

"Daaag. That's some real live Jesse James stuff there," Adena said with a mesmerized expression. "Okay, yeah . . . Momma was a big-time bank robber and all that, and she's famous now—been on the *America's Most Wanted* show. Been on them other Court TV cop shows—all that. But when it comes down to it, Momma was a rollin' stone, girl. Plus, what I got to show for it. She's locked up till infinity plus infinity, and I get to live without a momma in my life. She's famous in jail, while I was miserable in foster homes and been switched around from broken family to broken family."

Adena looked apologetic for the dogging she'd done. *There I go again, screwing shit up in a relationship.* Adena was about to share a common thread they had, but, as if Loween could read Adena's mind, she went with her story. And left no stone unturned.

"Naw, it's all right, you was curious. It's cool, really. I'm tellin' you. I done pulled all the good outta all my situations. Even Momma left me with jewels that'll always hang in my mental. Like . . . Momma used to get me ready for school the rough way. I mean rough! Like, *Nigga, get up out that bed an' wash yo' face.* That was what my bum-ass brother had to hear every morning. And me? Momma called more bitches than a kennel of female dogs. *'Bitch, clean them dishes . . . bitch, vacuum that carpet and don't mess a' inch!'* "

"Whoa, whoa, whoa," was Adena's open-mouthed response.

"Oh yeah, no shit. We had it harder when she was home than when we hit the orphan circuit. And plus, they separated me and my dog—my brother was *my dog.* And shit with me just never been the same since."

"I would've never known you had it like that by lookin' at you, Loween. You carry yourself real slick. *Word.* Like you grew up as a princess or somethin'!"

"The girl with the silver spoon in her mouth, I'm not. But I *am* a princess," Loween said. "In my mental, I was always a great person underneath the hard shell. That's why I never stop grindin'. That why I didn't stop to cry on nobody's shoulders or take handouts, or welfare. I'm a goddammed trooper. Gimme some boots, *bitch."*

Adena laughed until her eyes teared. She was seeing some of herself in Loween. And she didn't have to pour out her own history of abandonment and the foster care system or the abuse . . . she didn't have to tell Loween any of that because she knew Loween had lived it, too. The two of them, she swore, would be cryin' fools up in the diner.

*Pick it up, Adena. Pick that conversation up!*

Mason's words were stuck in her mind, something she would lean on from time to time when she needed to turn a negative into a positive.

"So, where you livin' now?"

"Here, still. But I just put a down payment on a studio in East Stroudsburg. I had to find somethin' close till I get my hand on some wheels. Don't think I ain't seen that pretty lil' Lexus you got out back of the hotel."

"Hmm . . . that ain't shit. Don't let the brand name fool ya', matter fact, I'm tryin' to sell soon."

"What's wrong with it?"

"Not a thing. It's just . . . my man and me live up high. And the winter's right around the corner. I swear I ain't tryin' to see another winter without no Jeep."

"Oh, okay. Y'all be gettin' a lotta snow around here?"

"A lot ain't the word. Mother Nature's big-ass dump truck be backin' right up to the Poconos in Pennsylvania, and she be droppin' it like it's hot!"

It was this latest laugh that found the two women looking deeper into each other's eyes. Even if it was for a second, it was a half-second longer than usual.

"Okay," Adena said. "I guess this is where we go back to work for the man."

"I'm right behind you."

The connection between Adena and Loween only got stronger with time. They became an inseparable team, always sharing information, wishing each other the best in good times, and consoling each other during the misery. If schedule changes came around, both women got a jump on the competition and easily made arrangements so that the team would be together. An eight-hour shift could be torture if you didn't spend it with people you liked.

It was because Adena *liked* Loween that she invited her home for dinner with Mason. It didn't have anything to do with sex. Just a friendly get-together for Mason to meet Adena's new friend. And, of all people, it was Mason who opened up Pandora's box. It happened after dinner and before dessert.

"Am I too nosy if I ask what you do in your social hours?"

"Social hours? *Whoowee.* What is social hours? But then again, what's a social *minute*? I can't lie, Mason. After Katrina hit, I became a nun! I ain't met nobody that thrills me, nobody who can pay my bills, and nobody who can rock my world in this town. For real. The men at work all got the same goals, they want to flash fake chains, they want gold and platinum in they mouths, and they even got the nerve to— Do you know I saw some fool-ass nut with chrome spinners on a beat-up, unwashed, discolored Lincoln Town Car?"

The three exploded in a chorus of laughter.

"And it wasn't like the car was partway through some body work. It looked like it was one of those everyday cars that this idiot *depends* on. And you know he thinks he's impressin' somebody with that *ignant* ride!"

Mason weighed in: "You think he had DVD players in the headrests?"

Laughter.

"Now, that's not cool enough for him. His DVD player gots be on the dashboard, plugged into the lighter!"

"And don't forget the hydraulics."

"Oh, *hell* no," said Loween. "Ain't possible! 'Cuz I seen the fender hangin' by its last wire. One more bump in the road and that nigga gon' lose his pants, his shoes, and his ego!"

When they were done laughing, Loween recalled Mason's original question.

"But the reality is that there's not a lot of good men to choose from. I mean, I know they're out there, but how many of the good ones live out here in the Poconos? And then—let's take it a step further. How many of the good men in the Poconos are black, with dental benefits—?"

Adena jumped in with the "hellooow!" and the high-five.

"—And a sense of security? I met a dude a few weeks ago, yeah, I'm not gonna lie; I go on the hunt from time to time—and he was claimin' this and claimin' that . . . he was in law school, played football in college, ran two or three businesses at once, ain't got no kids, and he was drivin' one of those nice shiny red Mustangs, *oooh chil'*, he swore he had it goin' on. But we went to a movie and this nigga got close for too long—long enough for me to get a whiff of that foul breath! *Jesus!*"

Both Adena and Mason traded a sour expression, both of them perhaps interpreting what *foul* might mean.

"But not to judge, not to judge, I gave him the benefit of the doubt. Plus, there was a movie to see, so I went on with the date. I ain't gonna pull the curtains on my evening of entertainment so fast. Anyway, we did dinner after the movie. Nothin' special, just fish-fry night at Perkins Restaurant. But the road to the restaurant was the last time I was gonna get in that jalopy of his. The last. No, I didn't say a peep on the way; a girl was mad hungry, and, again, no sense in pullin' the curtain on my good time. Only thing is, if a nigga's teeth ain't right, if his car is out of order—like there coulda been a ham samich hiding under the seat . . . ham *and* pickles—then do you think for a minute that his house is in order? Or, let's take it two steps further . . . do you think his future is in order?"

Mason and Adena were both wagging their heads in perfect understanding.

"But, let's take it *all* the way there. He's at least thirty pounds overweight, okay. And I'm not judging a book by its cover—fat, skinny, or one-eyed, I'ma give the nigga a chance. But with all that mess I was lookin' at . . . the gingivitis, the funky car, the wicked table manners . . . show of hands, does anybody think for a minute that this nigga washes his ass right?"

Mason and Adena busted out laughing.

"I'm just saying. I really couldn't tell 'cuz I didn't get that close, plus he had some tangy cologne on. But I'll bet every nickel I got that the boy needs a steam cleaning."

"Loween, everybody isn't perfect," Mason said once he stopped laughing.

"But, okay. I'm with you on that. Come to me with your imperfections and I can work with you. I can change a man. *I know I can.* But you comin' to me with a fly ride, a résumé this fuckin' long about how you was in law school, had businesses, whatever. *Nigga, I can ride, I can ride. I'm a trooper!* But I can also see through the lies, fam. Men got game, women got game, too. But if I can see through you lies on the first date? If your picture is getting foggier and foggier by the minute? I ain't trying to deal with it. Too many cons in the world for me to be that next victim. Too many. Plus, I don't know if Adena told you about my background, but Momma was hard-core. She was so hard-core that I'm like tree bark—"

Suddenly, Loween pulled out an inhaler from her purse. She shook it, and turned away from the table to use it. Her measures seemed drastic. Mason and Adena respected the moment, suddenly realizing that Loween was asthmatic and that the device she had was what folks used to keep their breathing normal. It was instances such as these that kept life in proper perspective; where the globe and everything spinning with it came to a screeching halt for some other most-relevant priority.

"Sorry, my condition. When I get all worked up, ya know?" Loween said. "As I was sayin', Momma didn't raise no fool. And I can't afford to lay up with no moron nowadays with all I got on my plate already." Loween scooped up some more food, then drink. "You two all right?"

Mason and Adena were stiff, caught up in their house guest's raw footage.

"Oh yeah—just . . . ahhh, that damned Mustang man."

"Exactly."


Once Loween left the Fickles' home, Adena and Mason resigned for the evening. They talked about Loween and what a strong woman she was. And then Adena came out of nowhere with:

"She's your type?"

"*What?*"

"She is, Mason. I know your taste. You like them pretty, thin, with big tits."

Mason laughed. "Go to bed, Adena."

Adena cuddled up to Mason and whispered in his ear, "Okay, but you're the one who's gonna be dreaming about Loween tonight."

Without turning to face her, he said, "You are *definitely* straight trippin', boo."

And because Mason didn't dispute with Adena about how Loween was his type and how he'd be dreaming about her, Adena caught the bug. She decided that Loween would soon be girl 11.

# eleven

When Mason came home that Sunday night following the Chicago convention, he had no idea what was in store for him. Maybe Adena would have on some sexy lingerie with the peek-a-boo slits; maybe she'd pull out the fur handcuffs after so many months; or there could be an even bigger surprise. Mason had long ago mentioned to Adena how he wanted to revisit that night when she became a belly dancer for him. She'd even taken lessons for the occasion!

Those images of the outfit she wore, the belly necklace, and the way she worked her body never left his mind. And she took it all a step further by incorporating some street dances into her act that really got Mason excited. There was no telling where or how far Adena's imagination would stretch, since their relationship more or less allowed for no limits. They could watch triple-X porn together, they could play master/slave games, and take turns becoming the meal on the dinner table. They even indulged in some bondage episodes that included a degree of torture and pain.

However, none of that could've prepared them for this night. Or the morning after.

"Baby, I'm home! Sweetheart . . . *Daddy's home!*"

The Fickles were living large these days, thanks to Mason's strong financial expertise, and because the Poconos, for a long time, had been an attraction for home buyers to leave the big city and live a better life. Homes and the plots of land they occupied were spacious, with ample front and backyards and infinite views of forests, rivers, and streams. The roads to these homes were smooth blacktop, winding, long, and threatening to swallow a stranger, but embracing expected visitors just the same. Frogs, skunks, raccoons, squirrels, chipmunks, and deer are what you'd find here. You'd sight an eagle or two if you were lucky. All the other animals—the two-legged ones as well—were indoors.

Walking farther into his warm home, Mason focused on Loween, who was standing in the candlelit living room holding a flute of champagne in each hand. He dropped his bags and shed his coat before he could call out to Adena and ask her *what the hell was going on.* The house was feeling a lot like a labyrinth—a darkened, mysterious atmosphere where anything could happen and no one would know. Even the incense was stronger than usual, the candles were livelier, and the air was tighter and more intimate.

"Okay, somebody's got some explaining to do," Mason said. "You're Loween, right?"

"One of these is for you," Loween said as she swept across the carpet toward Mason. She urged him to unhand his travel bag. And he did as she suggested without hesitation. "And yes. It's Loween. And I expect that after tonight you won't ever forget it."

In his other hand was a wardrobe bag, occupied by two suits from the weekend. Loween took that from him, too.

"Make yourself at home," she said, and Mason thought, *It is my home.*

Except, something in Loween's grin, in her strut as he followed her, and by the sheer nightgown she had on, all of it told Mason that indeed, *he* was the one about to be possessed.

"Did my wife put you up to this?"

"Shhh," Loween instructed, raising the flute to her lips. "Just come along. Take a sip. You had a safe flight, I expect. Now it's time to wind down."

Mason stared at Loween. It was as though he were looking at a different person—different from the woman he had met some time ago. And maybe it had something to do with that evil sensuality in her eyes. She was sexy but somehow dead serious about it. Flight or no flight, Mason's dick began to throb.

"Can you at least tell me if my wife is here, safe, somewhere? You know that's something a husband looks forward to after his trip."

"Don't worry. She's fine," she said in that sultry voice. "Now, have a seat . . . let me drop these over here . . . and . . . you don't mind if these come off, do you?"

Loween knelt down in front of Mason and slipped his shoes off. She fondled the bottoms of his feet. More. His dick throbbed *more.*

"I'm sure that you expected to shower this evening, so we've already prepared that for you."

"*We?*"

"Adena and I, silly. Now, relax while I loosen that shirt." Loween removed Mason's glasses and helped him with another sip of champagne. She also took one herself. "See, down in N'awlins, we like to keep things mysterious but lively. And by the look of things," she smoothed her hand down Mason's neck, inside of his partially opened shirt, then down to his . . . "it's quite lively already."

A sigh seeped out of Mason. She had his stiff dick in hand.

"Mmmmm, that's a good boy. Close your eyes and relax. Think of nothing at all. Not business . . . not today . . . not tomorrow. Just be free and let go. Let your mind wonder and imagine and let it say whatever it is you're feeling."

Mason felt hypnotized. Whatever Adena had planned—*I got a surprise for you*—was working like magic. "Okay, easy does it. Easy . . ." One last, slow stroke and she let go of Mason. And it was a good thing because, even with the pants still on, he was about to make a *big mess.*

Loween took Mason's empty glass and discarded it with hers into the blazing fireplace. The breaking glass only added to the intense mood. Then Loween led Mason up and out of the living room.

Even with the jet lag and the champagne buzz, Mason could see that these women had set this up lovely. There were candles everywhere, all of them flickering ever so slightly since there was virtually no movement, none except for these two. Candles on the stair steps, through the halls, and leading through the bedroom, where Mason expected to see his wife.

"Adena?"

"Shhh—not yet," whispered Loween. She was still leading Mason to the master bathroom, where the shower had been running.

Mason smiled, thinking that Adena was in there waiting. He was still while Loween undressed him from head to toe. She slid the curtains back some to guide Mason into the shower. She secretly dropped her gown and followed him in.

In a mellowed-out tone, Mason said, "Adena?"

"Shhh . . . she's comin', Daddy. Let's get you cleaned up first."

And Loween's hands worked even more magic, expertly scrubbing Mason until she was entirely familiar with his body. She also directed his hands along her curves and cavities, and now he was working alone under the warm, constant shower stream. The two were slippery against each other, her back to him, reaching over her shoulder to pull him into their first kiss, allowing his hands to fondle and grope her private world.

She started to jerk him, then stopped. She started and stopped again, and then her foot found a place up high so that she could open herself for Mason, and Mason behaved accordingly. After all, he knew this was all sanctioned by his wife. This was also beginning to feel less foreign with every thorough thrust.

"Take me, Daddy. It's yours," Loween moaned.

Mason let this strange feeling overcome him. If this was *supposed* to feel so wrong, it was working, because it felt like he was cheating. It felt like Loween was taking something that wasn't hers. But indeed it *was* hers. Again and again. He pounded her longer, with that slick, soapy tool he had, until he was on the balls of his feet, reaching for the farthest depth of her.

And then just when it all started to get crazy, the shower curtains were swept open.

"You *bitch!*"

Adena was standing there, angry faced and fully clothed.

"Get the fuck away from my husband!" Adena shouted, but she also reached under the shower's rain and grabbed a handful of Loween's hair.

All Mason could do was stand there frozen. First, the draft had him shivering. Second, his wood-hard dick was throbbing, swollen, and twitching with want for release. *Fuck!*

In the bedroom he could hear Adena and Loween scrambling. There was a smack followed by another smack. Some *bitch this* and *bitch that* expletives. And it sounded like some furniture fell over. All the while, Mason was rushing to rinse the soap and sex from his body, and then he rushed into the bedroom to try to stop hell's fury.

"What the fuck! I thought you two were friends. I thought you had a surprise for me. Adena?"

The two women paid no attention to Mason while they wrestled on the floor, one with hair in her fist, and the other with her neck in a choke hold. The screams and other guttural shrieks were filling the room with just as much violence as the visual drama that progressed before him.

"This is fucking unbelievable!" Mason shouted.

He ran to rescue the women from each other, prying apart

clenched fingers, wedging himself between the two, until he eventually had them propped on the bed and an adjacent armchair, respectively.

"Listen, I don't know what the fuck is going on here, but you two are freakin' me out. And *you*! You oughta . . ." Mason was chewing his words and only threatened to raise his fist at Loween, but some powerful force seemed to hold him at bay.

"You *tricked me!*"

Loween was checking herself, Mason guessed, for any serious injury. Adena, meanwhile, had her face scrunched up in rage.

"How *could* you?" she asked Mason.

"But, *baby*! I didn't know! I promise you! I just came home and—"

Adena held her palm up: *Talk to the hand.*

"Don't say another word," she said, and Mason immediately surrendered control.

After fixing herself, Adena turned to Loween.

"You low-down dirty bitch. No wonder you said it was an *emergency* that you got a new inhaler. You just wanted to get me out the house. You knew exactly when my husband would be coming home and that's how you do me? Your *friend*? I let you use my car, I lent you money, I cover for you at work, and this is how I get treated?"

Mason started to say something.

"No, Mason, you shut up. I don't blame you. I don't. You're just a weak-minded man when it comes down to it. Put a pussy in front of you, and you lose your mind."

"Wait a—" he started to argue.

"I *said*, sit down and shut up!" Addressing Loween again, Adena said, "You wanna fuck my man so bad? Huh? Is that what you want? You want *married* dick?"

Adena went to the corner of the bedroom and knelt down to open a safe. Then she pulled out the inhaler from her purse.

"Now . . . there's your inhaler. If you really need it bad, you'll do as you're told." Adena locked the device in the safe and spun the dial.

Loween looked frantic. "Adena, you didn't. You *know* I need that!"

"Mmm, I know. And I know you'll need it soon. But don't lose hope now. You help me . . . I help you."

Adena had changed from a mad black woman to a mad scientist.

"Help you *what?*"

"Well, shit, you're gonna finish the job you started. Now stop talking, and go fetch me a glass of champagne."

From the expression on her face, it was clear that no one had ever spoken to Loween this way.

"You heard me, bitch. Fetch me some goddamned champagne."

Loween lifted herself up and headed for the kitchen with her naked, scheming ass. In the meantime, Adena began to shed her own clothes.

"Adena, what are you up to? You're gonna *force* that girl to have sex?"

"Why would I have to force her love . . . my loving, faithful husband?"

Mason frowned, at a loss for words.

"Cat got your tongue?" Adena asked, with her clothes now in a pool by her ankles. "See, Mason, tonight you're gonna see how much I really love you. So much so that I'm gonna watch you fuck another woman. And you're gonna do it. *Why?* Because now you owe me. I caught you cold, Mason. Give me this fantasy tonight, and we're even. And you better follow my every instruction, husband."

Adena's words may as well have been restraints holding Mason down on the bed. He was floored by the twisted circumstances, but even more dumbfounded by the way she was controlling everything. And then she had to go and wink her eye as Loween returned with the glass of champagne.

"Your champagne."

"Right . . . and that's the way you serve me? With an attitude?"

Adena made Loween stand there and wait while she dug in her dresser drawer for a wife-beater shirt. She wiggled it on over her perky breasts, her nipples creating stiff, excited impressions through the fabric. Then, Adena turned to Loween, took the glass, and tossed the champagne in her face.

Ignoring Mason was easy. Keeping Loween in check was the challenge here.

"Now, fetch me a glass of champagne, bitch, and do it without the fuckin' attitude."

Loween was wet and shocked. However, her nipples were just as wet and shocked.

"What are you doing, woman? You're buggin'! You are definitely gone, gone off the deep end," Mason said. "I can't believe how you're humiliating this girl! And she needs her inhaler. Adena, don't play."

Adena made a face that said she was about tired of Mason's mouth and Loween's disrespect. She went back into the drawer and pulled out the leather belt. Lord knows, Mason had seen *that* before.

"I'm waiting, Loween. Big, bad, pretty-ass Loween. Bring that pretty ass in here, I got something for ya."

When Loween returned, she seemed apprehensive about giving Adena the second glass of champagne. Her body was still glistening from the first glass. Adena took the glass from her.

"Oh, I see you been wiping it off, huh? Who told you to wipe it off? What if I wanted to see my husband *lick* it off?" Adena gestured as though she were about to toss bubbly number two.

Loween flinched, anticipating the worst. But instead, Adena just gulped the champagne down.

"Psych!" Adena laughed so hard and loud she almost choked. Then she pointed to the bed. "Now, you obedient whore, you wanted married dick? Well, there he is. And you didn't even need to sneak around like the devious bitch you are. You can go ahead and fuck him right in front of me. Go fuck 'im."

Loween went to climb onto Mason, but Mason wasn't ready. His dick was far from hard.

"Oh, don't worry, boo. His dick has a mind all its own. Give it a little taste and watch it rise, watch it rise, *watch it rise!*"

Mason wagged his head, wondering if Adena was up to something.

Meanwhile, Loween grabbed Mason's limp meat and began to massage it. She wasn't watching Adena, so she didn't notice her ready the leather belt. Adena's arm cocked back as if she pulled at the cord on an outboard motor, and her contact with Loween's bare ass was just as abrupt.

"Ouch!" shouted Loween. And she moved right out of her position, how her knees had been curled up under her with her ass exposed and facing Adena. Now she was rubbing her sore spot.

"Uh-uh. Keep strokin' that dick, girl. Ain't nobody told you to stop."

Mason had quickly grown an erection. Whether it was the Loween touch or the sight and sounds of the belt, Adena couldn't tell. But there was so much more to come, so much more for Adena to get off her chest.

"I see you don't want your ass facing me no more. I thought I was your girl. I thought we could trust each other." Adena reached over and pulled N'awlins' finest so that it was back in position. "And a nice ass you got, too. I never got to see you this way, Lo-Lo . . . *Hey!* That's a nickname! Lo-Lo, for how low down and dirty you are." Without warning, Adena went from caressing, touching, and stroking Loween's ass to her second strike.

"Ouch!"

"Well, shit! What do you expect? A fucking award? You expect me to award you for tryin' to snatch up my husband? Huh? Aw, no you don't. Get that ass back here. I'm not done witcha. And don't forget . . . the inhaler is a few feet away," Adena whispered close to Loween's ear. "I can get that lickety split." Still with a hand stroking the hot spot on her victim's behind, Adena raised the belt again. Loween flinched.

"No, boo . . . I'm just kiddin'. Psych! I don't wanna hurt you, ma, I just want you to be our plaything tonight. I want you to pay dues. Now . . . take that dick in your mouth."

Loween's expression was still a nervous one, but she did as she was told, and not an amateur with it, either.

"You like that, Mason? You like the work she's doing, or the work I'm doin' on this ass?" Adena, without the belt this time. She smacked Loween on the other cheek, the cheek that had yet to be assaulted. No cry this time, just a whimper as Loween's mouth sucked up and down on Mason—Adena's property.

"Sorry. I couldn't resist. It's just, your ass is so hot. Like, I'm sure every man on the East Coast would wanna work with something like this all-chocolate pleasure I'm lookin' at." Another smack. Another strong whimper.

"How's she doin' over there, hubby?"

Mason had this confused look about him, possibly seeking more assurance from Adena. *Tonight you're gonna see how much I really love you.* But those words were almost forgotten now, with how Adena pushed things up a notch with the belt, the blow job, the psychotic instruction.

"Or should I ask her? How's it goin', boo?"

Loween pulled her lips form the job at hand and a rich *pop* resulted.

"It's going good," said Loween.

Smack!

"That's what I'm talkin' 'bout! But keep suckin' that dick, ain't nobody told you to stop. Now I asked you—" again with a smack on Loween's ass. Then she went to hold her head so she wouldn't stop sucking to reply. "I can't hear you, Lo-Lo."

And Loween answered Adena as best she could with a mouth full of Mason meat.

"What was that? It's what?" Adena still held the girl's head in place, so the reply was both distorted and gobbled.

"Don't you love that, Mase? She can talk and suck dick at the same time!"

"Adena, you're buggin'!" Mason tried to speak casually, but he stammered with his speech. And that was all his wife needed to hear.

"Get off a him. I don't need him to come yet. There's other things to do."

Loween wiped her mouth and asked, "Please, can I have—"

"*Hell no, bitch.* You get it when I tell you can get it. Now. On the floor. Hands and knees. Do it." Adena, the drill instructor, fixed the leather belt around Loween's neck as one would a leash on a dog.

"See, when I say bitch, I mean bitch, You are a bitch . . . a *dog* . . . and . . . now you're my dog. Now—" Adena pulled the belt tight, surely in control of Loween's head and neck, and so the rest of the body followed as she walked her bitch around the bedroom, then the hallway and through a portion of the house.

"You need to video this, Mason!" Adena's voice carried through the residence, her arena for this torture. When they returned to the bedroom, master and slave, Adena pulled her pet so that she was back on the bed.

"Where you goin'?"

"The bathroom," Mason said. "I gotta pee."

Adena wanted to say something and stopped Mason with her hand to his chest.

"Wanna pee on her?" Adena laughed, laughed, and laughed some more, but she also let Mason proceed to the toilet. At laughter's end, Adena said to Loween, "I'm bein' a sweetheart right now. Trust. Things could get a whole lot more wicked tonight. Best thing for you to do is obey, get your inhaler, and then you can get the fuck away from my man, for good. Until then? You're mine."

Mason heard all of this over his stream of urine—the champagne leaving his body. He shook and wiped himself, flushed, and was back in the bedroom standing over these two warped women.

"What now, baby? Let's get this over with."

"It's far from over, baby. Plus, we need him to be at attention again." The leash was jerked and Loween was on her knees.

"Suck it."

She did. And like magic, Mason became a hard rock again.

"This is gettin' boring," warned Mason.

"Oh it is?" Adena chuckled. "You ain't seen shit yet."

Within minutes, Mason was laying face-up on the bed. Loween was sitting on him with his dick filling her wet spot, while Adena straddled his face with hers. All the music that was created came from skin slapping, tongue lapping, and Loween's cries, whenever Adena twisted her nipples or smacked her face. Face-to-face the two women sat, both grinding away at Mason's mouth and nether region. Whenever Loween appeared to shudder, Adena pulled the choker to snap her out of it. If anybody was gonna come first, it was the master!

Meanwhile, Mason was eating rough times from Adena's pussy. Of course, the two had been here before, with the wife sitting on the husband's face. But this was nothing like that. Nothing sensual or erotic. More like demanding and raunchy. Loween was about to come again, it showed in the way her face was twisting, and her eyes fluttered between open and closed.

"No-no. *Hell* no. Get off of 'im," commanded Adena. And she emphasized with the pull on the leash. But Loween didn't seem to want to get off, so Adena smacked her face. No attention was paid to Mason, whose face was one step from suffocation. Loween lifted herself so that she was in a squat, dripping wet over Mason's dick.

"It's good you're wet, baby. Because now I need your *ass* on his dick." Adena looked behind her, back at her husband. "You cooperate back there, you hear?"

Loween lowered her squat and didn't seem to mind about the ass fucking she was about to receive, since all she could've wanted was for her empty cavity (*any* empty cavity) to be filled again. It was a different face now, a tormented face with some pain and agony showing.

"I like this; I hope it hurts *real* good. I hope his dick is too big for your tight ass. I hope it reaches up your ass to your throat, you triflin' tramp! Fuck her asshole, Mason."

And then something must have popped in Adena's head, because she began to shiver and her body froze and shook and broke into a fit of rage. Back and forth, she was working her grind on top of Mason's mouth, nose, and chin. His whole face was a wet mess, her rapid movement punishing his lips and tongue.

"I'm—coming! I'm co-om-ing!"

More rapid grinding, like a race had to be won, like life or death was the issue. Like . . .

"Oh my God! Mason, Mason, Mason!"

Adena's ranting was no less than a wild pony ride, until she fell forward, her face lying against Loween's chest. She seemed satisfied and exhausted; both. There was a fixation on Adena's face as she moved her pussy from her man's mouth. It was a moment that made for an uncertain near future. Was this the end? Would Loween be dismissed?

"Did you come yet?"

"I'm lucky if I can still breathe," replied Mason.

Adena sucked her teeth. She wasn't trying to hear that shit.

Meanwhile, Loween was still—still, with the peg in the hole. The wincing on her face had eased, maybe that she was comfortable right here and now.

"Loween, my man didn't come yet."

Mason interrupted, "I'm good, Adena. Really."

"No, you're really not, boo. This night isn't about me. It's about you two!" Adena got off of the bed, let go of the leash so that it fell to Loween's side and still hung off of her neck. "So, I'll appreciate it if you both can finish while I watch. I want you to come first, Mason. You *have* to come, and I *have* to see it. That's the only way I'll get satisfaction, baby. Don't you understand?" Adena reached for the glass, still with a smidgen of champagne left. When she got up the energy, she went to fetch her own bubbly.

"And I wanna hear you! Sounds effects are important!"

"Be easy, Mason. I'm sure we're about through," said Loween. "You know the combination to the safe, don't you?"

Mason nodded.

"Maybe I can—"

"*I can't hear you!*" hollered Adena in her wicked singsong voice.

"Shit. She's coming. Come on, Mason. Work with me here. Can you come?"

"I'm trying. Trust me," Mason grieved.

Loween began to get more into it, working her ass in circles, up and down, heaving forward with her breasts dancing against Mason's chest. Her hair hiding his face. Her face hiding the pain.

"Good. Good. Good! I like! You two were really made for each other. Really."

"Fuck me, Mason. Fuck me!"

"Oh, shit now, Momma. This is lookin' too much like pleasure! Get down!"

Loween must've been too caught up to realize that Adena had ordered her to stop. Then she pulled on the leash.

"I said, off, bitch." The choke hold on Loween's neck had her fall over, off the bed and onto the floor. Now, there was a different kind of pain.

"Ow!" Loween had fallen awkwardly, and her leg was somehow gashed by the heel of Adena's shoe.

"Oh, shit. Do I see blood? Oh, okay. Better not get no blood on my carpet. Mason, come rub her leg."

And he did, crawling off the bed to where Loween was curled on the floor.

"You are blowin' my fuckin' high, girl. Mason, stand up." Adena finished her drink. "STAND THE FUCK UP!"

"But I hardly touched her leg. She's still hurt!"

"Okay, so I guess what. That's the name of this game, Mason—she hurt me, you hurt me, and now I hurt you both. Now, if you love me, you'll stand there. And you—" Adena with the choker again. "On your knees!"

There seemed to be a renewed anger in Adena. A new fit of rage. Mason wondered if she didn't have something else with her champagne.

"Now, Lo-Lo. Suck his dick." Adena knelt there beside Loween, inspecting the blow job. She even took Loween's head in her hands and forced her mouth over Mason so that his wet and nasty dick went where it was supposed to.

"I can't do this," Mason said. And he backed up out of reach. The two women remained there on their knees, listening. "I just can't do this. You're committing a *crime*. First of all, forcing this woman—this beautiful woman!—to perform sex."

"I don't think she's that beautiful," Adena said.

"Shut up. SHUT UP! Second, this shit is gettin' gross. You whipped the shit out of her with the belt, you got me fuckin' her pussy, her ass, now her mouth—"

Mason didn't catch this, but Loween and Adena shared a long stare, altogether ignoring him. And while he was carrying on recalling the rough evening *he* was having, the two embraced in a steamy, sloppy tongue kiss.

"What the *fuck*!" Mason just about lost his mind through his words. Like he was spitting out his brains. It was obvious that this kiss was a willing one, with Loween's hands smoothing Adena's ass, and Adena's hand combing through Loween's hair. A moment later, the two were hee-hawing, laughing, and pointing at Mason with the whole *gotcha* grins across their lips.

"OH, YOU MUTHAFUCKAS!" Mason's eyes were tearing. He couldn't believe he'd been had and tricked. In his mind now he was rewinding the tape, jumping to conclusions as to how things had progressed and how he'd fallen right into the trap!

"And you even hit the nail on the head, Mason. Right after you stepped through the door—*Did my wife put you up to this?* You said it and I almost kissed your ass for figuring this out so soon, 'cuz I didn't think it would work!"

Now, Adena cackled.

"But she convinced me. Your *loving wife* was correct. You fell for it. The whole inhaler plot. The safe. Wow." Loween's eyes now teared from the excitement.

"You two seem to be forgetting something," Mason said, suddenly no longer entertained. "You're forgetting to SUCK MY MUTHAFUCKIN' DICK!"

# twelve

The pretending was over with. Of that Mason was sure. Now he was in charge. Another glass of champagne for everyone helped to raise the threshold of anything-goes excitement. And no sooner did Mason order both women to their knees, taking turns with his dick brushing their gums and tongues.

Now, he could be the disgusting one. Now, his acts were sanctioned and warranted and justified. Now, he felt good and full of himself and, of course, engorged as these two healthy, able women sucked and gobbled. Back and forth he drove his stick, in one mouth, then the other.

"Okay, you first."

Now it was in one pussy, then the other. Relentlessly, he pounded Adena for being naughty, and then Loween—Lo-Lo—for being conniving. This was payback! Earlier, all the devious acts had prevented Mason from having an orgasm. But not now. Now, he intended on shootin' a load that would drown these two for their sins against him. There was an instant when Adena was challenging Loween—who could give the best blow jobs. And the mood changed from Mason's want for revenge to a contest between two very capable vixens.

Adena's mouth was a gutter. She washed Mason's dick with everything she had, swabbing it generously, and gagging when she took his full length down her throat. But Loween had a trick for this occasion. She took Mason's dick down her throat for twice as long. And to add a soundtrack to the pleasure, she was humming and depraved, making underwater gurgling sounds with her mouth.

The challenge went on for at least another thirty minutes, until the defining moment. Mason's head was spinning, but he was at least aware that his dick was submerged deep in Adena's pussy. At least, he thought it was hers. Hard to tell, with all that was happening—his orgasm threatening to push out of his body. Loween licking his ass like the juicy lollipop it became. Adena panting and mooing like a cow as Mason drove his dick into her asshole. Loween on her knees under the married couple, working Mason's ass, then his balls, then slipping his dick from Adena's hole until the only thing Mason remembered was gagging, gagging, gagging. It made him force it—the sounds, the excitement, the euphoria. It was all he needed to explode—a mile-long river of his cream surging through him into some warm, wet, wanton receptacle. He came so hard it felt like peeing.

Lights out. Darkness. An abyss pulling him ever so deep into a world beyond his own. Lifeless, thoughtless, nothingness, and numbness—Mason was all of these at once, drifting from satisfaction all the way into the dead zone. The dead zone. The dead—

A dena screamed.

"Oh my God, oh my God, ohmigod!" Her hands and arms were everywhere, flailing about with enormous energy.

Mason was still groggy. "Would you stop yelling? God!"

Again, Adena screamed.

"She's dead, she's dead, she's dead! Ohmigod!"

Mason finally opened his eyes and was jolted by what he saw. Loween's frozen face was turned toward him, blue and purple bruises flushed her skin. Her mouth was open as he remembered from the night before, like she got stuck on the first note of "Amazing Grace." On her lips and face was his semen.

Adena was curled up in their bed, sobbing within her upturned palms.

If Mason was dizzy earlier, he was delirious now. *What the fuck!* He could never imagine something like this happening.

*How did this happen, Mason? No, you can't just shrug this one off. What did you remember? What part did you play in it? Did what—? Did the excitement go to her head? What a question! It doesn't look like her fault, Mason. It looks like your fault, to tell you the truth. It looks like you choked her, Mason; no, Adena didn't choke her with your come! Jesus Christ, nobody chokes to death on come! And oh . . . the belt around her neck, the life-saving inhaler locked in the safe? You murdered her, punk! You and your sex addiction are goin' to the pokey, punk! See if they like your candy cream in the slammer. Better yet, see if you like theirs!*

He remembered Bill Clemons's words: *You're a grown-ass man doin' teenage things, Mason. . . . Too much of anything, even sex, can kill you.* And there was the bell-ringing, flag-raising advice that *really* stuck in his head: *Do something now, before it's too late . . . before it's too late . . . before it's too late.*

Mason wanted this to be a daydream, but it wasn't something he could make disappear, Loween's dead body was very real.

Adena was no less than a frightened cat curled up in the corner. Her nerves of steel had fled. For God's sake. Loween—her friend for a month—was dead in her bedroom. That woman, so full of life, hope, and drive, a woman who had climbed up from rock bottom to a place in the world where she could see again. Where she felt she could belong. She was now gone from the world, never to experience the success that was destined to be hers, never to have the children she so wanted to bring into the world, into a better life than she'd been dealt.

Plagued with those dreams and goals that Loween had shared with her, Adena felt marked, just because she was somehow responsible; because she was the closest association Loween had in all the world. And she felt guilty to have set this whole mess up—the ménage à trios, and bamboozling her husband to the degree that he would avenge himself, however unintentionally, with the blow job of death. All of this weighed on Adena's mind until it felt as if she were spinning mercilessly.

"We have to do something, Adena. We have to think. We have to plan."

Adena's eye twitched. She couldn't even think.

"What's there to think about, Mason? She's dead. My friend is dead. I can't believe it." Adena collapsed into more sobs.

"Calm down, baby. Please. Crying can't help us now." Mason scooted over on the bed, held his wife and rocked her shivering body.

Adena mumbled into his chest, "Does she have to keep lookin' over here like that? It's like she's takin' it out on us with her eyes or somethin'. Somethin' like, you both know you wrong for this!" Indeed, Loween's eyes had yawned into their wide, frozen state. And she happened to be positioned in such a way that she stared at the couple with intense depth.

"Okay, that's enough." Mason snatched whatever sheets he could get hold of, and he threw them over the body. If he was the one in control now, then that ghastly blue and purple face would never be seen again.

"We gotta call somebody, Mason. We gotta—"

Mason put a hand over Adena's mouth. And this was the part of the marriage where love, honor, and obey was tested.

"Adena. It would help if you didn't think out loud right now. *Call somebody.* What're you, mad? Who the hell we gonna call? Po-po? So they can lock us up?"

"Us?"

"Yeah, us! What the fuck? You think they just gonna take our word about what happened? *Oh gee, mister officer, we drank, we fucked, and she chocked to death.* OH HELL NO, Adena! They'd have our asses in handcuffs before the next raindrop falls. And if you didn't notice, it's raining cats and dogs outside."

"Well, what then, whadda we do, Mason?"

"I'm not sure," Mason said, staring into space. "That's why I say we gotta have a plan. Gotta think this out. But you—you gotta think to yourself if you're gonna come up with an idiotic suggestion like that again." Mason got up. "Lemme get a quick shower. In case you didn't notice, you and I smell like four hours of sex."

Adena sat there, listening to the ticking clock on the wall, the constant rainfall beating on the windowsill, the infrequent truck or car making its lone journey down or up the single lanes of Route 409. Folks would be heading to work about now, or they'd be off and running on that serious commute for those who merely laid their heads in the Poconos but who worked in Jersey, New York, or Philly. Adena considered work; her first day of the week would begin tonight and she wouldn't have her buddy to work that "system" they worked so well.

Another shiver, and Adena thought about the forest right outside their home, stretching almost endlessly.

Breaking Adena's spell, Mason hollered from the shower, "I'm just about done! Come on. Get ready."

Mason knew there was no time to waste. He went into the bedroom and was already pulling on his pants. "I'll be right back," he said.

"Where are you goin'?"

"Outside for a minute. No big deal. Just get that shower on, please."

Mason then slipped on his Phat Farm sneakers and left the room to do what he did best.

An assessor by trade, Mason often calculated situations and people. If you answered one of those ads in the *Daily News* about living in your "brand new home" for "little or no money down," then chances were that a percentage of you would be directed to Mason Fickle for that very first home loan. And once you'd explained to him what the combined annual salary was for you and your significant other, then bip-bap-boom, Mason would tell you what you could and could not qualify for. Right before he accepted your application fee, then got you qualified for the loan. It's what he did.

However, one possibility he would never rule out was the most impossible of occurrences, such as all things that might be considered absolutes. That was what kept him thinking and solving problems. It's what kept him curious, and what challenged him to sometimes take risks outside the box he lived in. Outside the box: like moving away from the big city without a plan, but then easily achieving his dreams. Outside the box: proving himself to be an "earner" so that he could be promoted to a top executive position with a major corporation. Outside the box: moving into a quarter-million-dollar home and finding the woman of his dreams.

And yet, so "outside the box" was Mason living, so comfortable with achievement and progress and living his dreams was he, that he got caught slippin'. The risk taker, Mason, with his contentions that *anything was possible,* was the very vise grip that held him captive today. And it was also the very consideration that he neglected to consider when he came home from Chicago—when he stepped through the door and saw Loween in her sheer nightgown. Bottom line: This could've been avoided.

It was a little chilly outside this morning and the rain didn't seen to want to stop. It had been raining for three days straight already; rain-related deaths were reported on CNN. The Fickle home sat high up on a hill, fortunately, a distance from the busy roads in town, and even from civilization, it sometimes seemed.

Mason did little to brave the weather as he strolled out on the yard, his footfalls soaking into the soft earth, and he assessed the surroundings. The rain didn't stop the broad daylight, the cricket that was singing solo, or the faint hum of traffic that Mason knew came from I-90. And yet, no matter how peaceful and serene, these were the elements of this mysterious morning, the haunting melody that ushered in a woman's death and the scene of a murder.

*"As far as the eye can see."* The sales pitch that Mason remembered hearing from the real estate broker when he first came to view the plot of land where the house was being built. That quote sounded amazing then. Only now, considering how a dead woman was in his midst, this "spacious" piece of land, as well as the colonial built on it, had sudden limitations. Properties to the left and right, and even the property being built across the street, were all too close for comfort. Was anybody out here last night? Did someone happen to be strolling along, trespassing in the yard, and maybe overhear the screams, horse howls, cries, and commands during the twilight hours?

However unrealistic, Mason couldn't help but come up with a list of unforeseen possibilities. Even the deer that infrequently called the Fickles' lawn its home and the two eagles that could sometimes be seen were all suspected witnesses. Yes, these were all crazy, insane ideas and possibilities, but how crazy and insane a possibility is it for a man to kill a woman with his dick? And besides, there had been many nights when Mason was hard at work at his dining-room table, crunching numbers for some dreaded deadline, and he happened to feel someone watching through those patio doors. Sure, it was a sense of paranoia. But it was black as ever out there beyond those patio doors. And even though his motion detectors were supersensitive and would glow up his yard the instant there was any substantial movement out there, Mason still couldn't help imagining the worst-case scenario. He still couldn't help thinking that someone was out there looking, plotting, and hating on his success.

## Mortgage Banker Wins Award and Promotion
## at Allentown, Pa.

The annual C. Rene Chester Award was conceived as a means for recognizing the one person of the Mortgage Bankers Association of the Poconos who has contributed the most for the advancement of both the homebuyer and the mortgage industry. This year, that award has been given to Mason Fickle. Mason, a thirty-two-year-old Philadelphia native, moved to the Poconos area just over five years ago, and in five years' time he has earned an enormous amount of respect from his peers industry-wide. As a MBAP board member, as well as an area sales manager for East Stroudsburg Mutual, Mr. Fickle has almost single-handedly changed the practice of mortgage lending with his skills in coordinating hundreds of loan packages for minorities who have had difficulties acquiring their first homes. He has also strengthened government relations, initiated financial collaborations between private lenders and local governments, and has launched the ever-popular Poconos Living Expo, a yearly event that draws thousands of home owners from the tri-state area. Mason Fickle has also earned a recent promotion to Executive Director of Mortgage Acquisitions, a position that will give Fickle even more leverage in his quest to help home buyers find affordable housing.

To Mason, the story in last year's *Pocono Record* performed like more of an announcement than good reporting. But Mason was nonetheless overwhelmed, thinking the article was a good thing for local notoriety. At least the locals, whether they were bikers who heard a rumor, or candle makers whispering behind his back, would know who he was and what his constitution was. Not that it would encourage others, whites especially, to look at him any differently—like maybe he was indeed a contribution to the neighborhood and not a liability. No, it might take some sensitivity training for that to be a reality.

Meanwhile, the locals weren't the threat Mason was keeping in the back of his mind. Who he had in mind as a potential threat were the haters from his past, or the high-tech burglars of today—both of them groups of smart alecks whose job it was to research newspapers, and to red flag a comeuppance of a person like Mason. And maybe they'd dig further into his personal records, find his prestigious home, and zero in on the best time to execute a home invasion. Was *that* so impossible? Of course, much of the Poconos was unsettled, a kind of final frontier with plenty of acreage that had yet to be occupied. And such expansive, isolated roads were the only means to get to or from these areas. But, in the words of the legendary Glen "Golden Boy" Cooper, "You never could know."

# thirteen

Back in the bedroom, now with a clear idea about what he might do, Mason deliberated about handling the body—wood chipper or burial?

"Baby, that you?"

"No, it's Loween. She's lookin' for part two. Of course it's me. Open up."

"You don't have to talk to me that way."

"Well then, don't ask questions you already know the answers to." Adena peeked out of the bathroom enough for her head and breasts to show. All she gave Mason was the look. "Watch it there, we already got one dead body in here."

Mason pursed his lips. "Glad you can have jokes at a time like this, Adena. She's your friend."

"Was."

"Whoa! What was in *that* shower?"

"Listen, I cried my cry. And I really do feel bad for Miss Loween. But ain't nobody goin' to jail, or even close to it, just for one night of fun. For real."

"Well, all righty then, I have an idea. Let's get the fireplace started. Let's gather all her things"—Mason was already going for the clothes on the corner chair and the purse underneath—"and adios."

"Hold it," Adena said. And she went for the purse.

"Now you are just too minority for me," Mason said.

Adena sucked her teeth as she picked through the purse.

"I'm just curious, Mase. You picked through my purse many times when we first got together, so, don't front."

"What? And how would . . . how *could* you possibly know that?"

"Mason, you were so insecure when you met me. Please. And then, soon as I put it on you—I mean *really* put it on you—you got all comfortable. You started dressin' better, takin' better care of yourself with the workouts and the noni juice. . . ." Adena had Loween's wallet now. She peeped at her ID. "Damn, she got a ugly high school picture."

Mason was ready to shout back at Adena about the idea that she was responsible for his personal growth, but: "We're gonna continue this conversation where it left off," he said in a warning tone. And he now looked at the photo.

Adena sucked her teeth and mumbled, *"Whatever,"* under her breath.

"High school photo ID card. Why would she still have her high school ID in her purse?"

"Beats me. I ripped that shit up the day I graduated," Adena said, and she snapped her fingers in a circle.

"OH SHIT! Oh—no."

"What?" Adena asked cluelessly.

"Look at the birth date, Adena. No wonder she still had her ID from high school! She was barely out of high school herself! Plus, her name ain't Loween. It's Cynthia." Adena did some quick adding in her head, but Mason cut through all the red tape. "She's seventeen. Adena. Seven*teen*. Lord heaven's mercy."

Adena stared at him in wide-eyed shock.

"This shit is bananas! Adena, how could you?"

"I *ssswear* I didn't know, baby! You gotta believe me. Please, please look in my eyes and tell me you believe me. I did—not—know. She carried herself like a grown-assed woman. I mean, we talked nearly every day and she *never* said she was seventeen."

Mason did more of his deliberating, hand under his chin and staring into outer space. For now, outer space was that painting of Miles Davis on the bedroom wall.

"Baby, we gotta do somethin'. I'm gettin' the creeps with her layin' there. Plus, something is startin' to smell stink."

Mason pulled his wife to him.

"I thought I had before," Mason said. "But I *definitely* have a plan now. No police, no morgue, nobody can know about this except you and I, Adena."

Adena nodded.

"No. Now, you gotta promise me better than that. This is our lives on the line. Our futures. You gotta swear on everything you love. You can't say a word to friends at work, not to Barbara at the salon—*nobody.*"

"Okay, okay. God. I got you, boo." Adena put her arms around Mason. "I swear I got you."

"You betta. 'Cuz this here? This counts as a sex crime. No matter how you slice it, Adena. And if you tuned into any kind of news broadcast today, you'd know that it's a rap—it's over for you even if you're *charged* for a sex crime. Never mind if you're found guilty. They got it so your name and face are all over the country. And nobody, not even *me,* wants sex offenders livin' near them. Plus, plus, *plus!* Do you know what that would mean for my job? My awards and all the hard work I put into getting people homes? Do you know what that would *mean?*"

Mason grabbed his wife's shoulders in his firm grip. His eyes turned apologetic.

"Adena, it's *over* for me. For us. We'll lose our jobs, the house, the cars. Our lives are finished." Mason shook his head. "I can't believe how one minute I'm an honest, hardworking citizen . . . all I do is help people. And the next minute I'm duckin' a lynching." He sat on the bed.

Adena pulled his head to her chest. "It's gonna be all right, Mase, you gotta believe that, 'cuz I need you. I need you in my life and I need you to be strong."

Mason shook his head again.

"Yes, yes, yes, Mason. Take some of your own advice. In control, not *out* of control. That's right, baby. Breathe in—breathe out. Things are gonna work out fine."

Mason eventually turned toward the late Loween Brewster.

"Finish getting dressed so you can help me," he said.

The two of them pulled the bedding together so that it wrapped Loween's body. Adena made a face. "*Ewww*! Now I know what that stank smell is." She pointed to a dark spot that had soaked through the sheets. "It's a *shit stain*, Mason." Adena's body appeared to shiver, maybe shaking the image from her mind.

"Come on, wrap it tighter," said Mason, trying to keep his wife focused. "Now, pull the blanket."

The Fickle conspiracy was off to a blazing start. They carried the corpse to the kitchen, near the patio door.

"I'm gonna go get the truck ready."

"We're gonna bury her, right, Mason?"

Mason stopped dead in his tracks. He looked Adena over with the most incredulity he could muster. He mumbled, "It's no use," as though Adena were a jug head and would never quite get the point. Mason then went about the task at hand.

A lone in the kitchen—alone with the body, that is—Adena's hungry stomach began to grab at her.

Encouraged, she went to the fridge. It was a full house in there, and still Adena couldn't decide on anything satisfying. In the back of her mind had to be that question: *What food feels right in the presence of a dead person?* She inevitably decided against anything too filling—no meat, nothing crunchy or slimy—and settled for a small branch of seedless grapes. Fruit is mostly water, Mason had explained over and over again. And here she was, following his advice. She didn't even like grapes, which goes to show what one will do while under the gun.

"We're under the gun here, Adena." Mason only now realized Adena was feeding her face. "Oh, excuse me for interrupting breakfast. Will there be a second course?"

"Oh, shut up and let's get on with it."

"Okay. Here's the plan. We're gonna move her to the truck. We're gonna—"

"Do you have to call her a *her*? She's an "it" now, Mason. *It* is a corpse. *She* died last night."

"Are you quite through?" Mason asked.

And Adena flashed a phony smile.

"Okay. One, two . . ."

The doorbell rang. They locked eyes and nearly dropped the body.

Mason whispered, "Get down," and she pulled the patio door closed. "Stay down, Adena."

Mason duckwalked through the house in an effort to see and not be seen. There was a short shadow rocking in place behind the stained glass to the right of the front door.

The bell rang again.

Mason cursed at the idea of having so many windows. It had been a good idea at one time. As if the person behind the door knew just how to zero in on Mason, the shadow moved for a nearby living-room window. A person would have to walk through the immaculate landscape and flowers in order to do that.

Mason cursed his visitor.

"Hello?" A man's voice, muffled, deep, with a hint of sugar.

*Maybe it's the phone company,* Mason guessed. The lines had gone haywire since the strong rain, and the phone company had posted notices. Besides, who else would have the *audacity* to walk through the flowers?

"Who is it?" Mason asked without opening the door.

"Sid Williams. Er, uh, may I talk to the owner of the house?"

*A salesman. Only a salesman asks for the owner of the house!* Mason didn't mind opening the door to chase the guy away. Plus, the truck was still running out back—work to do.

"Listen, my friend. Don't mean to be rude. I'm sure you have some fine product or service to sell me, but—" Mason looked down.

"Um . . . I'm sorry to intrude. But, well, I feel a little uncomfortable about this—"

Mason couldn't believe he was facing a man in a wheelchair. That was number one. Number two, he didn't walk through the flower bed. *He rolled?* Mason wanted to curse the guy out so bad, but there was a compassion that overcame him, despite the issues at hand.

The man softened his approach when he saw that Mason was uninterested in letting this unwanted visitor in from the rain.

"Okay, well . . . I have this friend? Uh . . . well, she might've come to visit you recently. I was wondering if—"

"Who *are* you?"

"I told you, Sid. Sid Williams. And I have this friend, Cynthia. You might know her as Loween, like everybody else. But she's always been Cynthia to me. But sometimes when we're actin' silly—"

Wheelchair Sid just kept talking and talking, but Mason could only think one thing: *Loween. Loween, who is sometimes Cynthia? Jesus fuckin' Christ. The shit keeps getting deeper.*

"—So, I call her by her nickname. That's her nickname, Loween. Hope I'm not interruptin' nothing real important." Wheelchair Sid poked his head left, then right, trying to get a peek past Mason standing in the doorway. "That would be a shame, wouldn't it. Can't have that, a stranger knockin' on your door. When you're busy. Hope Cynthia's in, 'cuz I sure can't seem to find her nowhere else. Cynthia, you there? *Cynthia?*" Again, Wheelchair Sid attempted to poke into the house.

"Uh, mister? Mister?" Mason took a much-needed deep breath before he said, "Really, you have the wrong house, wrong number, wrong *everything*. Really. Now, I'm sorry, but I gotta . . . a . . . a pot on the stove. Go on like a nice man."

"Name's Sid." And Sid's eyebrows cut into a V. Mason done got Sid upset.

"Okay, Sid. Well. I'm sorry I can't help you. Hope you find your friend, whatever her name is. Bye now."

Mason was almost rude. Sid had rolled his wheelchair forward so that the front wheel would cross the threshold. He leaned forward some in his chair, trying to get a better look-see. Mason wanted to kick the man, wheelchair and all. But he realized the guy was a bit disturbed, not to mention legless.

"Listen, dude!" Mason, with the tough talk.

"Raise up, lover man. I ain't here for no trouble. If you want her you can have her. I just wanted to tell the bitch good-bye. That's all. No harm done. Nothin' ventured, nothin' gained, and all that. Holla."

Sid backed up like some robot on wheels, and he swung his wheelchair around, popped a wheelie and everything. Then he pushed himself back to the driveway. Mason only now realized there was a truck in the driveway. A big, black, ugly truck at that.

*A driver? Was the guy alone?*

More than immediately, he rushed back to the kitchen. Adena. The body. It was all as he had left it. Confused as ever.

"Be right back," Mason said. And he was the through the rear patio door again to get to the Yukon. He hadn't even turned the corner yet before he ran into Sid again.

"You!" Mason said with a growl.

"Me? What up, son?"

"I don't know who you are, what you want, or why you're here, but this is *my* house. You are tres*passing*. . . ."

Mason approached Sid and Sid started backing away—Sid and his whole buzzy cut, leather outfit, and ears too small for his face. And his forehead had that Frankenstein thing going on. All that, coupled with his nasal voice and wheelchair acrobatics, was enough to bring the champagne back up from Mason's stomach. He reminded Mason of an Oscar Mayer hot dog, only with clothes on.

"And you need to get some business before—"

"Before what? Before po-po comes? What're they gonna take, an hour to get here? And when they do, I'm outta here already. Ghost. I'm with the deers in the forest."

Mason looked around, wishing somebody else could witness this freak of nature. *What up, son? The fuzz. Ghost, with the what, in the who? Holla?*

Mason could've laughed, but this was absolutely not funny. He had a body to dispose of, a woman to keep calm, and (it felt like) a world of burden to get off his shoulders. Curling his lip in for a bite, Mason was trying awful hard to observe better judgment.

As though Sid read further than the eye could see, he spoke up. His voice turned more demanding.

"Look, man . . . I know my girl was here, 'cuz I seen her—"

"You seen *who*?" Mason came to figure out, he was serious about this. Convincing enough to start pulling his pants down from his waist.

"Hold it! Hold it! That's somethin' I really *don't* need to see, Sid."

"Okay. Well, I ain't scared. *Shyyyt*, I done shown a million peeps this tat."

"No problem. Don't need to see it. Uh . . . you said you saw her?"

"Course I saw her. Last night she came over here. I followed her."
Sid pointed at his truck. A Ram Charger.

One of those mammoth trucks had transported this pip-squeak
with no legs in a wheelchair. *Where am I at when this dude is on the
road?*

Sid's head dropped some in a moment of shame.

"And I saw *you*."

"Me? Really. Okay, so you saw me come home. So what?"

"Right. So what," Sid said. And he didn't mind looking Mason in
the eye before the next revelation. "I'm not no Peepin' Tom. But I
was curious about who my girl was cheatin' on me with. Now I
know." Sid popped another wheelie in his wheelchair. He wheeled
back to his truck, and Mason wondered who was there to help him.
But nobody was.

Sid reached up with his strong arm to open the passenger-side
door. He locked the brake on the wheelchair and manage to pull
himself up into the truck. Then he reached down with some kind of
hook and fished the wheelchair up and into the vehicle. Through the
windshield, Mason could see the wheelchair disappear into the back
of the truck. Eventually, Sid worked his body into the driver's seat
and the Ram was charged up.

"Sorry it gotta be this way, homes." Sid had lowered his window
and apparently had some lasting impressions to leave. "But I'll fight
you if I have to!" he shouted.

Pip-squeak-no-legs-wheelchair-Ram-Charger-Sid revved his motor three times and some music began to blast: "Try, try, try to
understand, he's a magic man."

Mason couldn't quite hear Shorty over the loud music, especially
since it seemed to now entertain the entire Delaware Valley forest.
But still Sid was singing or screaming, one.

*Try try try to understand*
*He's a magic man . . .*

And now (in Sid Williams's words), he *was* the ghost.

Mason shut off the XL's engine and went back into the house.

"What was all *that* about?"

Mason's eyes were bugged out, bloodshot, and lost.

# fourteen

Yes, sir. It should be no later than Wednesday. Yes . . . I hope so, too, sir. Thank you for understanding. See you then. Okay. Bye."

Mason hung up, but he picked the phone right back up.

"Now, it's your turn, Adena. These are sacrifices we have to take, come on, dial."

"Should I tell 'em the same thing? Wednesday?" Mason was staring again. "Mason? You okay?"

"Uh, yeah. Wednesday. Unless you have any *other* homecoming surprises to give me. In that case, we'll need even *more* time off from work."

"Oh. Now I get all the blame— Hi. Um . . . Kelly, please? Thank you." Adena placed her hand over the receiver and said to Mason, "Just remember, I wasn't the one to dick her mouth so hard she choked. Yes, hi . . . this is Adena Fickle. I have a problem at home . . . it's my husband . . . he got hit with a *virus,* and we're trying to find a *cure,*" Adena said with sarcasm. "I need till Wednesday to get things in *order.*"

Adena cut her eyes at Mason. In a minute, if Mason wasn't careful, there'd be a second body up in here.

"Thank you, Kelly. I'll let you know the progress. Yes, yes, huh? Ah right. I guess Loween can take my place. Good idea. I'll talk to you later."

Hand to her chest, Adena tried to collect herself. It got to her to know that this was more than just what went on in the house. Loween obviously meant something to someone, somewhere. It wasn't as if her existence would simply vanish without folks recognizing her absence. All of these second thoughts began to tug at Adena's insides, but then she had to get back at Mason for what he'd said.

"Hope you don't think that just rolled past me, Mister Mortgage Man. I can't believe you're blaming *me* for all this."

"Put it this way: I would be at work now if you hadn't set this up, okay! I would be at my desk. On the computer, helping some goal-oriented clients with getting into their first home . . . getting them on the road to wealth—and look at me! I got a dead *freak* in my kitchen, and her *boyfriend*, her fuckin' boyfriend in a wheelchair, knockin' at my door! I was at a convention just hours ago! I was being productive and faithful and learning about the growth in my industry! Now I'm a wreck! Because of one night of lust with *your* friend! Your plan!"

Adena up and left the kitchen. So what if there was a life-altering priority at hand. She was not going to stand there and take any more shit from the man who she went out of her way to please.

"*Bastard,*" Adena fumed from the hallway.

"What? *What was that?*" Mason went after her but then fell back. Space and time were resources that they probably needed to make use of right now, even if they weren't their *best* resources.

Mason squeezed his hands down his face and strolled the length of the hallway. On these walls were portraits of successful business ventures and of his own home when it had finally been completed. And there was a wedding photo that at one time he felt was his greatest accomplishment. Of that, he wasn't so sure now. There was more on that wall that was productive and enriching and spoke to Mason's consistency and contribution in life. And all of that was jeopardized by what the one photo represented. Mason stared hard at the photo to see if he cold change it; to see if he could see himself as a Clyde and Adena as a Bonnie, and if his was a biased conclusion, then so be it. However, seeing himself as Clyde was not even possible. Yet, seeing Adena as Bonnie? Now, that was a cinch.

The best guess was that a clock was ticking. A clock that was forcing Mason's actions. But, now that he thought about it, there was more than just one clock. What about the clock that ruled Loween's decomposing body and the stench that it would inevitably emit? What about the clock that was guiding (or misguiding!) Wheelchair Sid? Lord knew what was going through that nut's mind, or how soon it might be before he returned. Mason humored himself, wondering if there was a posse of these guys—all friends of Sid—who all wheeled around on their own in monster trucks and chased after women who really didn't want to be bothered.

*That would be a trip,* Mason told himself. But there were still other clocks. There was the employment clock, which the two were able to stop, if even for a short time. And what about the other people who might claim Loween as their own. Mason recalled hearing a story about Loween from Adena, how she had (despite her obstacles) pulled herself up by her own bootstraps in order to forge a new life for herself. Surely, there were dozens of others who were attracted to this sort of energy and constitution. And even if there was a slower clock, surely there was a measure of time that would mark their tolerance of her absence. And wasn't that another ticking clock for Mason to be mindful of? So many clocks in life: when to sleep, when to get hungry, when to use the bathroom, when to take the car for an oil and lube. Silly little clocks, many of them, directing you to know "when." But why in the world did Mason adopt *these* life-threatening clocks? Of all the things to have rule one's life. Of all the thoughts to have weighing on one's mind, these had to be the closest you could get to a firing squad.

There had to be some type of normalcy for the day, thought Mason. And the only way to get *that* clock ticking was to at least get the body out of sight. For now, he dragged the corpse on his own, down the few steps into the two-car garage that he had converted into a home office. It was what real estate people would call an "unfinished" or "converted" basement, the unfinished portion of the house. Except, Mason got it to a warm and cozy status with the heavy carpeting, the couch, the pool table, and the service bar. It was only when Mason got into this room that he smoked his head. *Why didn't I think of that?*

Minutes later, Mason was scooping up papers from the top of the pool table and putting them into a box. He shifted some other goings-on, like his wardrobe of coats and Adena's wardrobe of "other things," and eventually he found room to move the pool table. There was some other light cleaning, just to make room, but when it came down to moving without the damage, he was going to need help.

A dena, I'd love to sit and talk with you about what was and wasn't my fault last night. Really. But we can't use this time catching attitudes and erasing speaking terms. We need to communicate and keep it movin', because things don't get any prettier from here on out. Not until you apologize. Not till you say it right here. Right now, that this wasn't all my fault."

"Okay, is that what you want? It's not all your fault. Satisfied? Now let's—"

"Now kiss me. Bring me back to life. Please."

"Oh my God. Woman, you're buggin'."

"Okay then, I'm not movin'."

"All right, all right already." Mason kissed his wife tenderly.

"More, better than that," she instructed.

A slight chuckle. But Mason pressed his lips more and better.

"Now hug me."

"Jesus, Adena. I feel like a teenager with his teacher."

"Good. That's how you *should* feel. That's how you should *always* feel around me. First-time jitters. Brand-new beginnings. Don't you ever get too comfortable with me and start talkin' to me any old way and takin' me for granted, Mason Fickle."

"All right all right. I'm sorry. It was all my fault, and I'll never do it again," Mason said.

Adena smiled, kissed his cheek, and was the first to step off.

*Works every time,* thought Mason.

B ack in the converted garage, the two muscled the pool table over and out of the way until there was room for the XL.

Mason wasn't so sure the coast was clear outside, so he went back out into the drizzle. He was quiet enough not to frighten the deer in his front yard. But he was still wondering about that deer as a witness. The deer sprinted away, as if reading Mason's mind.

*Whoa.*

On to more important endeavors, Mason more or less circled the house, wishing he had some binoculars, but he was ultimately one satisfied conspirator when he saw his property was Sid-less. He operated the remote for the garage door and backed the XL inside. The door was closed again. Another blanket was tossed into the back of the truck, then the body, and then the lump was covered again.

"This'll buy us some time," Mason said, considering the situation. "We need to think smart and practical about this. That means cleaning up the bedroom sheets, carpet, all of it."

"Carpet? We just had that shampoo job done two weeks ago."

"Adena, stay with me here. Our bedroom is now the scene of a crime. After we clean it up, it will be our bedroom again. You understand what I'm sayin'? There's a dead girl's DNA in our house, and we need to erase it. Seriously."

"Then what?"

"The body. No one can ever find this body, Adena. I know what you're thinking."

"No, you don't."

"Okay, well, what were you gonna say?"

"Just . . . well, why can't we bury the body behind the house? Far back. At least it'll be a respectable burial and I won't feel so guilty."

"Is that how you wanna do this?" asked Mason.

"I think it's a good idea. We'll always know where she's at, and that nobody's touching her."

"Hmm . . . never thought of that. You sure you want it that way?"

"It's just my idea, Mason. What was your idea?"

Mason with the sly grin. "Actually, that was it. I just wanted you to bring it up." Again with the grin.

Adena sucked her teeth.

"So, why is she in the car?"

"Back there is a corpse, Adena. *It*, not *she*, remember?"

"Anyway."

"Well, I figured when we're positively sure the area's clear—like maybe tomorrow, early morning—I'll be able to drive the truck to a spot."

"In the woods?"

"It's what this truck is made for, baby. Rough ridin'."

"So, what're we doin' in the truck now? We need to be cleanin' the bedroom."

"Because I wanted us to do our normal routine this morning." Mason checked his watch. "It's nine thirty."

"Okay."

"What would you an' I be doing at nine thirty if this was any other normal day?"

Adena let her mind wander.

"Depends," she said.

"On?"

"On . . . if we fucked last night. If we did, you'd be asleep curled up behind me."

"If we didn't . . ." Mason said with an expression fit for a disciplinarian.

"Maybe food shopping, or little errands. Last week Monday we had breakfast at Perkins."

"There it is there."

"What?"

"Breakfast at Perkins." Mason started the truck and depressed the button on the garage-door remote at the same time. Then it was down the five-mile stretch to 402, to the 209 crossing. With no serious traffic to slow them, Perkins Restaurant was but a twenty-minute drive.


A country-style atmosphere, with a country menu, Perkins was busy with locals, tourists, and staff. The Lumber Jack Expo had just concluded the day before, and it was clear that some strangers had been left behind.

Because food wasn't the Fickles' focus, so many other sights and sounds consumed their senses. The waitresses gliding back and forth. The older folks talking about every possible thing there is to talk about, and the music feeding the air with everything and anything you ever wanted to know about love but were afraid to say.

*Somewhere down the road, our roads are gonna cross again. . . .*

A waitress approached.

"Welcome to Perkins. May I take your order?"

So cheerful an attitude that the couple could almost forget their troubles. Almost. And that was just the thing Mason was trying to achieve.

While Mason had flapjacks and Adena an egg with ketchup, so

many other worlds were swirling in their midst. A little girl with long, straight hair slumped down in her seat. It made Mason wonder.

"This must be an off day for school."

"It's Columbus Day. Of course they're off," Adena responded.

Any kind of "normal" debate; Mason said, "Like you celebrate Columbus Day," and he twisted his grimace.

"I celebrate lo-ve, baby." Adena had the whole neck roll in her words, although a cute determination to go with it. "Love don't have a day or a date. It just"—she snapped her fingers—"happens."

*Oh Lord,* Mason grieved.

"But you know what holidays matter to me, Mase. Columbus Day is not one of them. Speaking of holidays—Halloween is coming up. Remember last Halloween? You were Dracula and I was Little Bo Peep?"

Mason looked into Adena's eyes, asking her, *You really wanna go there?*

Apparently, Adena didn't read his mind, and she went on babbling. And Mason's mind now wandered.

The little girl's eyes were closed, with her hand reaching across the table.

"Touch me if we're goin' to the movies today," she said to the man, probably her dad, at the table. He did, and she kind of jumped for joy in her seat. In the booth next to them was a quartet of four golden girls, all of them white women, wrinkled, and proud.

"Decaf for me."

"And more of this Sweet'N Low, honey."

"Of course, ma'am," said the waitress.

Somewhere behind Mason there were other conversations.

"A judgment? *Really?*"

"Should we just split it three ways?" asked another.

"Ninety percent of life is what you think it is . . ." said another.

The little girl again now *eating* orange juice with a straw until:

"Touch me if there's orange juice left," she said, eyes closed and hands extended.

The music now: *There'll be sad songs to make you cry.* . . .

At least, Mason could follow this song in *his* mind. Anything to get past Adena's never-ending boredom.

"So, why ain't you talkin'?" she asked.

"I don't know. Nothin' personal. Guess I'm just a little tired, that's all."

"Niggeritis. You get that after you eat real good."

Mason nodded in agreement.

"But then. You didn't get much sleep last night, did you?"

"Can we not talk about last night?"

"Know what? I'm gonna head for the bathroom, and when I come out, have the bill paid. I'm outta here. And honestly? This whole normalcy bit *ain't* working." Adena kept her voice low enough for their ears only. But you couldn't help thinking people were trying to read lips.

Mason exhaled and signaled for the waitress. It was cute how she tried to play it off, like his breakfast mate hadn't just vacated the table.

"Will that be all, sir?"

"Keep the change," Mason said. It was a twenty—probably fifteen or more over and about the cost of the meal.

efore they got in the truck, Mason and Adena stood out on a walk way to the side of the restaurant entrance.

"Something wrong, Adena? I mean, a minute ago, you and I were all lovey-dovey. Now you're snappin' at me."

"Excuse me for saying this but—" Adena fell against Mason's chest. "I'm scared, Mason. For the first time in my life, I'm really, really scared."

Adena wept and her tears spilled onto Mason's top.

"All right, all right. It's okay to cry. Come on, let's get out of this drizzle."


A dena curled up in the passenger's seat. She was a nervous wreck, spilling endless tears. As if the rain were somehow in the truck with them.

"You gonna be okay?" asked Mason.

"I'm tryin'," Adena answered with a trembling slur. "I'm tryin'. But every time I think I'm strong, I think of what I did, and . . . I'm so sorry, Mason. Will you ever forgive me?"

This was a huge change of heart for Adena, to go from having confidence, to losing it again. Her confused emotions all obviously fucking with Mason's brain.

"We're gonna put an end to this once and for all," Mason said. And his foot grew heavier, with the XL truck sweeping up 402.

"Whatcha gonna do?" asked Adena.

"I'm not gonna wait till tomorrow. We need to bury this body to-day. Right now."

# fifteen

They called him Juggler, ever since he had been a wispy, wiry basketball player at the New Orleans YMCA. But things turned sour when he couldn't keep his grades up. Even worse, he dropped out of school at age seventeen. Juggler-the-dropout became Juggler-the-hustler virtually overnight. And what did Juggler hustle? Women. He won them with his charm and his ill-gotten finances. He wooed them with his promises, dangling expectations of jewelry and clothes and, if absolutely necessary, cash. But, he also purchased them from scouts with well-trained eyes who hung out in pizza shops and candy stores and even libraries to identify the most incorrigible ones. These scouts would "accidentally" bump into candidates; they would inconspicuously even break up a fight to earn their immediate confidence.

The scheme worked so damned well for years, turning the most innocent girls into prostitutes on film. Porno princesses, they were called. And the fishnet stretched as far down as Mississippi, and all the way up to the French Quarter of N'awlins. The names are now a part of porn legend: Lisa-Lisa Clark, Gina Tonsils, Measure-mouth Mary, Six-inch Suzy, and, of course, Tina the Tongue.

And while they were the most notable of the Silver Dollar Club, there were so many others—hundreds of now-willing lassies who learned to love or hate what they considered the world of porn.

If Juggler was considered N'awlins' prostitution king, then Sidney (aka Sid) Williams (aka Wheelchair Sid) would more than likely be his first lieutenant, wheelchair and all.

Their scheme, however, came to a screeching halt when Hurricane Katrina hit. The cash flow that had netted Juggler $20,000 a week, and sometimes more, dropped to zero, and all of his stock, the girls, the warehouse of videos and DVDs that had been mass-produced, along with the building itself, were all history now. Restoring the business, locating the girls, and remaking new masters, which were used to duplicate more product, were tasks that were out of the question if not altogether impossible.

"I'm goin' to Houston to stay with family," said one of Juggler's top girls. Another was headed for Phoenix, and another to San Diego. But it was the advice of Loween Brewster, his number-two girl, that persuaded him to try again up north. "The Poconos is sweet, Juggler. You can get your grind on one, two, three."

Juggler knew anything was possible, especially since he and Sid weren't doin' too hot in New York City, where they first relocated. And he also felt that his appearance—the fair skin, the sharp facial features, and the ease with which he could blend in with white folks—would turn into more of a benefit in the Poconos. In Harlem, the Bronx, and in other boroughs, people were *not* feelin' his country ass, with his pimp ways. And besides, the name Juggler was getting laughs instead of respect. A few times, Juggler had to fistfight to get that "jug head" title out of a dude's mouth.

"This just might work out for us, Sid. That Loween actually did us some good," Juggler said.

"Maybe so," Sid said, navigating his Ram Charger by hand controls, an accommodation that the Silver Club's proceeds had paid for.

The two were driving through East Stroudsburg, checking out possible handouts and looking for a motel where they could initiate plan A of the Silver Dollar Club's comeback.

"But don't git that shit twisted, I'm fittin' a put a foot 'n 'er ass the minute I catch 'er. Straight up. How the fuck she gon' tell me *it's over*? Juggler changed his voice. "It's over, Juggler. I can't do that no more . . . I want a few-cha ahead a me!" And now Juggler was heaving and panting, pretending to experience an asthma attack. Juggler the jokester.

The Ram Charger was filled with riotous laughter.

"Wait'll I git that bitch," Juggler said, along with that habitual sniffle of his.

"I'ma give her a inhaler that'll reach so far down her throat it'll tickle her asshole. Ah ha ha ha ha!"

"No doubt," Sid agreed.

The easiest place to find a room to rent was at the Days Inn, just off of Main Street. And, as fate would have it, Sid was at the end of the hallway one night, smoking a "funny cigarette" (he called it), when he overheard a Days Inn staffer mention Loween's name. Something about the "next shift" and "she'd take care of it."

" 'Scuse me. Did I hear you mention the name Loween?" Sid inquired after sniffing out the weed and wheeling closer to the employee.

"Yeah. You know her?"

"Shoot, that girl is my sister's best friend. The last name wouldn't be Brewster, would it? 'Cuz I know there's not a lot of Loweens in the world, but there's sure in hell a lotta Brewsters. I got another friend named Brewster, but he's—"

As Sid babbled on, the two Days Inn workers looked at each other with disbelief as they suddenly found themselves held captive by the wheelchair guy and his never-ending chatter.

"So is that her name?" Sid finally asked.

Coming from their brief trance, one of the workers agreed that Loween might be the best friend he spoke on.

And there it was: the wild idea of confidentiality gone right out the window.

The inquiry at the Days Inn led to Sid keeping late hours the following night; and he was damned if Loween wasn't working the third shift there at the very hotel where Juggler was setting up.

*Wait'll Juggler finds this out.*

But then, to go a step further, Sid tailed Loween one night, and shit if it ain't her steppin' up in some rich folks' house! *Wait'll Juggler finds this out!*

It was more than curiosity that brought Sid to camp out across the street that very evening. He found a good spot across the way where a new home was being built. All the elements seemed to support him; nobody living there yet, the night was dark, and so was his truck. And so he sat awhile to see what else he could learn. Not until a woman left the house and jumped into a white Lexus did Sid begin to wonder, *Who's that?* He was so sure that Loween hadn't yet left the house—he'd know that tall, sexy body anywhere.

*If Juggler didn't wanna punish that girl so bad, I'd love to get a shot at it,* Sid amused himself. And he was even tempted to leave the truck and wheel closer to the house. But now there was a second person, parking a Yukon XL in the driveway. *A man? First a woman, now a man. Wow, Juggler is gonna love this.* And, just as Sid was shaking with excitement, the Lexus returned. *The girl is back. Okay . . . where you at, girl? Where you at? Where the party at?*

There was a long wait before the woman left her car. Before she eased up to the house. Oh *shit, shit, shit!* From Sid's position he could see the preparations: the lights shutting off and someone moving about the house with a lighter, igniting candles throughout. Oh *shit, shit.* And now that there were three persons (as far as he knew) in the house, and that the candlelit mood was in effect, he was *definitely* gonna get a close-up of this!

A nd then I got as close as I could to try and see what was up."

"I got a fuckin' Peepin' Tom for a lieutenant. Well, shit, nigga—tell it, *nigga!*" Sniffle, sniffle.

"Okay, well . . . the rest I couldn't really see. I woulda had to climb the house—"

"Well, shit, Why ain't you—oh. No legs. My bad." Juggler was snickering at his joke. Sid merely twisted his lips. *Corny.*

"But, what I was gittin' ready to say is, I heard some crazy shit up there, Jug. These houses up here must be made a paper 'cuz that shit was clear, like in the movie theater—word to motha!"

Juggler had never been more concentrated on what Sid had to say. Never.

"First I heard a whole lotta shoutin', like I think our girl Loween had the dude cheatin' on his girl or sumpin'. Then there was more screams. I think there was a fight."

"What?"

"Yup, then yo, check this. Outta nowhere I'm hearing 'suck his dick' and 'eat his ass' and all kinds a freak shit. Yo, my dick was like a rock, I ain't gonna lie."

"Day-um. What else, what else?" Juggler almost spitting the words faster than they could leave his lips.

"Yo! I heard somebody's ass—I don't know who. But somebody was getting their ass whipped! Like a belt or a whip or somethin'."

"Word? They was on some sadomasochist-type shit?"

Sid kissed his fingers twice, touched his chest, and raised the same fingers in the air before he said, "I put this on everything we lost in N'awlins."

"Yo. Here's what I want to do. 'Cuz they fuckin' wit' *my* bitch. That's my fuckin' money that was invested in this bitch, and they just gonna reap rewards? Oh, *hell no!*" Juggler was a mass of jealous rage.

"Okay, Juggler, before you go on . . . there's more."

Juggler waited, holding in so much anxiety, having heard all he could take.

"I know you woulda wanted me to take the next step: to do what I had to do to bring her back to us. So . . . I stayed up there. I even slept in the truck."

"Fuck you do that for?"

"Jug, the—"

Sid's words were interrupted. Juggler had popped him upside the head with an open palm.

"Nigga always think they boss!"

"But, Jug—"

"But-Jug-what? I coulda got Yap, Ace, and Pooh and we coulda ran up in there while it was dark. Now whatcha got? Go 'head, tell me you got my bitch tied up somewhere waitin' for me! Right, I fuckin' doubt! Go head. Tell me what fool-ass shit you did that gotta clean up after."

Cowering, Sid was hesitant to speak.

"Come on! You 'bout to tell me shit I already know, Sid. YOU FUCKED UP! Now, tell me how."

Sid eventually explained things. The knock on the door, the introduction, the liaison around the back of the house. And he didn't forget to mention the drizzling rain, which he laughably thought might earn him the boss's sympathy.

Not.

"Okay, okay, okay! Enough talking. I shoulda had you shut up the minute you said a word!" After the sniffles, Juggler took a deep breath, as though his clear thinking came from his lungs.

"I want Yap, Ace, and Pooh to get the fuck out their beds. We got work to do."

This rain is actually gonna be more help than harm. Now, you hold down the house, Adena. No calls in or out. We gotta control every move we make, okay?"

Adena nodded. Her ghetto ass was as soft as cotton now, especially since her crying jag.

"And don't answer the door, either. Whatever you do, please don't do that. I need to go dig a hole." Mason kissed his wife's forehead and took up his shovel. Then he hiked out into the backyard, beyond the fifty yards of trees that made for the gateway to a much wider, broader forest.

The earth was soft and agreeable each time Mason thrusted his shovel down into it. It also helped that he had boots on, so that he and the shovel could make that perfect team. He moved rapidly, like a soldier on a mission, driving that shovel deep and keeping the pile close by so he could quickly cover the body when the deed was done. With each thrust, Mason also surrendered to his thoughts about the past and the future. With all he knew about what he called "a man's contribution in life," digging a hole to hide a dead body was not a part. There of. Somehow, he was gonna answer for this; of that he was sure. It was that well-known law of the universe that promised to give back to a person exactly what he or she gave. He had experienced the good feelings of that law many, many times over. He went out of his way on many an occasion, and because of it, there were dozens and dozens of families—hundreds, if you counted each individual—who were now the lifelong beneficiaries of his deeds. So many happy-faced people, with their happy tears and their joyful praises, filled his peaceful nights with self-gratitude and self-appreciation. Sure, there were the awards, the certificates, and all the political alliances he was now forming. And there were mortgage bankers and real estate agents across the region who held Mason in high esteem, turning to him for whatever resources he could provide.

And the comments of his comrades were bells that were meant to ring forever: *We are honored to recognize Mason Fickle for becoming one of the most informative resources in our industry today. . . . We are so grateful to be working with Mason, who has been doing such a fantastic job with people relations in the Poconos area.*

These acknowledgments droned on during Mason's laborious digging.

*Do you, Adena Woods, take Mason Fickle as you lawfully wedded husband . . . Congratulations . . . you may kiss the bride!*

*Congratulations, Mr. Fickle. Your loan has been approved. If you'll just sign here . . .*

*Mason Fickle, your work at our company has been exemplary. Our board of directors had decided to promote you to Executive Director of Mortgage Acquisitions. Congratulations.*

These were the most important turning points in Mason's life in the past five years. They had propelled him into position of respect where he could feel admiration from the people he worked beside every day. Not just superficial acknowledgment, but the deep-rooted sort that would touch people's lives instantly and perpetually. It was the type of work that he could feel proud of, but it also served him with a sense of redemption for a past that he'd rather forget.

Digging this grave, he wondered, might be the past coming to haunt him. If it was true that a universal law returned awards for good deeds, then that had to hold true for the bad ones. But Mason was confused for a time as to who or what decided what was a good or bad deed. Or, was it simply a person's heart and common sense that decided? Mason's contention was that he'd done the right thing back in Philly. He had been arrested in conjunction with a statewide financial fraud—a check-kiting ring that was draining tens of millions of dollars a day from the economic infrastructure of a Philadelphia banking system. The scam had been ongoing for years, but the investigation got stronger and stronger.

The principals were eventually targeted. Bobby Fickle was one of them. The feds had mistaken Mason for Bobby. But when they realized the truth—that Mason and Bobby were both suit-wearing bots with the banking industry, but that Mason was the good seed and Bobby the bad—they couldn't wait to play poker.

"Mason, we got you guys cold. Lemme tell you how your scheme works and you correct me if I'm wrong. First, in that underground laboratory over on East River Drive, your crew manufactures the bogus bonds!"

"You're wrong. I don't run with a crew! I don't manufacture bonds!"

"But I'm not done! Listen, see if this sounds familiar. . . ."

It was the dreaded interrogation room. Every city has one—every television studio, too. And Mason was just as familiar with the games that investigators played as the next couch potato.

This nameless shirt and tie in Mason's face, tobacco breath and all, was trying to paint a picture for Mason, trying to get him to feed into images on the gray wall. But Mason saw only a gray wall. There was nothing to agree to. Nothing but a wall.

"Once you've manufactured the bonds, you ship them to Tom, Dick, and Harry, who in turn deposit these bonds for you—"

"No no no! I don't create, distribute, I don't have anything to do with this."

"—Oh, here's the best part. From the Tom, Dick, and Harry accounts, you get pretty certified bank checks that you then ship to the Cayman Islands. And the account keeps growing and growing and growing—"

Another shirt and tie jumped in: "Mo' money, mo' money, mo' money!"

Mason interrupted the cat-and-mouse game.

"Listen, I don't mean to disappoint you two, but right now? I'm missing a hot date, a hot movie, and a hot night in bed. Now, you're either gonna stop wasting my time, or you're gonna make somethin' happen."

Mason considered his response cooler than 007 could've imagined, or any TV gangster, for that matter. But what Mason didn't know was how deep this actually was.

"Well, okay. You ain't gotta spill the beans, Mason. We'll letcha go. No sense in holdin' this man up anymore. *Charlie!* Come get these cuffs off."

Mason felt this was too easy, but he wasn't about to argue.

"And let's get the next suspects in here. . . ." The shirt and tie looked at his clipboard. "Hmph . . . this should be a breeze. Says here that she suddenly came into a house, a car, a *substantial* increase in her bank account. . . ."

Mason wasn't paying too much attention to the investigator, already rubbing his wrists and ready to leave the police interrogation room. Only when he raised his head to focus on the entrance to the room did he see her—the "she" that the shirt and tie was claiming suddenly came into a house, a car. . . .

Mason nearly collapsed; or at least he wanted to. His feet became cinder blocks. His head and heartbeat drummed inconsistently.

"Well, lookie who's behind door number two."

Mason did hear *that* remark, an in some kind of wicked slow-motion gesture he turned his eyes to the left, where the investigators stood with their arms folded. Mason's eyes turned to slits, blades to cut this man's heart out. But there was no use. He realized that this was a game he couldn't win; one that these men were practiced at and probably gloated over how easy this was time after time after time.

"Mason? I'm sure you know this fine woman here? Let me introduce you to your mother. Mrs. Zanobia Fickle."

Mason's game turned away from the joker and back toward his mother. His head went from proud and upright to ashamed and depressed. This wasn't the time or the opportunity to cry or to apologize. This wasn't time for excuses or blaming. Mason wasn't that little boy anymore who got bruised from a fall from a bike, only to run hone for Mommy to fix it. Mommy wouldn't be able to fix this. This was the big leagues. This was life, where one mistake or one false move could get you a life-altering experience. No doubt.

----

W hat's it gonna be, Fickle? You and Momma walk right now. Today. No strings attached. No more legal worries. Your lives go
back to normal and nobody knows a thing. All we want is Bobby."

Mason looked up at Momma. She'd spent all her life just to see
her sons progress and achieve.

She was there at every step of he way: school trips, bag lunches,
the clothing store, sore throats and fevers, teenage pimples and
heartbreaks. She was there for the driving lessons. The school grad-
uation, the cuts after the fights. *Momma was there for it all,* Mason told
himself. *Only when we became men did we need to make our own choices.
And these choices cannot endanger the woman who gave birth to us and
care for us. These choices are choices that we must stand by, and if necessary, suffer the consequences.*

"What do you want me to do?" Mason asked. Only, it wasn't a
question. It was a submission.

*Game over, Bobby.*

# sixteen

Is it deep enough?"

Mason nearly jumped out of his skin at the sound of Adena's voice, and his glasses almost slipped off his face.

"Don't you *ever* do that again!" commanded Mason. He didn't see the drink that Adena held. He didn't care, either. Where Mason's head was at right now—Adena was a reproduction of Bobby, how his brother had done wrong, and it eventually pulled everyone else in for the fall.

Same with Adena.

"Fuck you, Mason!" And Adena tossed the cup of apple juice at him before she spun off on her return to the house.

Angry-faced, Mason seceded, kept himself from chasing after her, and he continued digging. The juice would have to wait, and so, too, would his apology to Adena.

*Damn, I was in a zone, too.*

It would take some time for Mason to get back to that state of mind, how all kinds of thoughts were whizzing about in his head. Nothing made labor manageable more than memories. Good or bad, a person could really lose themselves.

So, he kept digging and digging. A rock here and there interfered with his rhythm, and by now even his boxers and socks were wet.

But this was an important job that his future relied on; the rain would eventually go away; the body, however, was a weight on his shoulders that would remain for a long time. It made Mason quietly wonder if these events would *ever* leave his mind and permit him to go back to his productive routine. Doubtful, he muscled on until he figured he was five or ten minutes away from the desired depth. As though this were the last lap of a race, Mason went at it feverishly. Images flashed through his mind: his mother, Bobby, Adena . . . the women who had shared his bed, then Loween . . . the real estate brokers, the buyers and their new homes . . . on and on these pictures appeared and vanished, over and over until Mason heard a crackling sound. Hoping Adena was sneaking up on him again to apologize, Mason turned his head. Three of them were in his yard, just past the edge of his grass, and now making their way over rocks, branches, and brushes.

"Hey, now," said one of the men. Mason could only assume these were hunters, since two of them held shotguns directed at the forest floor. But there were a few things wrong here.

"Fellas, what's happening? Ah . . . the property line is where the orange ribbons are, way back there, in case you're lost." Mason pointed away from his hole in the ground and stepped out in front in case the strangers were nosy. "And then, according to the permits, you can only fire five hundred yards away from any homes, so . . ."

The men looked at one another for some clarity, no idea what Mason was talking about.

"And you know y'all need those orange vests, to hunt out here, don't you?"

One of the men, the bald one with the fare skin and light features, began to chuckle. Then, as if to lead the others, he turned so that his laughter was contagious. And now all three of them were carrying on.

"Get that? He thinks we're hunting," the leader said. But then he suddenly stopped laughing to say, "Actually, we *are* huntin'. We're huntin' for *pussy!*" The hee-hawing began again.

With no room for games, Mason said, "Excuse me, gents . . . you're on private property right now. So . . . if you don't mind, I'm gonna have to ask you to leave." To discourage any possible curiosity, Mason eased away from the hole, sidestepping toward the house.

"And if we *don't* wanna leave?" The leader stuck out his rifle so that Mason was stopped in his tracks. He didn't point it at Mason, but held it as somewhat of a roadblock.

Mason assessed the situation.

"Fellas, I don't know who you are or why you're here, but I think you're mistaken. I'm Mason Fickle? Ah . . . this is my house?" As if any of that might matter right now.

One of the tagalongs said, "Fickle? Fickle? You mean, you're the one and only Mason Fickle?"

"Exactly," Mason said, expecting that *now* they would see the light.

"Oh, man! Lemme shake your hand, man!" The guy stepped past his buddies and reached out for a shake. Mason was encouraged, and he extended his hand. A split second later, he felt an extreme pain in his thumb, then his wrist, then his arm. His entire body was thrown into a somersault, and the next thing he saw was red and black. Red was the fiery pain that shot through his body. Black was the extent that his eyes and mind would allow, since the body slam knocked him out cold.

There was fire around him for as far as he could see. He realized it was the forest and that the blaze was closing in on the house. He tried to get up to find the hose to extinguish the flames, but he found that his arms and legs were bound, tied to the wood planks of his outdoor patio. Somewhere behind the flames those three men were laughing, clapping, and blasting off their shotguns.

"Adena! *Adena!*" Mason felt his cries from his gut. He felt like Rocky crying for Adrian. Then, he *knew* he was delirious because while all of this was becoming his fate, Adena pulled open the patio door, dressed in the negligee he remembered Loween wearing, and she had a champagne glass in each hand.

"Adena, hurry! Cut the ropes! The ropes!"

"Are you yelling at me, Mason? The woman you love? The woman of your dreams?"

"Adena, be serious! The fire's gonna kill us! Cut the ropes!"

"I will. Just relax. Have some champagne."

"Relax? What the—"

The flames were closer now and Mason swore he could feel the heat tickling the inner soles of his bare feet.

"Adena, cut it out and get me out of these ropes before I burn to death!"

"I will," she said. "But first, for once, do as I ask. Now, sip some champagne with me, honey. Congratulations are in order."

Mason would have done anything to alleviate this torment. He reached for the glass.

"We're toasting what *important event* while my toes fry?"

"I need you to do to me what you did to Loween. I need you to *slay me* with your dick, Mason."

"Okay, I figured you were gonna freak out on me. Get me OUT of these ropes!" Mason shouted.

And Adena took the glass and poured what was left of it on Mason's head. She laughed. Then she said, "Get out of them yourself!"

And now she was laughing along with the trespassers.

"Lord, no!" Mason cried. Please, somebody . . . anybody!" The flames got so close, Mason snatched his legs back, and that's when he became conscious again.

Mason's dream immediately became a nightmare as he opened his eyes to see Wheelchair Sid.

"'Sup, homey. Good to have you back with us."

Mason realized it wasn't just the no-legged freak; those trespassers were all now occupying his living-room furniture. A couple of them were lounging on his new sectional couch, while another was sitting up on his kitchen counter.

Suddenly, the dream of flames and Adena wanting to get her final freak on wasn't so bad after all.

"Hey, Juggler. Look who's back up in the heezy!"

*Juggler. Juggler's the baldy,* Mason realized as he watched the TV go off and the terrorists approached.

"So . . . you're the famous Mason Fickle," noted Juggler. He had obviously peeked at Mason's accomplishments, those framed credentials hanging in the hallway.

"Maybe if you woulda cooperated with me yesterday, you wouldn't be all outta whack right now, homey," said a suddenly sympathetic Sid.

"Sid, go get you some business," ordered Juggler. "You talk when I say talk. Not before." By the way Juggler looked at Sid, it seem as though he felt the same way Mason did about the man being a no-legged freak. Point for Juggler.

"Now . . . you. Buddy, listen . . . Sorry we had to get rough outside, but as I always say, *you never know.* You looked a little paranoid out there. A little scared. And although I wouldn't a took it as far as my man Ace here did, I still woulda had to contain you ass somehow, 'cuz you look like you was about to git in some feelings. And scared people do crazy things. Trust me . . . I know."

"Ain't nobody scared a you," Mason said. "It's your gun that's a threat. Without your gun and goons, I could take you easy. Bullies are wimps when they don't have their support team around. Even I know that."

Juggler's face wrinkled with concern and he began pacing back and forth in the living room.

"Mason Fickle, you surprise me. An accomplished real estate man like you gittin' all tough all a sudden . . . like you gangsta or something." Juggler broke into a sadistic laugh. Then he shut the laugh off as if by a switch. He got up in Mason's face close enough to be nose-to-nose.

"You don't really wanna take me on, Mr. Fickle. So I suggest you watch your mouth!" Juggler backed away and his voice changed again from angry to soft. Of course, there were the sniffles. "I didn't really come here to argue with you, big dog. Nothin' like that. What I'm here for is my property."

Mason raised his body some on the La-Z-Boy chair and realized some pain in his back. There was that color red rushing through his brain again. Aside from his brooding, Mason asked, "What property?" even if it didn't sound like a question. "This land is mine, this house is mine, and—*where's my wife?* Adena!" Mason with the pain in the ass.

"She's busy right now. Our friend Pooh hurt his thumb out in the woods—you know, you're not an easy one to carry. Carried you all the way back to the house, sure did."

Juggler seemed to be concealing something—Mason could feel it in his aching bones.

"But what I really need to know is about your relationship with my girl Loween."

Eyes ready to roll back in his head—*her again*—Mason bought some time for his reply by agonizing over the sore back and head.

"Oh, my head."

"Yeah, *oh my head* is gonna turn into *oh my head is split open,* if you don't answer me."

"I don't know what happened to your girl, man. She was here. She left."

"She left. Is that right. Did she drive? Take a cab? Hitch a ride?"

"*I don't know,*" Mason said, more concerned now about his wife and some guy name *Pooh.*

"Okay. I guess we'll just hang out awhile—wait'll she comes back. *She's never coming back,* Mason thoughts shouted.

"In the meantime, don't you have a bruise that maybe the Missus can fix for you, Yap?"

"Hey—ho—wait a minute. What—? Adena! *Adena!*"

Juggler approached Mason and put his hand to the left shoulder. Then he squeezed until Mason winced.

"I just need you to not yell for Adena. Right now. Trust me when I tell you, she's busy."

Mason's lips pursed into an unforgiving frown.

"Now . . . you sure you don't know where my Loween is?"

"Ask 'im what that hole's about outside, Jug."

Juggler pointed at Wheelchair Sid. His forefinger could've been a rifle the way he used it.

"Did I tell you to get some business?"

Sid's head shrank below the neckline.

"Well? You heard 'im. What's the hole for, Mister Wonderful? Looks like it's big enough for a coffin, if ya ask me."

*Tell him, Mason. Tell him, so he and his band of fools can spill tears and get to steppin'. Don't tell him, Mason. These dudes look like they're ready for war. Better not upset them. Stand your ground, Fickle. They'll get tired of this pseudo-interrogation, and they'll disappear.*

The many minds of Mason Fickle were only just emerging from hiding. He couldn't put a finger on the time the voices last showed themselves. He was sure it was in a time of great crisis. Some real estate deal about to sour. Or was it the snowstorm that pummeled the Poconos, forcing him and his wife to hole up in a motel?

*My wife!* Mason suddenly came to his senses.

"Juggler, the hole is just for oil."

"You're diggin' for oil?" guessed the guy named Yap, nodding his head, matter-of-fact.

Then it was the third guy, Ace, who said, "We rich! I *knew* it! We fuckin' rich!"

Mason didn't want to read too deeply into the terrorists' comments. But if he had to, he would swear the guy had just said *we*, as if something that belonged to Mason was somehow up for grabs.

"Oil, huh?"

"Of course. Oil from my truck," Mason said, glad to be a disappointment to the guy they called Yap. *Yap? Who comes up with these names?*

"Oh, right. That XL of yours—whaddya gotta change the oil, ev'y week?"

Mason couldn't believe they were falling for his cock-'n'-bull. But he sure didn't mind playing along.

"Yeah, Somethin' like that."

*Stupid, and since you believe that, I also got a bridge to sell you.*

Juggler had been rocking there on the part of the couch *not* made for asses. But Mason quickly decided to keep his mouth shut, to consume the desire of losing these guys. And now the band leader twisted his neck to and fro, as though he was preparing for a more intense encounter.

Mason fretted that this guy was about to speak again. He could almost feel the recurring pain about to rise from his back, a pain motivated by Juggler's intentions.

"*OIL from the XL.* And I thought I heard it all." Juggler rose to his feet and approached Mason. "You must think we too country to be smart, don't cha—" The shotgun that was wedged under Juggler's arm and pointed at the floor was now level with Mason's chest. And the quarter-size nose was at an angle, parked right there in the pocket under Mason's Adam's apple.

"Go 'head."

"What?" Mason's pleas came just as quickly as the hands did. Juggler's goons restraining him. "What?"

"I'll tell you *what*. We gon' start hearin' some facts around here. And in my mind is this meter—call it my living meter. If I even *think* you telling a lie, I pull the trigger and the story ends. Even if *think* you tellin' half a lie, game over. Now—"

Juggler pulled back the shotgun, cocked it like it was a natural reflex, and he planed its nose back there in the pocket of Mason's neck.

"Now, I'ma ask you one mo' gain, Where is Loween?"

S o, that's the truth, man, That's all of it. I didn't want no beef wit' you, Mr. Juggler. And, I sure as hell didn't mean for things to turn out this way, But, it was all in agreeance with the girl."

"Her name is Loween. Stop talkin' 'bout her like she ain't matter. Like she ain't even got no name—"

"All right. I'm sorry. Loween. Loween was a willing participant. She—"

Juggler hadn't stopped talking. "I mean, sure she ain't no highfalutin' businessman or a property owner in the burbs . . . and she sho' wasn't no bourgie brand. . . ."

Mason was certain that Juggler was referring to him and his wife, maybe assuring that Adena was just as accomplished as—

"But, I'm tryin' hard to see if you even gave two shits about my girl. I'm thinkin' how you actually was diggin' a hole! You was gonna give her the most unrighteous end—just to see her ass buried in the backyard! Nigga, what was you thinking? You ain't put nary value on this girl's life, 'bout to just write her whole shit off . . ."

"It's not like that," Mason appealed. "You gotta believe me. I—"

"Nah, fuck that, you knew what fuckin' time it was. That's why I don't believe she was your willing participant. If she was so willing, how come my peoples hear y'all fightin'? How come there was shoutin' 'n' shit, wrestlin' 'n' shit? And now my girl is dead?" Juggler got hot enough to raise the Mossberg shotgun again. This time, it was a sure bet that he meant more than to threaten.

"Wait, wait, wait!"

Up until now, Adena had been out of sight. But it was clear that she'd returned in time to catch the worst of the tension in the living room. "Please, Juggler. It was all my fault. Loween, I mean Cynthia, was a friend of mine, a good friend. We worked together every day. Shared stories and had mad laughs. She'd be the *last* person I'd ever wanna hurt. Especially after all she'd been through."

Juggler seemed to cool down some, enough to want to hear the rest of Adena's testimony.

". . . We got to talkin' about sex and havin' fun, and well, one thing led to another, and she agreed to come home and do my man. He didn't even know about it. It was a show, man. That's the truth. But regardless of what it looks like, you gotta know that, first, we had no idea she was underage. Second, I never even knew her real name was Cynthia. And, three, the asthma thing caught us by total surprise. I mean, I knew she kept an inhaler, but I never thought sex would . . ." Even Adena got choked up about the truth and how her friend was dead as a result of an out-of-control blow job.


Eventually, Juggler asked the couple, "Where is the body?"

Mason and Adena looked at each other, likely the both of them thinking about the music that had just begun to thump loudly from the garage. Obviously, somebody was toying with the XL.

# seventeen

A bass-heavy rap song by the Ying Yang Twins was loud enough to rattle some of the yard tools that hung along the walls of the garage. Through the corner of his eye, Mason caught Juggler shaking his head as he followed the Fickle couple down a step into their garage. It was too easy to read Juggler's thoughts, how he must've been cursing Sid in his mind.

Juggler had already yelled the name once. Now he knocked on the driver's-side window and barked the name louder: "Sid!"

The music died down enough for Sid to hear the gang leader.

"What're you, a *moron*? I can't even believe I got you handlin' money for me, stupid as you are."

Sid was left with that dumb look on his face. And that's when Juggler pivoted off toward the back of the vehicle.

"Any cripple fuck for a best friend let be the first to know."

And that might've been a funny comment to both the Fickles, but for the gross sight they were about to witness once Juggler opened the rear hatch of the truck.

Mason could already see Loween's face in his mind, how her mouth was frozen open, as though she were ready to get it on again. Only this time there was a surprised look about her, with her eyes swollen, glassy, and gleaming, and her cheeks drawn in as if she'd lost twenty pounds in just as many days. All the imagery in Mason's mind, and Juggler hadn't even opened the hatch yet. When he eventually did, it was preceded by a deep breath, maybe to brace himself for the worst.

The next thing Mason knew, his own insiders erupted. The stench was so god-awful that it could've been smog, with odor thick enough to chew on. But for sure, it was at least disagreeable enough to have Perkins breakfast spit out of Mason's mouth in a kind of discolored lava. The others, Juggler, one of his henchmen, and Adena were merely jolted, all but Adena turning away in a rush of upset expressions, coughing, and searching for clean air.

"What gives?" asked Sid, just about back in his wheelchair by now. "Ewww," he uttered once he saw the vomit.

Surviving his coughing and hacking, Juggler turned to Sid with a pair of wicked, watery eyes. "You mean, *you ain't smell that shit?*"

"You know I can't smell shit wit' how my nose is all burnt out."

And then, as if some explanation were required, Juggler turned to Mason and said, "He went from painkillers, to weed, to blow. His nose ain't been the same since." But Juggler soon revisited the project at hand: the dead body of his former number-two girl.

The blanket she was wrapped in had come apart some— something Mason hadn't given much thought to once he and Adena returned from breakfast. He never considered the curves and the turns that made heading to and from the house no less than a roller-coaster ride. Maybe he was also in denial about the whole affair, daydreaming and hoping that this would go away.

"Couldn't even wrap her proper, huh? Just some baggage to unload in a hole."

"I swear we wanted to do the right thing—"

"So you called po-po?" Juggler asked.

"Not *that* much of a right thing. If I did that, I'd be all over the news by now," Mason said, recovering from the upset stomach.

"So, you save *your* ass, while Loween gits her ass tossed in a hole."

"Listen, I don't know where you're from, but up here shit like this doesn't happen. Especially the *way* it happened. And—"

"What that gotta do wit' where we from?" mentioned another Juggler cronie.

"If you let me finish makin' my point, I'm looking to say these hillbillies don't play up hers. We ain't too far from all-white here in the mountains, and what *is* black will no doubt jump right in on the action."

"What action?"

"THEY HANG MY ASS!"

"And they wouldn't waste no time," Adena said. There was moment of deep thought as the various sets of eyes drifted into the truck, where the corpse lay awkwardly.

Feces had escaped the body and smeared about the covers and the carpeting. Loween's skin had lost some of its brown and was now digressing to a clammy gray hue. And the stench was still very strong, even as it mixed with the cool garage air.

"I still can't believe you ain't smell this shit," Juggler said, maybe searching for a place to take the conversation besides this dead end. "Whatcha waitin' for, Pooh . . . Yap. Wrap that girl up. We got a burial to finish."

And just like that, the men made a mummy out of Loween with a canvas drop cloth from the corner of the garage. They went back out to the ditch, finished the digging. And if this wasn't a burial that was cheesy enough, a handful of weeds and daisies were set across the top of the corpse before the soil was replaced.

"Spread the rest of that dirt over these, and get some leaves and twigs and shit to cover the raw area so it's like the forest floor." Juggler, the general.

The rain that had turned to drizzle was now wind. And while the entire bunch was now indoors, Adena offered to make lunch. Mason was about to make a face in response to his wife's sudden hospitality, but one of the goons—the quiet one, named Ace—was watching Mason's every move. There was still a dilemma here, something Juggler was ready to address in depth: "And the dilemma is that your secret is no longer *your* secret, it's now *our* secret. Meaning, we all have a lot to be concerned about. More you than us, for sho'. But I'm thinkin' there's a solution to all this. A solution, where you win, I win, we all win."

Mason took a deep breath before he said, "Let's hear it."

As if he had a choice in the matter.


If you asked Mason, Thanksgiving had come much too fast, even if his days had felt like weeks. There had been some memorable holidays in the past. Intimate dinners at lavish restaurants. Serving dinner to the needy in nearby Harrisburg, Pennsylvania. That occasion had also been conveniently featured in the local papers, another feather in Mason's cap. Mr. Do Good Fickle. On other occasions, he and Adena had just stayed home to do what they did best. Fuck.

However, this Thanksgiving was likely to outdo every other, whether in the past or the future, because the Fickle house, for the first time, was inhabited by nearly a dozen people. Most of them absolute strangers who didn't leave room for a dull moment.

"What choice do we have?" Mason had said to Adena, on the evening of Juggler's now-famous "solution" speech. "They got me by the balls. They either stay here a few weeks and get their so-called *business* off the ground, or I tell them to all go to hell, and suffer the consequences. And I don't even wanna *think* about the consequences.

A media circus, a tragedy, and, oh, the *suicide*. 'Cuz for real? Life really wouldn't be shit once we got that rubber stamp—"

Adena was lying close to Mason in a sheer teddy, when she ordinarily came to bed naked. Her hand was on his bare chest, stroking the calm into him.

"What's the funny look for?" Mason then asked her. "You know what I'm talking about. The whole thing with being marked as a sex offender. It's not even the worst part that I'd have to do time, get probation, or whatever. That's the easy part compared to the public stoning, the loss of my status in the Poconos real estate market, and you know my competition would have a field day. Competition? Listen to me talkin' about competition like that would even matter. Shit, I'd be lucky if I could hold a job at McDonald's flippin' burgers."

"Mason, you shouldn't be so hard on yourself. You always came out on top. Every time you have a big closing you get like this. And I know you're not an insecure person. If you were, you'd never be that accomplished, successful husband I married."

Mason chuckled and said, "That all sounds so impressive until you add a dead body and a bunch of New Orleans thugs."

Just ten weeks later, those New Orleans thugs had their enterprise in partial swing, operating from the home of Mason and Adena Fickle. Sid was up to his old tricks, luring the cuties from their after-school encounters or the local public library, the library being his most successful spot. He'd play needy, like when he asked one girl if she could reach a top shelf for a magazine that was out of his reach. She'd never know how he was staring at her stretching her young body to help him out. She'd never second-guess as to why he parked his wheelchair directly across from her, close enough to hear her giggles and the comment, "I know, but he is kinda cute." And she never saw it coming, the charm that Sid could turn on and off at a moment's notice. Once the girl's friend stepped away, Sid made his move.

"So . . . I'm new around here. Where can a guy go to hang out and have fun?"

"Fun? Here? In the Poconos? There's no fun here. Nothin' but deer, tourists, and, well, the flea market."

Sid coughed up a laugh.

"I know. Big deal, right?"

"Well, I'm sure for some people."

"I actually work here. It's the only place I can get a job at my age."

"Oh? How old are you?" Sid guessed her to be sixteen or seventeen.

"Sixteen. You?"

"Oh, I'm nineteen. A little more facial hair than the average college hunk, but still I gets my compliments."

"College? Oh yeah? Where?"

"Er . . . uh . . . St. Agnes."

"Huh? Neva heard a that. Where's it at?"

"Uh . . . really high up in the mountains, closer to Delaware, ya know. A private institution."

"Oh. Okay, neva been to Delaware."

"Bet you never been a lotta places."

"Oh, I would go. My parents let me use the car now and then. I just neva had no reason to."

"I see. And you live here, right?"

"Yup. Near the Shawnee Village. Dad does construction with them at Shawnee. Mom's a clerk at the post office."

"That so?"

"Yup."

"Ever, ah . . . think about modelin'?"

"Modeling? Me? Lord, heavens, no."

"Well, I think you should seriously consider it. You're not exactly an ugly duckling."

"What's that s'posed to mean?"

"Don't take it the wrong way. I was just complimenting you. Just sayin' I think you're kinda fly. Definitely attractive enough for fashion. Maybe even movies."

This was Sid's softer sell, the bit about modeling and possible movies. The softer sell he reserved for the pushovers, those young girls who hadn't seen much of life but for TV, movies, and magazines. The hard sell he'd save for the city girls, since they'd been there and done that. They wouldn't easily fall for the average line, which was why Juggler didn't make out too well in Harlem. Sid just couldn't deliver the bodies. However, here in the Poconos was a different story. He'd already run this same line more than two dozen times and was never more successful with his numbers. Altogether, the New Silver Dollar Club had six and soon to be seven (if Juggler had his way) girls turning tricks to help build the new enterprise. Of those six girls, four of them were down at the Days Inn, two per room. The latest two were sharing a room at the Fickle home, and already they had become part of the day-to-day activity—the cooking, cleaning, and clothes.

With Thanksgiving Day's arrival, the large group all lent a hand in the chores. And again, one of the girls was all up in Adena's business.

"Is your man always away like this?" one of the pros asked Adena. "Pro" was the title Juggler and his boys had given to their working girls. It was also something of a sarcastic moniker, obvious that *pro* was short for *prostitute*, but more so since the girls were definitely *not* great at what they did—like a pro golfer or a pro baller. These girls were bicycles with training wheels, bound to one day ride on experience, but still stumbling along the way.

Martha, Bones, Stormy, Neva, Raven, and Trixx. They were either birth names or nicknames, all of which Adena came to know quite well. Adena had taken on tasks that included everything from arranging discounted rooms down at her job, to getting the others comfortable in her home, to food shopping for thirteen people. What once was a life of solitude with her soul mate turned into a communion of seedy characters; a small army, which depended on the whims of a bama named Juggler, whose intentions were three inches over the line of wrong and risky.

"Basically, he's into real estate up to his neck. Always at an open house, a closing, or a negotiation. It's always something."

"So, when does he make time for you? I hardly see him."

"Oh, he *makes* time. Trust me. 'Cuz if he don't do nothing else, he gotta have me satisfied."

"Right, right. I don't think I could keep me a man for too long, 'cuz I always gotta try something new."

Adena laughed. "Is that why they call you Neva?"

"You laugh, but that's the truth. I can't get enough. I need dick every day, at least four times a day. And if I only get it three times, I'm gonna be at least playin' with myself to make up for that missing dick. They used to call me Neva-Enuf, just 'cuz I was even crazier when I was younger. I used to jump everything moving."

Adena mulled that over. Crazier? She used to get it more than four times a day?

"They had to kick my horny ass outta high school when a school monitor caught me in the boys' room."

Adena smirked, and glued herself to Neva's every word. It was as if she was being exposed to so much more than what the eye could see of these visitors in her home and their backgrounds.

"It wouldn't have been so bad," Neva continued, "except they caught us dead wrong, all half dressed, and out there like two sweaty freaks. I couldn't even play dumb with how I looked—hair all messed up, a breast showin', and, oh, I was on my period when we were fuckin', so of course it was nasty."

Adena made a face. As much as she was curious about Neva, there was still such a thing as TMI—Too Much Information. But if Neva-Enuf was hot, Stormy was blazin'. Over Thanksgiving dishes, Adena learned just how raunchy a young white girl could be, despite a good family, a high school diploma, and an impressive intelligence. All that didn't stop Stormy from having multiple partners in a Harrisburg playground, or her exhibition at a local movie theater that turned almost everyone's eyes away from Tom Cruise *("Tom who?").* Stormy had joked when describing how intense her theatrics were and how much attention she had received before an usher showed up. And when that encounter didn't seem to impress all the women in the Fickles' kitchen, Stormy detailed a "dare" she'd accepted.

"I just didn't give a fuck," Stormy said. "And I had every last one of those stiffs jerkin' off in front of me right in the same glass. Okay, so it sounds crazy, me swallowin' that mess—but it all went past my tongue, so I didn't taste nothin'. Plus, I took their three hundred dollars, just had to listen to them cackle like asses. But *they* looked more like freak shows than I did, since all I did was head for the bathroom to gag it all back up from my throat; and you *know* I gargled with Listerine, brushed my chops, and drank like a gallon of water. Still, ya girl basically pulled off the big magic trick," claimed Stormy, putting up a high-five for the few listeners who understood and agreed. Meanwhile, Adena and one other stood dumbfounded by Stormy's audacity as she summed things up: "Bottom line is, ya girl paid her rent with that money, ya heard?"

While Stormy and Neva had the seedy side of the Silver Dollar Club covered, there was a softer side, a void that Raven filled. Raven was the quiet one with the petite body and honest eyes. She had that appeal and seemed agreeable to everything. She was also becoming the "in demand" member of Juggler's stock. Quiet as it was kept, hardly around, and almost always working. If not turning tricks down at the Days Inn, Raven was at least serving as an escort for someone on the growing client list. For a few of her escort jobs, the clients didn't even want to take the date to the distance. In one case, a client would see Raven as "too sweet," and he continued to date her with hopes of developing a relationship in the truest sense of the word. Little did that hopeful know that Raven shared these desires with Juggler at every opportunity. Not only did this information keep her boss abreast of things, but it also had him laughing till he was nearly hoarse. At the same time, he applauded Raven for her honor and dedication.

"You keep on selling him the fantasy, Raven. And if that moron takes it too far, you tell him, point-blank, your pussy is too precious to belong to any one man. And if that doesn't work, just tell him the truth, that your pussy belongs to me." Such a claim had Raven turning bashful, more or less agreeing with Juggler and his cold comment. And yet, this was the reality in Juggler's world. You did as he asked, he kept you comfortable, and life went on as usual.

Adena got to see all of this firsthand, got to hear all the twisted stories adjusted to all the mannerisms and idiosyncrasies, too. "It's like I'm squeezing all of these different lives, these different characters, with all their ways and dreams into my own," she told Mason while in bed one night. In bed was the only private space the two had left in their home, the only place that their secrets felt secure.

"It's like my own life has been multiplied, I'm doing more, hearing more, and seeing too much all in one day. And I get that all without even leaving the house."

Mason let out a frustrated sigh before he said, "It won't be too much longer, boo. At least they're doing what they said they'd do. They got their bullshit business going. More and more they're leaving the house, right?"

"Mason, you're blind. Yes, their business is booming. I always see one of these guys counting money on our kitchen counter, mind you. But, hell no, they're not leaving the house more. On one or two occasions I've seen strangers stepping out of the bedrooms, the bathrooms, even the garage door. Sometimes, when you're gone, I want to call and cry, but I can't stand to make this any more miserable than it is. They've turned our love nest into an orgy, Mason. Half of 'em don't clean up after themselves. The other half is rude and disrespectful." Adena's eyes watered with her testimony.

"Easy, baby. Easy. This'll soon be over."

"You promise, Mason?"

"I promise. But as of tomorrow, that stuff about strangers in the house has got to be addressed. I'm sorry you didn't say something sooner." And Mason kissed his wife with whatever passion he could muster. Mostly it had been missing ever since this nightmare began.


Mason's morning routine used to see him up around four thirty, on the StairMaster for a half hour, and out of the shower by six o'clock. But things had changed. Pooh and Yap were housed in Mason's garage now, with the electric heater always on high to keep it warm with the rest of the house. No more big breakfasts at home, either. He spent most mornings at Perkins now, making it a point to try out their entire variety just to keep things interesting. He was usually the first one in the office. That early it was still quiet enough for him to lay his head on the desk and grab up a few more winks since his time at home wasn't exactly peaceful.

Music was thumping on one side of the house, the TV blasting all night on the other; a loud card game was escalating into cussing and arguing. The Fickle home, it seemed, would never be normal again.

But this morning he had to confront Juggler. He came into the living room and cleared his throat, trying to awaken Juggler from his slouched position on the sectional. He went for the remote and turned off the TV, which was blaring the most recent *Girls Gone Wild* video offer. Mason cleared his throat loudly again.

"Uh . . . Juggler?" Mason had gathered up all this confidence to address the bandleader, and now he couldn't even wake him. Mason's eyes swept the living room, brushing past the litter of beer cans, pizza boxes, and half-empty fast-food containers. It was a pleasure on the one hand to know that his wife had given up the hospitality insofar as cooking dinners and doing clothes and such; but on the other, this group was nearly destroying his property and its value—everything from the oil slicks out on the driveway pavement to the carpet stains indoors, to the cigarette nicotine and fingerprints on his walls, to the sudden emergence of insects. Sure, they lived in the woods, and a certain amount of buzzards were expected. But as much as these visitors opened doors and went in and out of the house, the Fickle house could've just as well been a welcome wagon for fleas.

Now, Mason nudged Juggler. He got some movement and a grunt, but not much more.

" 'Sup, homey?" Mason spun around, half scared out of his mind, and his attention dropped a few feet to where Wheelchair Sid sat bare-chested in boxers.

Lanky, tattooed, and scarred, Sid seemed comfortable in his shell, although handicapped and menacing to look at.

" 'Sup, y'self."

"Juggler knocked out a couple hours ago, after he goddamned cleaned everybody's pockets."

"That so?"

"You tryin' a holla? 'Cuz I don't think he's much about nothin' right now. Last time I saw 'im this way was down home; we had some po' boys, a fifth of Henny, and it was a wrap for him until late the next day."

"What's a po—never mind. Sorry I asked. Just could you tell Juggler to call me when he wakes up? I got somethin' important I need to talk about." The way Mason carried his request had an air of warning to it.

Sid merely whimpered before responding with a lazy, unconcerned, "Riiight." As if to say, *Sure you do*, or *Sure, what you say will matter.*

In response, Mason's expression firmed up, and he said, "Just tell 'em to call me. I don't need the extra shit."

"Oh-ho-ho-ho . . . Nigga tryin' a get tough now, huh? You bet I'ma pass him yo' message. And I'ma love seein' you bitch up when my nigga hollas back. Now one y'self." Sid did this whole wheelie with his chair, spun around, and whistled in a way that promised trouble.

In the meantime, Mason's face was still twisted with the *one y'self* comment, bringing him (once again) to wonder how in the hell he got himself into this quagmire with these idiots.

All that day Mason maintained that hard-nosed approach at work, on his business calls, and with his clients, while in the back of his mind he awaited that important call. Somehow he had to be firm with this guy, to let him know he meant business. But at the same time, he had to be cautious, considering the variables, the what-ifs, and the consequences of a potential falling-out between the parties.

At eleven o'clock Mason took lunch. He called Adena as he wolfed down a turkey sub.

"Everything okay at the ranch?"

"Hmm . . . okay as it will ever be, I guess."

"No word from our boy Juggler?"

"Should there be?"

"I told you I'd have a talk with 'im. Did you cross his path?"

"Well, it's kind of hard not to cross his path, dear. I mean they're only all over the place."

"So nothing unusual. No hostility or nothin'?"

"The only hostile thing here is me, Mason." Mason could hear Adena lowering her voice and perhaps speaking through clenched teeth as she said, "Get these people out of here."

"Okay. Okay, boo, I'm working on it. Trust me. Would you? Just don't do anything or say anything crazy to push his buttons."

"*Whatever,*" Adena said. And she hung up.

Mason stopped chewing and starred at his cell phone with that stupid, stunned gaze of his. *No, she didn't jus'*— He would've called back and addressed that little 'tude of hers if it were any other time.

However, things being as "special" and sensitive as they were, he dared not to take it there.

After a sigh, Mason's resolve was to forget about things until the call came. How many times had he told himself to stop pushing anxiety to the limit? To stop buying and selling fear before the objective came to pass? And yet, saying something and doing it were two different things—the space between a dream and a dream come true. A space that Mason found himself trapped within, trying to guess his way around, conjuring answers to so many loose ends.

So busy was he that time raced by without that important phone call, carrying him right into rush-hour traffic and up those winding roads until he returned home once again.

At once Mason realized the trucks were missing, and he thought about that best-case scenario: *Maybe they packed up and left?*

M ason came home to a dark, quiet house.
"Adena!" he called out.

No answer. It was half past seven and Adena would usually be home to welcome him. Even if she had to make a run she'd leave a note, or she'd call him from her cell. The two might even catch each other on the main road as they drove in opposite directions. But not today.

Mason immediately grabbed up his cell phone and hit the speed dial. His worrying would begin once he reached Adena's voice mail, or if the phone rang without an answer. Instead, his worst fear became a much greater nightmare.

"Yo!" was the answer—a man's voice, when Mason called his wife.

"Who dis'?" the voice came again. But Mason simply disconnected the call and redialed, only to hear the same voice.

"Yo, who dis', man?"

"Jesus. Is this Adena's phone?" Mason asked.

"Dee Dee? Oh, yeah. She up in her job hookin' sump'n up."

Mason's trembling, exhausted response was, "Really?" *Dee?* He even lost track of his intentions. Why had he called his wife in the first place? What the hell just happened? As though his whole world turned upside down, all of a sudden, Mason became dizzy and he forced his vision to blur as he stared at a wall of his dining room. Had things gone that crazy that these vagabonds were answering his wife's phone? *They're at her job? Maybe even driving together.*

The phone call Mason made may as well been a final warning to show just how deep these people had gotten into the Fickles' lives. They were in the house, sharing the kitchens and bathrooms, using (and abusing) bedrooms. And now they were on Adena's phone? Down at her job? Doing who knows what? This had to stop! He had to think of something.

Again Mason hung up the phone, only now it was desperation pushing him as opposed to anxiety. His first desire was to find anything he could get his hands on, and to smash it in a fit of rage. But within minutes he found himself in gym clothes working up a sweat on the StairMaster. Stress relief was his only recourse for the time being, that is, until he'd come face-to-face with his adversaries.

Ten minutes into his workout, Mason knew there was only one solution.

He had to move Loween's body.

# eighteen

More than half the clan had returned by the time Mason finished his shower. He was feeling so goddamn good that he was almost singing to himself. He easily put out of his mind the rage and hostility he felt toward the visitors and couldn't wait to confide in Adena.

"So where'd you guys go?" Mason asked Adena as he dried himself. She had come up to the bedroom to put away her purse and keys.

"Still showin' 'em around town. They needed to get a set of keys cut and they recruited a couple of new girls that had to be put up at a motel."

Mason's response was most instant. "Keys?"

"Not for the house, babe. They found some apartment where they do—well, ya know. And they needed some copies for all the girls. I'm tellin' you, these guys *are* about their business. Even though I'm tired of seeing their faces, you at least gotta respect their game."

"Respect their game. Since when did you start respecting the prostitution business, Adena?"

Adena sucked her teeth. "It's not like that, Mason. I just see what I see, that's all."

"That so? And while you were seeing what *you were seeing,* did you happen to ask these *fledgling businessmen* for a month and a half rent and lodging fees for having used our home, running up our bills like they've been doing? Betcha didn't remember that." Of course, Mason was being facetious about the room and board. No way that was gonna happen.

"Mason, don't get salty with me. You're the one who said yes to their proposition. If you want their money, you ask 'em. Don't lay that on me."

The argument was just getting off to a start when the bedroom door was pushed open.

"Hey there!" Juggler said to Mason. "Heard you wanted to see me?"

Mason wanted to lash out at this man's gall, barging into their bedroom like he did, but he held his tongue. He had bigger game to bring down and it started with his plan to get himself unstuck from the muddy mess they were in.

"Nah—I, ah . . . I had—or I *thought* I had some exciting news that could help you with your enterprise." Mason, the liar. "But the deal went belly-up this afternoon. Long story, short, it was a vacant house that I thought I could get you with no money down. Something that could've worked real good for what you all are doing, plus it was closer to town."

"Oh really? So what happened?"

"An investor came through and scooped it up."

"Just like that."

"Oh yeah. Happens all the time here in the Poconos," Mason said. He was careful not to look toward Adena for fear that she might shed light on his lie.

But it seemed that even Juggler was disbelieving as he said, "Well, why would I wanna go into a vacant house anyway? We're all perfectly happy right where we are, right?"

"Of course," Mason said quickly. "You guys are more than welcome to stay as long as you like. I just thought you wanted your own space . . . your own world." Mason was next to Adena now, hand around her shoulders to pull her into his way of thinking. In his mind he was saying, *Play along, love. I'll explain later.*

"The main objective is to keep them thinking that things are fine," Mason later explained. "As long as they think we're agreeable and content, they'll never expect us to slip the rug from under their whole scheme."

"But what happens after you move the body? What if they go to the police anyway?"

"That's just it . . . there is no body, so let 'em tell all they want. No body, no crime. You've seen enough TV to know that."

"And the body? Where you gonna put that?"

"Haven't figured that one out yet. That's why we gotta leave things alone. Let me work that part of the plan out in my head. I'm a good troubleshooter, so I'm sure I'll think somethin' up."

"So how much longer do we deal with this?" Adena asked, dressing her body for a good night's sleep. Mason was still in the bathroom, at the final stages of high day-ending hygiene.

"I would say for as long as we have to, but I know you're stressing here at home. So, I'll give it till Christmas. New Year's at the latest. But tell me . . . how often are they *all* out of the house at the same time?"

"Well, I can't say after tomorrow. I'm moving from third shift to first. So, I'll be leaving the house with you for the next three months."

"Okay . . . then, at least guess for me. How often have you seen them all out at once?"

"Sometimes it's the guys going out and the girls are home with me. The girls are always going in and out. Other times, it's just Juggler here with me. To be honest, Mason, I really don't keep tabs like that."

Mason made a face, as if to say, *You could've fooled me.* Adena took that as foul and curled up under the blankets. Her body language said, *No sex tonight, Mr. Fickle.* Still, Mason cuddled Adena from behind and promised her things would change soon.

F or the whole week following, Mason made it a point to work from home. The negotiations he conducted by phone were behind closed doors—both the bedroom door and the bathroom door. The Internet and the other computer activities he had no choice but to take care of in the garage. He did this while Pooh snored like a wild beast, or while Yap took his turn at the StairMaster, or while both N'awlins goons lifted weights and stirred up a spicy funk. All the while, Mason carefully assessed his opportunities, measuring when the best time might be for him to excavate Loween. He anticipated that the job would have to be done at night, but he didn't discount the possibility of a daytime move since, at times, the property and the surrounding area could be as peaceful and out-of-the-way as a walk on the moon.

C hristmas was around the corner by two weeks, and the Fickle household was beginning to show signs of joy and goodwill; at least all the visitors felt that way. One of the girls invested in decorations and another put up lights in the first-floor windows. And when it was decided that a tree was needed, without Mason's knowledge, Ace went out and cut a tree down. It was only then that Mason realized that Ace wasn't the sharpest knife in the drawer, since the tree he brought into the house wasn't even green but a young oak that had yet to drop its first acorn. But to compound the ignorance, there wasn't even a base for the tree to stand in. So some brilliant-idea man thought to carry in a few large rocks that were positioned as wedges so that the tree could stand alone. Never mind if a soft wind blew and that the tree might topple over. The spirited ones still went on with dressing the forgery until it cast the new and improved definition of gaudy.

Mason observed all of the happenings from a safe distance, as though he were a guest in his own house. He also realized a strong possibility, an advantage that might help him with his plan.

The group of men, including Juggler, Ace, and Pooh, were developing a ritual of nightly spades games that always had them shouting and arguing. In the meantime, if Sid wasn't chauffeuring a pro to and from town, he was a couch potato, playing one of those Grand Theft Auto video games, cursing at the TV while the game progressed. And if the pros weren't out on dates, they were playing their own games with makeup, or chatting among themselves or else indulging in a movie. Altogether there were six girls in the house now; the four who had been staying at the Days Inn had complained about one thing or another. But it was obvious that they were bored and isolated when they weren't working. And besides, the control freak in Juggler would rather that everyone stay up on the hill since, one, there'd be money saved; two, it was convenient; and three, the girls were useful, when they weren't catty. After all, there was housekeeping to be done; and who else was gonna keep things running smoothly in the domestic area? There was no way Juggler was going to do dishes or clean clothes. Pooh and Yap were already doing their part, escorting girls and running errands for the boss. Of course, Wheelchair Sid was next to good-for-nothing, and Ace was a straight-up slob, never seen without his three packs of cigarettes in hand and a cup, which he spit in from time to time. No sense in him doing any cooking or cleaning.

So, the bulk of the day-to-day living and the menial chores that supported it were left up to Adena, Neva, Stormy, and Bones. Bones didn't mind a bit since she wasn't "asked out" as much as the others. Better to be busy earning her keep, or else face possible dismissal. Neva, on the other hand, was finding good conversation and companionship with Adena and Stormy. Adena was more curious than a

virgin, and Neva already had so much in common with Stormy—
how they both could claim, in many ways, that they'd been there,
done that. And so even if gender may have been coincidental to the
needs of the present circumstances, it was still the way things usually went with Juggler, always with the upper hand over the women
who worked for him.

"I pay you, you do as I say, and what else is there?" was one of
Jugglers quotes if there was ever a question as to how or why he did
things the way he did. And who would argue with that?

Even if Mason didn't show it, he was wagging his head all this
time, wondering how these women allowed themselves to be overcome and walked over by this guy from out of town. What was it
that was so special about this guy named Juggler and his want to suc-
ceed as a Poconos pimp?

Except, Mason didn't plan on being around this crew long
enough to find out. Whatever their business was was their business,
and none of Mason's business. And regardless of what these women
were doing to themselves just for one man's progress, there was no
way Mason was going to step in and play hero; nor was he gonna put
his bid in for humanitarian of the year. He had problems of his own,
for sure. And, no matter what, that came first.


More and more, Mason was becoming familiar with their routine.
Sid was the scout who went after new flesh, while the other
three performed either as chauffeurs, gofers, or security. There was a
voicemail for new inquiries and a cell phone number for established
clients. The important part of the business was the return clients
who wanted attention every week, or every other week, all according to how much attention they lacked back home. In any case, all
business phone numbers and client names were kept confidential.
Good business required that.

In the meantime, Juggler kept track of all the numbers, the hours the girls logged, and the money they earned. Mason guessed the girls to be making from $100 to $250 per day, while they in turn brought back $1,000 to $2,500 per day, per girl. Considering that every day wasn't the greatest, and that Bones was the "lackey" in the pack, Mason calculated Juggler's earnings to be anywhere from $5,000 to $7,500 per day, realistically. In a week's time the enterprise could account for $25,000 on the low end and $40,000 on a good week. In the end, Juggler wasn't doing too badly.

Mason had been bored and found himself doodling these assessments at the dinning-room table, taking a guess at just how lucrative the prostitution business could be, when the doorbell rang. He had to beat out (of all people) Wheelchair Sid to answer his own door.

"Expectin' somebody?" asked Sid.

There were so many times that Mason just wanted to kick this guy's chair over; now was another of those times. Meanwhile, in his mind, his reply was, *And if I was?* But instead, he chose not to respond at all.

"Hey there! Bill. What's good in the hood?" Mason's greeting was an attempt at normalcy, but even he felt a little awkward. It didn't help any that he stepped out onto the porch, as opposed to welcoming his friend and neighbor in; something he'd do under ordinary circumstances.

"Nice day, no?"

"Mason, it's thirty degrees outside. But if you call it a nice day, I guess I can't argue. How you been, buddy? The wife and I have been reaching out to you, but . . ." Bill noticed the presence inside the foyer. "Everything okay over here?" The inquiry was made at a low volume so that it was for Mason's ears only.

"Just dandy, Bill. Why ask?"

"Well . . ." Bill made a face, his realization that some eavesdropping was possible. He also pulled Mason's arm so that he'd follow

Bill back up the walkway until the two were roadside, just next to the mailbox.

"It's not just me, Mason. Barbara's been saying the same thing. You two haven't been answering our calls. Both the wife and I have come to your door at least half a dozen times over the past weeks; you're never home, and if nobody answers the door, then it's either one stranger or another."

"Oh, that. Well, it's been real busy, Bill."

"I see that," he responded with his eyes reaching down the driveway toward the group of SUVs. "Anything special going on? I mean, last time we spoke you were telling me about your, ah, problem. How's that going?"

"Oh, that. Um . . ." Mason uttered a chuckle, knowing how that was such a slight issue as compared to everything that followed. "We're moving close to a resolution. Real close."

"And your visitors? Mason, between Barbara and I coming to your door, we must've met five different people. At least. You never introduced anybody. So . . . what're we supposed to think? I mean, we've had that one conversation about the possibility of you two moving, or that you might be involved in a time-share of some kind. But, I thought we were friends? Wouldn't you tell us if you were off somewhere on vacation? You tell us everything else. Plus, you know we'd watch the house."

Mason put a hand on Bill's shoulder for some assurance. "Trust me, Bill. Everything is just fine. It is."

"It is?" Bill repeated. But his attention was pulled to some movement down the driveway. Two girls, both of them with high heels and fishnet stockings, shorts, and long, flowing hair, were leaving from the side entrance. They got into the black Ram Charger. Following them was a guy in a wheelchair, who proceeded to execute his do-it-yourself entry up and into the truck.

All Bill could do was stare, face frozen, while he repeated again, "It is?"

"Yes, Bill. It is." And the way Mason said this was more of an indication for Bill to mind his business.

"Okay, well, just so you know, most of the latest block-watch meeting was about you, buddy. And a friend can only do so much to defend a friend, until it gets obvious."

"Meaning?"

Bill was already on a roll with plenty to say, only the loud motor and the Ram's aggressive exodus from the driveway made him hesitate.

"Meaning, I'm your friend, Mason. For almost five years now we've been communicating. Now, all of a sudden, nothing. And then this," said Bill, gesturing toward the truck and the exhaust it left as it sped down the road.

"Gonna have to talk to you later, Bill. I was crunching some numbers when you showed up. Got a deadline I gotta meet."

Wagging his head, Bill held a defeated expression as he turned away from Mason. He also mumbled.

"I didn't hear you, Bill."

Bill didn't even bother to turn around. He just raised his voice and repeated, "Something ain't right. Something ain't right."


Mason eventually shook his neighbor's comments and returned to the house. He could feel how bad things must've looked, and how distant he and Adena must've grown from Bill and Barbara in the past month. But there was a dilemma here. What could he do? And what could a corrections officer do to help him? Not a thing.

*You're a good dude, Bill. But this one I gotta handle alone.*

# nineteen

At every turn, this was becoming more complicated. The answer to it all seemed easy—lose the body and force the houseguests out. But just getting to that space and all the clutter in the way made things tougher than it was meant to be.

What Mason really needed was a head doctor, and yet he had to settle for Adena, who was the only person he could confide in. She was the only person he could safely share his troubles with. If they didn't discuss these issues in bed, then they did so over the phone, until even the cell phones ran hot, or lost their charge. The phone calls were also that necessary link between the couple, since they spent most of their days apart and most of their nights catching up on much-needed sleep. There was hardly room for affection, except for maybe an impromptu visit.

Today was about to be one of those days. There was the visit from Bill Clemons, then Mason locked his bedroom door and watched a DVD—one of the porn flicks from the couple's stash.

All that did was to add anxiety to his frustrations, and his heartbeat began to act erratic. And his dick got hard. And before he knew it he was zipping down Blue Mountain in near-record time, recalling Bill's visit in its entirety. *Just so you know, most of the block-watch meeting was about you.* If those images weren't fighting for his attention, then there were the drops of information that he learned about the visitors in his home . . . two high school kids in the bathroom stall . . . another girl serving multiple partners at the local playground . . . a group of studs all jerking off into a glass . . . legs in fishnet stockings . . . Wheelchair Sid and his *one y'self* comment . . . some faceless client stepping out of a guest room, fixing his pants, and looking at Mason as though *he* were the one out of place.

All of those images flashing through his mind, only to rewind themselves back to the digging—back to the body in his Yukon, and back to the night of the accident. And it all blurred Mason's senses until he was driving down the median, unaware of oncoming cars.

Horns blowing, cars pulling to the shoulder to avoid the maniac with the big truck, none of that shook him from his stupor. There was an instant when he thought he was the corpse, and he pictured himself being unwrapped in the drop cloth, looking up into the dark cabin of the truck. Eventually, dirt was being tossed over him and then all was silent.

The Yukon swerved and took a sharp right before it came to screeching halt there at the junction of 207 and 409. Plenty of traffic, drivers awaiting the green light, and strip-mall activities were all suddenly facing him.

Mason was rattled and wide awake, aware that he'd almost taken his own life, if not merely wrecking his body. But why? He was getting close to a solution here. There were *options* now for him and his wife to escape from a trap that at first seemed impossible to get out of. For the first time since things took a turn for the worst, there was a way out. As if to preach to himself, Mason counted these blessings and eased his truck off the road into the nearest gas station. Instead of gas, he went into the convenience store for a pick-me-up. He figured something hot (like coffee), or sweet (like a chocolate bar), was the answer. After grabbing both, and then swallowing half of each down his gut, Mason drove off with renewed energy. Ten minutes later he pulled into the Days Inn parking lot.

C ell phone stuffed in his pocket and keys in hand, Mason swaggered through the rear entrance and down a hallway that he knew would bring him to the housekeeping office.

"Hey there," Mason said, unsure of the supervisor's name.

"Why, Mason Fickle. Heard so much about you. Happy New Year to you."

"Oh, I wouldn't push it so fast. Still got a couple weeks to go. When January first comes, I'll be a new man."

The supervisor chuckled. "So what can we do ya for? Need me to page the wife?"

"Oh, no. Thought I'd just surprise her. Where's she workin' today?"

"Over in the East Quarters I believe—" Checking a bulletin board. "Yes. That's exactly where she is. Sure you don't need me to page her?"

"Not at all. Somethin' special to surprise her with."

"Well, you know you're always welcome to our home, mister. Already got the keys to the city, don't cha?"

Mason remained humble and thanked Adena's boss before he wandered off.

There was so much that Adena shared regarding her job, only Mason never paid it too much attention, as long as he knew where she was and that she was safe. Otherwise, how exciting could a housekeeping job be?

Across the parking lot and into one of three buildings, Mason climbed a flight of steps and immediately smelled the mildew. The East Quarters was the least used of the motel's facilities, so Mason wondered, *Why is she cleaning over here?*

A set of glass doors partitioned the second-floor hallway from the staircase. But before Mason opened them he could see in the distance where a housekeeper was standing in the doorway of one of the rooms. It was an easy call to see that this was Adena, with her hair in a ponytail and her ass round in her maid's skirt.

*What's she lookin' at?* Mason wondered, and he crept along until she caught a glimpse of him. At first she seemed startled, but relaxed when she recognized her husband. Mason forced a smile and walked toward her. Adena reached for his hand and pulled him closer to watch with her. Mason turned and looked through the doorway. The room was heavily lit, there was a cameraman positioned by the bed, and two girls were undressing a guy. Mason knew the girls, if not by their names, then by the fishnet stockings they wore when they left his house earlier in the day.

"So, this is what you do at work?" Mason whispered. Adena put her hands on her hips and gave Mason the crooked look.

More watching led to the comments, as the two Peeping Toms began whispering back and forth.

Mason said, "This is almost predictable. After they undress him, somebody's gonna be suckin' somethin'."

Adena said, "It's what you guys like. Why wouldn't we?"

Mason said, "You know, I just got finished watching one of those amateur videos we got at home."

Adena said, *"Our* video? One we made?"

Mason said, "No. Something else. The one with that guy you like. Swingblade."

Adena pretended to shiver in excitement. He was indeed the guy she liked to watch. But her eyes turned back into the room where the live action beat out Memorex, any day.

"This is Juggler's stuff goin' on?

Adena nodded and said, "Pretty professional, ya think."

"What's professional about fucking and sucking on video, Adena?"

Adena cast the sour puss at her husband, as if to imply that he might be jealous.

Predictable or not, one of the girls was now down on her knees while the other girl sat on the bed. The stud, in the meantime, was standing between the two, stiff as a board, enjoying the two pairs of hands and two pairs of lips that worked him over.

T hen Mason remembered why he had rushed down to Adena's job in the first place. He wanted to tell her about Bill Clemons visiting; however, it had been a long time since he and Adena had been intimate and loving. Even longer since it got raunchy and seedy.

"Wanna play?" Mason asked, and he squeezed his wife's hand to show that he was serious.

Adena's glassy, wanton eyes turned up toward Mason, and the two kissed there in the doorway. It felt romantic, at first. Like this was something that they'd both been missing. But Adena, it seemed, was just as hungry as her husband. She tugged at Mason's hand, pulling him away from the open door and to the next room over. The room key slipped out of Adena's uniform and was swiped through the card reader as naturally as if she'd done it in her sleep. Once the door shut behind them, with the slightest bit of daylight to accommodate their actions, the Fickles nearly attacked each other.

Mason was at Adena's blouse. Adena was at Mason's belt buckle, prying it loose as if her life depended on it.

Mason's teeth found Adena's ear, her neck, and then her nipples. Meanwhile, his hands molded to her breasts and their bodies were clinging to each other's.

Amid the heavy breathing, Adena managed to say, "Here we go again, no romance. Just a quick hit it and quit it."

Mason knew she was right, but there was a time for everything, even romance. However, if you asked Mason, now was *not* one of those times. Mason finally pulled his glasses off and tossed them.

"Baby, we haven't been together for over a week. I'm not even *think-ing* about romance at the moment. Maybe later," Mason muttered.

And yet, even Adena's body contradicted her want for romance, clinging tighter to her man, drawing more of his kiss in with hers.

Her back was against the wall now, and both of them were huffing and puffing, fiends for penetration. Mason scooped up his wife and held her legs with his arms hooked underneath. He was rock hard and poking at her until she said, "That's my ass, Mase." At once he adjusted his target. And not that he wouldn't go there, it just wasn't the plan at the present.

He eventually hit pay dirt and thrust up into her, jackhammer fashion. Adena began laughing. "Is this what you saw on the DVD at home?"

"No," Mason said. "I've just . . . been . . . wanting to . . . do this for a while now."

And as if he'd heard and said enough, Mason drove his point home, evoking deep moans from her. She cried here and there and the thrusting graduated to pounding once Mason carried Adena to one of the twin beds. The two of them had to ignore the dust that jumped from their fall and the mildew smell that followed.

"Oh, yeah, that dick feels so gooood!" cried Adena. "Oh yeah, oh yeah, oh yeah!"

All that noise was forcing Mason's excitement to the limit. But this was a woman he knew too well. He knew how to make her scream and how to ultimately satisfy her. So, the screams were just the beginning. Now it was time to fold her legs back for a deeper penetration. And as if this was what Adena was accustomed to, her ankles crossed over her head and her hands grabbed Mason's ass until the two of them were giving and taking, moaning and groaning. Mason bit into her neck. Adena nibbled on his chest. Mason withdrew and climbed closer to her face. Adena naturally took his sloppy wet dick into her mouth. Mason fed her. Adena ate all.

Just about ready to blast off, Mason slid out of her lips and released his ejaculate onto his wife's chin and breasts. When he was done she said, "You didn't cum a lot. What's wrong?"

"You call that not a lot? Shit, speak for yourself."

And just as Mason rolled off to Adena's side, they heard applause.

"Bravo! Bravo!" said a man's voice.

"Woo-hoo!" followed a woman's.

"What the—"

Mason scrambled for cover while Adena proceeded to use a piece of the dusty blanket to wipe herself.

"But I have you to getting *way* more freaky than that."

Mason had come to his senses enough to recognize Juggler's voice. Two of his pros and one of his goons hung by his side.

There was no way to respond. It was all still a bit much to bear, these strangers violating them like this.

But it seemed that the violation didn't stop there.


**H**ey! Gimme that!" yelled Mason once he realized there was a video being recorded. He lost all concern regarding his naked body to lunge at the cameraman. Juggler was quick to respond. He sidestepped so that he'd be close enough to elbow Mason, and Mason fell hard.

"Not so fast, *playboy*. If there's any attacking in here it's gonna be by me."

"You have no right!"

"Mason! Homey! Do you *not* know who you're fuckin' with? I have *every* right, boss. Possession is nine-tenths of the law. That's number one. But, number two, I got the goods on you, lil' nigga. Did you forget? So don't gimme no shit 'bout rights and wrongs. 'Cuz so far I'm the wrong muthafucka in the right place."


**M**ason squinted, not from failure to see, but from pain as he managed to lift himself from the floor. Adena was already putting her clothing back on, and Mason started to do the same. In that instant Mason saw a different side of his wife: how she appeared so "with it" when they were out in public. Even after a day's work, not to mention the work he did with her, Adena managed to appear so cool and together, as if they didn't have a problem in the world.

"Still. I want to thank you for adding footage to my new venture, Amateurs on Tape. 'Cause you two are *definitely* amateurs . . ." Juggler snickered before he repeated Adena's utterances: "Oh, yeah, *that dick feels so good!*"

Juggler and the others laughed while Adena tried to calm her husband. There was no getting around the raw coincidental power that Juggler yielded. And to top that all off, they all had to live together under the same roof.


**M**ason waited for Adena to get home from work and they decided on The Private Table for dinner, their favorite restaurant. It was the treat they needed to give themselves for all the stress they'd been going through. However, good food and a good atmosphere did not erase their problems.

"They're in our house, our refrigerator, our cars, and our bedroom . . . now, they're in our *sex lives*? This shit is off the hook! It's gone—" Mason realized he might be getting too loud, and he stopped to lower his voice. "This has gone too far, Adena. We didn't come this far in our lives to fall backwards. All the sacrifices and this . . . all of the leaps of faith . . . our marriage and our commitment. All of that is being jeopardized here, not to mention our piece of mind and our sanity. Hey—aren't you gonna say anything?"

"What *can* I say? Once upon a time my husband was a man who was a rebel; you used to fill my ears with the issues you had, it didn't matter what it was. If you had a problem with it I had to hear about it day and night. But, Mason, can't you see what happened to you?"

Mason sucked his teeth, then pursed his lips as though Adena didn't know what she was talking about. But in her eyes, she was sure she did.

"Mason, this doesn't have as much to do with Loween, or these assholes that we're dealing with. It has to do with you and success. Your success softened you."

"Softened?"

"I don't want you to take that the wrong way, my husband, but the Mason I used to know would've done things differently."

"Oh, yeah, I guess my attitude didn't change once a dead body came into the picture? My attitude didn't change when I bought you that diamond ring, or that pretty little necklace, or your expensive clothes?"

"What does one thing hafta do with the other?"

"A whole helluva lot, Adena. If we want to live a certain way, we have to walk that walk. We can't act like we from the hood and live the lifestyle we live."

Adena made a strange face, very confused about what he said. The two even had to step outside to finish talking.

Exhausted, Mason elaborated: "What I mean is, if I'm going to achieve certain things in my life, I gotta think like an achiever. I gotta dress like an achiever and, dammit, I gotta *act* like an achiever. I don't think I could have come this far unless I changed my attitude, Adena. People ain't tryin' to do no real estate deals with no thug."

"You ain't a thug, Mason. Cut it out."

"And I never was, and ain't tryin' to be no thug. I'm trying to make a point."

Adena cocked her head to the side. "What's the point?"

"My point is, I can't be two people, Adena. I can only be me. If you want to call me soft . . . if you think that way about me, just because some crew comes in our house, waving shotguns, then I'm sorry you feel that way. But, just to be clear, while I'm not gonna stoop to their level, Adena, I'm also not going to be their victim. The only shot I got at these guys, except for becoming a mass murderer, and maybe killing them all off, is to move the body. Adena, I *gotta* move the body 'cuz these guys are driving me mad. They're drivin' us both *mad*. Look at us! You just called me *soft*. When did you *ever* say some stupid shit like that? We were lovers just over an hour ago—all up against the wall, I mean, wild like we always were."

Some of the sting had left Adena's eyes and she got to wagging her head with slight shame.

"I'm sorry, Mason. I just . . . I guess we're both a little nuts right now. You're right. I didn't mean all that, 'cuz how could you be soft? It takes a trooper to deal with my ass." Adena smiled finally and the two returned inside.

"Speakin' of your ass, you think they're gonna use that video? Or maybe they're just bullshittin'."

Shaking her head, Adena said, "I dunno, Mason. I've been watchin' these guys for a few days. Most of their work has been, whatcha call it? Imprompt?"

"Impromptu."

"Right. What *you* said. And all of a sudden Juggler be comin' up with these wacky ideas, and he uses this hotel room for one thing, and another for another thing. They even shot some crazy shit in the laundry room where the skinny one, Bones, she gets in one of those big front-loading dryers we have? So she's in there nice and snug, and—well, the guy they got now is some flaky white boy they use for some shoots . . . well, he stands there, ass naked with his dick in Bones' mouth while she's spinnin'."

"Get the fuck outta here!"

Adena raised her hand and said, "I put that on everything I've ever loved, Mason. On my dead grandmommy, I swear."

Mason turned his head in some form of calculation before he finally responded, "That's sick."

"I know, I watched it," Adena said, forking up some more salad. "But it makes good video."

"I'm sure. I just hope *we* don't become a part of their *good video*. I've got enough problems to think about."

———

**G**oing back up to Blue Mountain was an uncomfortable trip. On the way up, the conversation was all about what to say and how to act. Both Mason and Adena agreed that they'd try to act as though things were normal and that there were no hard feelings. In the worst-case scenario, they'd also agreed that they'd laugh it off no matter how painful.

Meanwhile, the focus now was to find that window when the others were either away or else too busy to know that the rug was being slipped out from underneath them. Only, it might've been a bit difficult to maintain focus with a house full of rowdies.

From the moment Mason pulled up into the driveway, he could hear it was rowdy, even with all of his truck windows shut. It was that same lawless activity that was permitted thanks to their remote mountain atmosphere. After all, who (besides the nosy ones) would see or hear this? Cars and trucks whizzed by; homes were far enough away that privacy was assured; and as far as anyone knew, there was nothing illegal about partying all day and night. So the eight vehicles parked awkwardly on the property, on and off his grass, and the music that could be heard many yards into the forest, was nothing too wild to anyone but the Fickles.

"For us to hear music in the car means they're blastin' our stereo to the holy heavens," Mason said. "So I know they're havin' another one of those crazy parties of theirs." Mason turned his eyes away from his home and grieved.

It was after five in the afternoon. The sun had all but disappeared from the skyline, and if there was anything worse to come home to, on this windy, weekday afternoon, it was a house full of people trying to imitate Babylon.

"I can't go in there, Adena. Call me soft if you want, but I got a hunting rifle, too, ya know. I can be just as crazy as anyone else with a gun and a reason."

Adena argued, "Don't be silly, Mason. You gonna let them chase you outta your own home? Not me. I'm tired as hell. I need a shower, and plus I'm workin' a double tonight. So, I need to get a few hours' sleep, at least."

"With a party goin' on?"

"Mason, I'm gonna get me a shower, and I'm gonna hit the bed like a sack a rocks. You know I sleep like a bear when I want to."

"Well, I hope you know what you're doing, Adena. I don't wanna hear you got fired from your job because you were caught sleeping."

After a second or two, she asked, "Aren't you driving in?"

Mason wagged his head miserably. "I'd just rather not deal with it," he responded.

"So . . . you're gonna hang out in the truck?" she asked.

"I guess. Or else I'll go somewhere and have a drink. Maybe at Caesars."

Adena screwed her lips and gathered her things.

"Doesn't matter. I'm not scared."

And before Mason could respond, she was gone, heading down the driveway. All he could do was let off steam and grunt to himself.


For at least two hours, Mason drove around the neighborhood. It had been some time since he'd done this, just cruising around without a purpose or a destination. And when he ran out of patience he headed back to his block and idled in the driveway across from his home. There was still construction going on here—a new house—but maybe the house building was suspended until after the holidays.

The holidays: That was whole other issue that Mason never got around to giving much thought to. And now that he'd found himself dozing, it was all he could think about.

One Christmas after the next, his momma did the best she could to make it work. Even with no father around, pulling the weight for her sons and their upbringing, always keeping them in top shape for school and keeping food on the table, as well as maintaining a job to keep the paychecks coming in. With all of that on her shoulders, it seemed like a painful victory to be able to put up a Christmas tree and to light it and decorate it and to have gifts under it.

And now that Mason had a chance to reflect on it all, and considering the direction his life had gone, it seemed like a damn shame that he had chosen not to maintain the tradition. And the one or two times that he had, it felt too much like a novelty act. His rationale was an easy one: That's a kid's holiday. It's a tradition meant to keep us joyful and righteous, even if only for a few weeks out of the year.

Those Christmas contemplations were tossed aside by the black truck that had crossed Mason's path. He was cruising along 409 and turned off the road down a trail. Sure, the sign said NO TRESPASSING; however, Mason could always assume the status of a curious neighbor; maybe he could lie that he'd recently moved nearby and stopped by to say a neighborly hello!

But as he took the dirt trail slowly, something in the deepest part of his consciousness told him that the black truck he had just passed out on the main road was operated by someone who might be more than just curious. He hadn't given it much thought, but (after all) Mason was a black in a white, rural area. This was a place a man like him could get lost, buried, and forgotten about, all within one day. Moreover, it might just cross someone's mind that the luxury truck he drove was not a sign of success, but an expensive means by which to break and enter and, maybe, rob one of these vacation homes that some folks need only seasonally.

Bottom line was any old excuse would do, under the circumstances. Only, Mason didn't follow his instincts. He didn't quickly make the U-turn to drive off of this private property. He instead explored the grounds, and he found what turned out to be a summer camp with cabins, recreational areas, and plenty of signs to guide or direct impressionable youngsters. CAMP DELEWARE.

Mason drove as far as he cared to, and his tires were muddied once he finally turned the truck around. But before he was able to take off and head back toward the main road, Mason stopped short, thinking, *Oh shit! This is the perfect place for the body!* And yet that sudden idea wasn't what really stopped him; in fact, it was that black truck parked right there, now almost bumper-to-bumper with him. His instincts were right. And then something else jolted Mason. There was a hard knocking sound at his window; something like a judge slamming his hammer down three times quickly. Only it seemed much louder since Mason's head had been resting on the glass.

It was only with the rapping at his window that Mason realized there was no cruise onto private property and no black truck with a suspicious driver. All of that was his imagination working overtime. Except, what shook him from his seat was very real, indeed.

"Whatcha doin', homes?"

Bad enough that Mason was going out of his mind; now there was this latest reality, Wheelchair Sid outside of his driver's-side window. "Why don't cha come in and have some fun, Fickle?" And Sid chuckled, maybe at his own inside joke. But this was no laughing matter to Mason as he watched Sid wheel himself away, across the street and back down the driveway where so many cars were parked. Of all places to cop a nap, to tuck himself away from the nonsense, he had to choose one that was accessible to the thug-wannabe-invalid.

Mason came to his senses a little while later and was relieved to see that there weren't as many cars in the driveway as before. Four vehicles meant that there couldn't be a house full of guests; fewer people to entertain, Mason guessed. Not to mention how his house might look after the likely abuse. That was another mental hurdle he'd have to cross.

Meanwhile, he admitted to himself how crazy this was, how he was unable, or at least unwilling, to relax at home when he wanted to. And he resolved to handle the worst, whatever it was. *What could be worse than what's happened already?*

# twenty

Adena had to laugh her way through the sights and sounds when she came into the house. All her hard work, planning, and decorating had suddenly gone to shit. And, instead of a tidy, organized, and fresh-scented house, Biggie Smalls and his rap song "Juicy" had taken over. The women who worked for Juggler were either dancing on a coffee table, lap dancing on the sectional couch, or sitting on her kitchen counter. Even Stormy (who Adena felt was becoming a closer acquaintance than the others), was acting up, with some stranger, probably a client, with her back against a wall while Stormy pressed her ass up into his crotch.

*Wall dancing? On my walls? Lap dancing on my couches? And, we fix food on these counters!*

Adena was fuming behind that phony smile, while at the same time trying to hold her breath. The weed smoke was so strong in the house; strong enough to make Adena an instant secondhand smoker. Strong enough to generate a buzz and to affect her senses.

So, then her senses were being affected in so many ways, to the point that she could taste that sour, funky body odor that hung in the air. To the point that the cheap perfume was fighting for attention. And of course, there was the litter that had her home looking like there was an ongoing block party. Bottles, cans, crumbs, and cigarette butts were everywhere. On the countertops, tables, in the sink and bathrooms. The refrigerator had been raided and someone had dropped a slice of pizza on the carpet.

*The carpet!* That was another story altogether. Someone had apparently tracked dirt into the house, and her off-white carpet was suddenly closer to off-brown. And why were the windows open as though the Fickles had intended on keeping the entire forest comfortably heated?

"Adena! Join the party! Joel, this is my friend, Adena. Adena, this is Joel. He's a doctor down in Harrisburg. A *foot* doctor," Stormy growled with that sexy voice that she used so well.

"Oh yeah? Hmm . . . wonder if he's a *wall doctor, too?*" Adena wasn't trying to sound bitter, just making mention for the two to be careful. Although, careful was kind of late.

"Sorry about the picture frame, boo. It was all his fault," Stormy said and stabbed her forefinger at Dr. Joel's pectorals and then at his nether region.

Adena forced herself to laugh again, maybe since there was little else she could do, considering how the damage had already been done. But, what really loosened her up was to watch Dr. Joel pull out his billfold to find five crisp hundred-dollar bills, which he immediately curled into Adena's hand.

"Any friend of Stormy's is a friend of mine! Hope this takes care of the damage."

Adena was frozen between a rock and a hard place. This was five hundred dollars more than she made in three days of working as a Days Inn housekeeper. But, did this guy expect that Stormy's friend would perform the same saucy acts? The wall dancing, the intimacy, and— *Did you two just drink from the same champagne bottle?*

Adena said, "Thanks, but I don't think . . ."

"What she means, Joel, is that she doesn't think it's enough. Give 'er five hundred more."

Adena swallowed hard while looking into Stormy's eyes. So much was said in that exchange, but Adena didn't dare miss how Stormy's hand slipped down to grab whatever Dr. Joel had between his legs, most likely something that was feeling stiff and encouraged since he coughed up that extra money lickety split without so much as a frown.

And now Adena said, "Well, hey . . . if you insist."

"Oh, I *more* than insist," Joel responded and quickly pulled Adena into a threesome.

Stormy had to read into Adena's mind now to whisper in her ear.

"Don't worry. I'm getting him drunk. You don't hafta do a thing."

Adena was confused, but she went right along with the fun. Minutes later, Stormy was giving Adena the finer points behind a wall dance. And somewhere during the tutorial, Adena caught sight of one or two of the others in the house, pointing and snickering about the debut dance. Encouraged by a handful of money, Adena went along with the charade. Why not? As far as she was concerned, her husband wasn't fighting hard or smart enough for their home. So, why should he care if she had a little fun?

Stormy poured Adena a drink as well, and before anyone could say Blue Mountain, the three were behind closed doors.

"I really need to shower, you two." Adena said this partially giggling, partially serious. There was a hiccup before she continued. "And I can't drink any more, 'cuz I gotta work two shifts."

"Whateva', bitch," Stormy said. "My man—my, uh, *doctor* can pay your salary for the night. Times two, right, doc?

"Bing, bing, bing!" The doctor pulled out three more dead presidents and the two laughed it up while Adena closed the bathroom door.

Inside, she couldn't help but stare in the mirror. She shouted, "You forgot, Stormy! I'm a sexy bitch, dammit!"

On the other side of the door, the two cackled in response.

Again, Adena was having the one-on-one. "Who are you foolin'? You ain't drunk, bitch. You just don't know what you wanna do right now. Your man's a punk, basically. But he's a successful punk—" The way Adena said it, the word sounded more like *shucceshful*, with the pronunciation slurring. "So whatcha gonna do? You know you're sexy," she said, and she kissed the mirror right before she took in another swig from the Moët bottle.

"Fuck it, baby. Let's celebrate. This nigga got a new, inspirin' empire, and my man ain't doin' nothin' but hatin'. Gotta respect that rags-to-riches shi—"

Adena almost slipped as she came out of her work clothes. Drinkers were the wrong people to try to multitask. Things were beginning to spin, even though she felt in control.

"Hey, Deena!" It was a loud whisper from the bedroom. Then, damned if the door didn't ease open. It was Stormy.

"Wassup, girl. Can't you see I'm 'bout to clean up?"

"He wants to know if we'll put on a show," said Stormy, slipping through the door so as not to surrender the rest of Adena's privacy.

"A show?"

"Yeah! Just a girl-girl thing. Nothin' major. I know how these guys tick. They just need to get their rocks off, and it's over. Like it never happened."

"I dunno, Stormy. I think I've gone too far already. Plus, if Mason found out I—"

"*Mason who?* Isn't that what you just said downstairs? What—you change your mind?"

"I just . . . I gotta be smarter sometime, Storm. He finds out, he divorces my ass and no more Jimmy Choo. No more Prada. No more fine dining."

"And besides all that? Is there still love?"

Adena cast a distorted expression, maybe to define her marriage.

"I'm with that. Totally. So, we do the next best thing," suggested

Stormy. "We keep our fuckin' mouths closed." Stormy was talking not to Adena but to her mirror image.

"Look at you. Fine as you wanna be. Still got pretty breasts . . . pretty face . . ."

Adena jumped some when Stormy smacked her ass.

"Don't be a fool, Adena. That man out there is an hour from dropping off to sleep. But before he does, I want that five gees out of his bank account."

"Five gees?"

"That's right, five thousand. And you can have half of what Juggler gives us."

"How much is that?" asked Adena, turning away from Stormy's mirror image to look at her straight on.

"Juggler processes all the credit cards. He gives us all but fifty percent."

"So that's . . ." Adena was taking much too long, so Stormy jumped in.

"That means you and I split twenty-five hundred dollars. And that's money I need real bad, girl. I'm not ashamed to tell ya. I gotta car note, my little court fee to pay for that prostitution case I told you about . . . I got bills, girl."

"What exactly would I have to do?"

"Oh thank you, thank you, thank you," Stormy exclaimed, assuming that Adena was saying yes.

"But I—" Adena began to protest. But Stormy went right on explaining.

Mason was close enough to the house to look into his dining-room window. It was dark out, and his movements would keep the deer away tonight. They liked it quiet and they crept up in secret. Except Mason was obvious, duckwalking through the yard like he did. For all the deer knew, he was plotting to shoot one of them.

But, in fact, Mason had another plan. Yes, he was tired from sitting upright in his truck, his neck was feeling funny from the way he rested his head. However, there was a job to do. And this just might be the time to do it.

From the shed, Mason pulled out a shovel and wheelbarrow. He hadn't forgotten how heavy the body was, and he was working alone this time, so he'd need the wheelbarrow to make things a little easier.

Only now did Mason consider how rough this might be. Number one, it was dark—even darker back here in the rocky forest where he searched. But this was home, and he could close his eyes and know where he was going, which made the dark the least of his problems. It was hard, but with some savvy he could pinpoint the where behind this task. Number two, the ground had surely hardened like a rock over the weeks, and he wasn't digging with a crew like before. So there was that. And three, Mason had never excavated a body before. How gruesome would this be?

The forest floor wasn't the easiest to navigate on, with large and small rocks, branches, and trees everywhere, but Mason was proud of himself once he felt the ground swell some. This had to be it. Loween's resting place.

*Sorry, Loween.*

After the apology, Mason looked back toward the house. Past the trees, after about one hundred yards, he could see the lights inside his house. The rest he could see only on his mind's monitor. Where Juggler and his friends sat around engrossed in their card game.

Juggler was likely sitting there getting his ego stroked by his underlings and their guests. By now, Mason guessed, Adena would be resting peacefully after a nice shower. Soon, after a nap, she'd be off to work again. And the only other person Mason had in mind (already knowing that the forest was the last place he'd seen this fool) was Wheelchair Sid. He'd have to work extrahard to wheel himself out this far, but it was next to impossible with all the obstacles. Still, Mason couldn't put it past that fool to try and make it happen. So, Mason had to keep and eye on the house, and he had to be extra quiet as he began to dig.

One thing led to another, and Adena was way past the part Stormy had suggested: *Pretend that you like it. He won't know the difference. Just make faces—I know you know how to make faces, girl. I heard some things.*

The pretending to "ooh" and "ahh" turned into an all-out battle for sanity. Stormy was down there between Adena's legs, touching everything and licking everything else.

The "oohs" had quickly escalated to "oh my God." The "ahhs" had become exclamations of "Oh shit! I'm coming! I'm fucking coming!" Adena could hardly control what was coming out of her mouth. Her body was another story entirely. It was heaving and bucking up and down, back and forth, riding with every flick of Stormy's talented tongue. Adena couldn't remember anyone—man or woman—ever doing it this good to her. And not only was Stormy so skilled at what she was doing, her lips were—

"Jesus, I love your fuckin' lips! Aaaaah!"

They were everywhere! There was even a moment when Adena looked down to see (at least it seemed) all of her genitalia captive within Stormy's mouth. And that vision was over even when Stormy looked up into Adena's eyes. Like she was saying, *I couldn't wait to get you like this!*

*She planned this all along?* Adena thought. *She was part of the coup to trap me in my own bedroom, a paid performance at that, with the philanthropist over in the corner jacking off?*

*Oh yes, talented indeed! Tricky, but I love this!* And Adena went from liking the spasms she experienced to loving the rush of pleasure that gripped her insides. She could see Stormy's one hand down there playing with herself, bringing her own pleasure to the surface, and that made Adena even wetter.

Mason wondered just what he was feeling for each time he drove the shovel into the earth. Would it be a softer dig? Would he hit a bone? And was he even digging too hard, where he might drive through the bone? There was too much to consider besides how deep and how wide he should dig. Not only that, he had to get every imaginable fiber of that body from the earth just to satisfy his own awareness about DNA and all that the authorities could piece together from such findings as flesh and tissue and blood. Mason basically had to be a pro, something his body and mind were not at all prepared for.

There was a crackle Mason swore he heard, and he spun his head around, shovel over his shoulder in a threatening, swinging position. His eyes worked hard in the dark; the house, the forest behind him and above.

What was that?

Still as could be, Mason didn't hear another sound, and as far as he could see, nothing had changed back at the house.

A deer? A raccoon?

The deep, trembling breaths that he took shimmered some, and he got back to digging. He was still many feet from his objective; still aware that this was a job for three or four men.

Another level indeed. Stormy had progressed from one opening, and she kissed her way up. To Adena's breast until she nibbled at her nipples.

"Ouch! Ouch! Ouch!" Adena's quick responses were accompanied by her body jumping. The painful bites were hurting, but somehow she didn't mind.

"You like that?" Stormy teased and growled like a pro. Adena didn't know how to respond to Stormy's question since she was already left speechless.

Furthermore, Stormy, it seemed, didn't even require an answer. She was instead kissing Adena full on the lips, then the tongue working its way around her own, across her teeth until it played with the roof of her mouth.

"I like kissing."

"I . . . I can tell," replied Adena.

"You all okay over there?"

Stormy's face turned from sensuous to irate as she turned to face the doctor.

"Didn't I say no talking? Now shut the fuck up, asshole."

The shaken client nodded like an epileptic while Stormy turned back to Adena. The sensual look again.

"They gotta know their place," Stormy said.

And the whole encounter was virtually turning Adena inside out. How amazing for Stormy to have such control over two people, a man and a woman at once. But she was focused, too, already kissing her way back down Adena's neck, breasts, and past her navel. It was something like a dive back into Adena's slimy pool, only that she was so obsessed about it, maybe looking for some hidden treasure with her tongue. Probing and digging . . . digging and probing . . .

A nd there was an instant when the digging felt different, as though the shovel reached something soft; maybe the canvas drop cloth that had been used to mummify the body. But there was so much more to do here, regardless of his having dug for two hours. The reality was that Mason hadn't dug deep or wide enough. As it was, he was cramming to get this far, with his body wedged in the ditch. And now that he'd taken a moment to catch his breath, by his latest estimation, he'd have to do at least two or three times the work he'd already done.

Six more hours!

Mason leaned back against the wall of earth, a wall that he'd have to inevitably dig out if he intended on getting this job done. No way was he gonna dig up a hand and pull on it until the rest of the body followed. Of course, the silly idea had occurred to him, but he had long erased it.

*I need a drink,* he finally realized.

And Mason reached up to spring himself out of the ditch until his ass was seated on the moist forest floor. The job here was beginning to seem impossible, not to mention how fatigued he was and how he wanted to cry to relieve some of what weighed on his shoulders. The idea about crying, however, was dropped when he recalled his wife saying he was soft. And then that was all the energy he needed to say, *The hell with the water.* And he got back to work.


If you do it, I'll give you both a thousand extra," offered Dr. Joel.

Even though the client had been ordered not to speak, the mention of money grabbed Stormy's attention. He had asked the two to perform on each other and he also wanted to join in; that is, he wanted to join in while the two went at it.

Adena's near-seizures came to a halt when she heard that. She had already considered giving back to Stormy, reciprocating her new friend for making her feel so good. And money had absolutely nothing to do with that. That was just a natural desire of hers, and an impulsive one.

But now this? Adena lay back to consider those possibilities while Stormy did the negotiating.

"One thousand, each?"

The doctor didn't need to respond in words. He simply pulled a plastic card from his wallet. Stormy turned to face Adena, her eyes immediately understanding the value in the man's hand—an American Express Platinum—and in that glance she said so much in so little time.

Adena didn't want to interfere with the cash flow here, but there was something evil about this guy's new demands; something sinister in his eyes.

"Absolutely not." Adena's words this time. And the response was a quick one, too, as though she'd done her own speedy calculating, all the variables being worked out in her mind. *Join in? Which means what if we're already busy? Where's he gonna put that rod of his while my mouth is—* Oh, hell no. And while these were Adena's thoughts, her lips weren't far behind.

"Not for a million dollars."

Sure, it was a party-pooping thing to say, and it took some of the spark out of the action, but Adena imagined that somewhere, somehow, someone was applauding her decision to draw the line and "just say no."

The doctor's face was already turning red under the lamp's glow, and this new level of things left an uncomfortable feeling in the air that threatened to commit the cardinal sin, her client losing his erection.

Stormy assessed things and shifted her attitude. She went from being a robbery victim to a troubleshooter, ready to compromise. She crawled off the bed and addressed her client face-to-face. Adena could still hear her.

"Okay, playboy. My friend is not going for it. She's not into dicks. Now, you just keep jackin' "—Stormy wasted no time snatching the credit card—"and keep my register ringin', while we do our thing."

Adena already knew the process, having witnessed Juggler's process here and there, and she quietly wondered if she would still get her share of this transaction. But for the moment, she was still captivated by Stormy's control, how she didn't waste any time closing the deal. And now she was back on the bed, slithering up to face Adena—

"Let's just keep doin' what we're doin'," said Stormy, and she stroked the beads of sweat from Adena's brow.

"And what exactly is it that we're, ahem, doing?" The way Adena said that was so cute, as if she didn't already know; as if she were Miss Innocent. There was no hiding those pretty eyes and how they beheld wonder and the urge for discovery.

Stormy purred and whispered, "Lemme show you."

Adena and Stormy flipped and folded and curled with each other's bodies like two unruly teenagers, leaving bruises about their breasts and their hair in a wiry mess. Both girls took turns in submission; however, it was Stormy who seemed to receive the most pleasure when Adena spanked her.

"Again. Hit it again!" cried Stormy. But she wasn't merely asking for a smack on the ass. No, Stormy liked to have her *pussy* spanked.

"Come for me, baby."

"I am! I'm coming. Almost there," cried Stormy.

"Your pussy looks so juicy," Adena commented, then she smacked it again between clicking and sucking.

The moans from Stormy began to build up to "ooohs" and "ahhs," and the cries of pleasure until she wailed, *"I'm coming! I'm coming!"*

There was a point when Adena was moaning as well, when the "oh my God's" wouldn't stop calling out of Stormy's mouth, and when both woman were lapping at each other's kisses. It was Stormy's pussy that squirted into Adena's face. Adena was surprised by this, having never been alone with another woman, and then actually having her come like she was—she came like a man! Squirting! Her pussy ran like a faucet for a brief time, and that even made Adena climax, until they were both panting with satisfaction. And why did the bedroom door just swing open?

# twenty-one

Mason was always the one to repeat the quote "You think you know, but you have no idea." Unfortunately, however, he needed to take heed of his own advice. Too late to *have* reservations now, especially with Juggler's goons tossing him through the bedroom door like a bag of rocks. He was still conscious, but barely so. Maybe it was the last blow to the left side of his face, or the boot that stomped his head during the fight—his fight—once he was pushed to the forest floor.

"Oh, Mason!"

Sure that was Adena's voice, *But that can't be my wife, naked, on the bed—OUR BED!* This . . . Even with his one eye nearly swollen shut and his vision blurred in the other, Mason could make out a third party in the room, the man over there in the corner trying to pull up his pants over his softened erection. And all of this was happening so fast that the challenges still triggered a new energy in him—some kind of heroic adrenaline that made him lift his body from the floor. Bruises or no bruises, Mason roared while he charged at his rifle-wielding captors with the vigor of a bull out for revenge.

"Mason, no!" Adena hollered, but it was no use.

The goon they had come to know as Jack was quick to throw a shoulder at Mason, a hard enough hit to take down a wide receiver.

Except, in this case, the counterattack sent Mason crashing into one of the dinner trays left over from the night before. The Fickle couple had been doing much of that lately, eating in the bedroom, since the rest of the house seemed to be up for grabs. And now those leftover potatoes, with the cabbage and chicken, were all over Mason.

His plan foiled, his body beaten, and now humiliated before his wife, Mason's head was heavy enough for him to shut his eyes and black out. Add to that the obvious activities that he stumbled on in his bedroom with his wife, a prostitute, and another man, made it all tragic enough to want to die.


**M**uch of what was said or done once Mason received the elbow and the leftovers went by as if a desert mirage. On one hand, he had a sense that there was movement in the room. But also, he could at least hear the commands from Juggler, he had the guy (whoever he was) get dressed and *get out*. In the meantime, Mason was still somewhat disoriented, somewhat battered and broken. His world had truly, and totally, slipped out from under him.


**M**ason? Mason baby?"
    Aside from hearing Adena's voice, Mason could feel a cold cloth held to his face. If not for the swelling, he might have been able to appreciate this. Only, he was swollen. And the only thing worse was that Adena—backstabber, adulterer, and cheater that she was— was doing the TLC. There was no way to respond to her. No reason.

"No sense in messin' with that punk. He's through, baby. When are you gonna see the light? When are you gonna make the best of that fine-ass body you got? You need to change ya game, boo. Git wit' us winners. 'Cuz that nigga there—?

"—This *nigga* that you talkin' about is my husband."

For a moment, Juggler gave that same thought. Then he said, "Six years, huh?"

"That's right. We got history together. We got love."

"Want me to show you how much that means? Want me to show you how much love he got for you?"

Adena looked confused. But Juggler apparently knew where he was going with this. He whispered something to his goons and they proceeded to lift Mason.

"Hey! Where are you taking him?" Adena attempted to protest, but her words and actions were interrupted when Juggler smacked her with his open palm, spreading Adena back on the bed.

"You bitches are all the same for real." Juggler went to shut the door once everyone else was gone. Then he continued. "You toss around words like *love* and *marriage* and *commitment,* but what it really comes down to . . . it comes down to the money." Juggler was so calm and calculating with his words, Adena crying behind her palms. "If a nigga got money and he can keep you happy, then you better be a good bitch. From head to toe, you wanna be a nigga's whore fo' life."

Juggler had circled the bed, and it caused Adena to scrunch her legs up to her breasts.

Unbuttoning his shirt, he said, "See what I mean about love, honey? I just smacked the shit outta ya, and what did Mr. Fickle do? He ain't do shit. 'Cuz I'ma tell ya straight up, if you was my girl, and a big nigga like me smacked you, I'da whooped some ass. A nigga would've had to shoot me. Word up."

Adena was still panting, still affected by the sting of this man's palm, as he continued to tell her fortune. And now that he removed his shirt and went for his belt buckle, she winced, and her eyes turned more afraid than they had been.

She had no defense at this point, weary from lack of rest; stripped of her security—the man in her life, violated and assaulted, all in one late afternoon.

"What are you *doing?*" Adena asked through her shortness of breath.

"I'm doing what you want me to do, baby. Look, a scientist this puzzle don't need. I mean, I'm just a dumb nigga from the Loo who likes Jimmy Dean Sa'sages and hangin' wit' my woadies. But I'm smart enough to add things up. You was fucking in the motel—got that on tape. You was already peekin' our movie shit for the past week an' some, so I know you a horny bitch. . . ."

Juggler now had his buckle loose and began to pull down his zipper.

"So, even here at the house, you leave your man in the truck, come in the house, and you can't wait to drink a little bubbly and eat one of my top-shelf pros. You know what I think? YOU LIKE SEX! That's what you like. But I'ma do you one better, just to show you how much you're ready to do as I say. . . ."

Juggler went into his back pocket and a thick wad of cash emerged. He opened it up and spread it on the bed in front of Adena.

"Now, that's my take from today. Gotta be seven grand, at least, and it's all yours." He lowered his voice to a husky drawl when he said, "Now bring your pretty lil' ass over here. This is more than you make in months, ain't it? I said ain't it?"

Adena nodded without really looking Juggler in the eyes.

"Yeah, I know. I speak to one or two of the maids you work with. They tell me everything. Don't take much to git what Juggler wants!"

Adena scooted closer. Indeed, this was more money than she'd seen in a long time. And it was calling her more than the life she had built for half a decade.

"Ain't any sense in looking over there. Door's locked. Plus, my woadies got you' nigga hemmed up. Fo' sho' . . . You just git over here and give me what I want."

Now, Juggler had his fully engorged dick exposed. "That's right. That's right, girl. I'ma show you how a bitch really needs to be treated."

Adena's hand was already moving up Juggler's thigh, getting familiar real fast. But there was that slight protest.

"Why I gotta be a bitch?" Her concerned eyes look up to this giant standing over her while she lay curled up close to the edge of the bed. The money was swept aside and Adena wiped her tears away.

"You see this?" Juggler grabbed up a bunch of money and held it in Adena's face. "This right here makes you my bitch. This right here makes you my whore. Now, bitch, put that fucking dick in your mouth and act like you love it."

Adena did.


Yap and Pooh had carried Mason down to the garage and they were now playing pool. It didn't matter what Juggler was up to, they just had to wait for additional orders.

"Dinner, fellas?" It was Martha who had popped her head into the garage. But when she saw Mason's condition, she uttered a gasp. "Oh my God."

"Go mind your business, Martha. We'll be in soon as we done. Gowon!"

Yap and Pooh exchanged glances before one of them went to close the door behind Martha.

"You know they gon' be talkin'," said Yap.

"But that ain't our problem, dog. Not unless they want it to be."

The two went back to their game. "Three ball, combination off the 'leven." "Oh, hell no! You can't combinate off my balls."

"Says who? Thas' what we did down at the club, 'fore the storm."

"Well, shit . . . it's a new day. These is the Poconos rules. That's how they kick it at Damon's."

"Nigga, whateva."

These two bamas arguing was all the leverage Mason needed to work his magic. Little did they know that his hunting rifle was just under the couch where he was lying. Problem was that the rifle was in a case; the bigger problem was, it wasn't loaded. Down, but not out, Mason planned his moves. If his wife considered him soft after this next move, then she surely had to be blind.

Playing victim, Mason pretended to hurt so bad, and he began wailing about his hip.

"Oh, man! Y'all broke my hip!"

Yap and Pooh shared a look of compassion, right before they got to laughing.

"Two ball, cross-side."

"Nigga, you ain't neva made a cross-side shot in your life." Mason heard a car pull up outside. Moments later, Trixx and Raven came in through the garage door. It was the household rule even before the N'awlins crew came into the picture, that the garage door be kept unlocked. There's no such things as burglaries up on Blue Mountain; and Mason agreed with his wife that convenience was more important.

"Oh, what happened to you?" asked one of the girls.

Pooh intervened. "He just had, ah . . . a little disagreement with a bear."

The two pros showed fear and amazement. But, before they had a chance to assess things, to figure out that the damage and the lie didn't add up, Yap said, "He'll be all right, ladies. Why don't you two go relax. He's good."

Yap had to go over and escort the ladies through the kitchen entrance. But this was just the godsend that Mason needed. He slid along the couch, still putting on the pain face in the event that Pooh got suspicious. And before anyone realized, he was on the floor, sitting up against the couch.

"Whatcha doin' down there?" asked Yap once he returned from ushering the women off.

"My hip. I need a hard surface to sit on. Please, my hip is killing me."

"Fuck 'im, Yap. He ain't goin' nowhere."

No, thought Mason. *I think it's more like fuck you.*


One flight up in the house that Mason Fickle built, things had already gone far past the point of no return. Juggler had called Adena every name in the book while he had his way with her. It only began with "bitch" and "whore." He even had Adena calling herself a whore and a bitch, and he had her claiming, however convincingly, that she loved sucking his dick.

"I love sucking Juggler's dick," she was directed to say.

"I'm a dirty whore, and I love this dick!"

"Louder! Until that faggot can here you!"

And Adena obeyed. But this she repeated all while she had a mouth full of meat.

"*Slur, slur, slur—*" was all that could be heard. But it was all that Juggler needed to get his rocks off.

"You want Juggler's dick in that nasty hole of yours, don't you?"

Adena nodded with her mouth full.

"I said, *don't you!*"

Again with the *slur, slur, slur*, with Adena trying to talk her way through this.

"Turn around. Hands on the bed . . ."

He reached over to scoop some money into a pile. "And put your face right here, right in the money. That's *your* money, you fuckin' whore!"

A minute later, Adena's reactions couldn't be faked as Juggler continued pounding her from behind. He was laughing when he wasn't giving directives. And when he wasn't doing that—"You're the *man*, Juggler! You the muthafuckin' *man*!" he hollered.

"Don't stop! Oh, don't stop, Juggler! Fill my fuckin' hole, Daddy. Oh yeah, I like that—ohhhh!" Adena's cries pushed out of her mouth like she was in labor. Shifting between loud and soft moans.

"Oh, yeah . . . oh . . . oh . . . feel so good . . ."

"You like that shit, ho?!"

"I like it."

"Scream it, bitch!"

"I like it, Juggler. Give me that dick! Give me more! More!"

"That's right, bitch. I want that nigga to hear me fucking his wife."

"Oh . . . oh God!"

"No, God ain't fuckin' you, ho. Juggler is. Now who's your husband? Wha's his name?"

"Ma—son."

"What is it?"

"Mason. His—name—is—Mason," she answered in between thrusts.

"But whose pussy is this. Huh?" Juggler smacked Adena's ass as he would a whore's with a leather whip. "Answer me! Whose is it!"

"It's yours," Adena answered while her hand played with her clit. "It's your pussy, Juggler!"

"Say it!" Juggler was hollering at the top of his husky lungs.

Adena followed Juggler's commands.

"Oh yeah. Oh, you are *serious*. Shit. I need this load in your mouth. Come 'ere."

Juggler immediately snatched a handful of hair and pulled Adena's head around so that her face was a target. And as if this was normal, usual activity, Adena grabbed a hold of his erection and began jerking at it. If he didn't know any better, Juggler would have sworn that she was taking and giving just as she would with her husband. There was no lying in her actions or her reactions. She was actually enjoying this! No bullshit!

I t was time to blast off. To shoot the shots that he felt would save his miserable life. After all, these guys were big and, no doubt, slower than a small man like Mason. So, as far as he knew, he had a good shot here.

He was on the floor. He already reached under and loosened the latched on the rifle case. He even grabbed four shells and hid them in his pocket. Good thing these guys were slow and stupid. There was no way a smart person would let Mason get this far.

Mason had been regaining his energies all this time; that, and prayer. Even if prayer wasn't at the top of his agenda, he now agreed with anyone who had ever told him that "one day you will." This was that day.

After a final deep breath and much calculation, Mason whipped that Mossberg from under the couch.

Yap had just announced, "Eight ball, corner pocket." And that corner was a far corner, one that required him to look away from Mason. Mason used those extra seconds to slap the shells in their chambers. *Click!* The rifle snapped open like an elbow.

*Clack!* The rifle was together again, ready.

At the first sound, the eight ball shot was disturbed. Pooh had turned some, unconcerned with whatever might be going on. But, once he did a double take, he realized the true threat. He lunged toward Mason, trying to stop the inevitable. But Mason had already loaded. There was no time to think about repercussions, or who might hear what. Any one of these goons was a threat. They were trespassing, unwelcome, and basically extorting Mason and his wife. So then it was decided. *What will be will be.* And the pool cue that Pooh swung at Mason was answered before it arrived.

The rifle blast was close enough to Mason's ear to create a ringing sensation that he remembered from firework shows, or from concerts after you've been much too close to the stage.

Although Mason hadn't intended on such carnal damage, his shot blew off the chunk of Pooh's face that joined his lips, chin, and cheek. The wounded man wailed and bled as he fell back onto the pool table. Yap's hands immediately went into the air.

"Ain't no fun when the rabbit got the gun, is it?"

"Hey, I don't want no trouble, dude. Whatever you say. I just go where the money goes and—"

"Yeah, right. And you do what the money tells you, too. And since money is still paying you, I'm gonna need to make some moves right now."

The wailing didn't stop as Mason went to a table in the garage that held rolls of duct tape.

"Let's start with the legs. On the table, and lay on your stomach. I ain't got time—jump to it."

Yap made a face, being that he had to be near the growing pool of blood, with his friend's face partially missing. Pooh was dying off now; at least his loud, agonizing wails were. There was panting, heavy groans, and then silence. Mason assumed that he was either dead or unconscious. At the same time, he wrapped Yap's ankles so many times he nearly mummified them. And now that the legs were done with, Mason ordered Yap to put his hands behind his back. Mason followed suit with the wrists.

"I'm gonna lose circulation to my hands, man."

Mason waited until he was certain that the goon was incapacitated before he began to fully speak his mind. "Well, that's just too fuckin' bad, ain't it. Shoulda thought about that when you stomped—on—"

Mason swung the butt of the rifle so that it smashed Yap's temple. He hit him multiple times.

"—My—fuckin'—head." With each blow, Yap became more and more of an unconscious heap of flesh.

"Okay," Mason announced to his other self. Now for the rest of the crew. He was sure that the rifle's blast was heard throughout the house, so he had to be ready for anything right about now. Mason the hunter.

He reached back under the couch, grabbed a handful of shells, and carefully pulled at the kitchen door. A TV was on in the living room, but the table where the N'awlins crew usually played spades was deserted. Mason could account for two of them, and in his mind he targeted three others; Ace, Wheelchair Sid, and (especially) Juggler.

On a mission now, Mason played SWAT in his own home, peeking in closet spaces, around corners, and eventually up the staircase where he knew his wife was. In his mind, he assumed the worse—that Juggler was up there raping her. There would certainly be a price to pay. Just before Mason climbed the stairs, he felt some movement in the dining room. He shifted gears and pointed the rifle toward the curtains behind the couch. It was clear to him that there were also three or four women somewhere in the house as well, and this was likely one of them.

In his calm voice Mason said, "Come on out of there!" There was a slight movement behind the curtains. It appeared to be more of a mistake than intentional.

"I'm gonna count to three, and then I'm gonna shoot regardless of who it is," yelled Mason. He was sure that this was a scared young girl.

"Please," was the whimper he heard after his one-count. "Don't shoot, it's just me, Raven."

"Aw, shit, girl. I ain't gonna shoot you. Where's the rest of them? Where's Neva and Trixx? Where's Martha?"

In that honest tone of hers Raven said, "Trixx was up in the shower last I knew, and Neva was up in her room with a client, but I think they went out a while ago. I think." Raven seemed to not want to look Mason in his face. Understanding why, Mason said, "Okay,

okay. What about the others? The one they call Ace. And the one who drives you guys around . . . Sid."

"Well, that's what I mean. Ace was supposed to drive Neva into town to hook up with a client, but—"

"All right, all right. So a couple of girls in the house, and you don't know where the wheelchair freak is? You lyin' to me?"

Mason made a face, but Raven was so pretty and harmless that he couldn't seriously be mad at her. She wasn't responsible for his bruises and bumps.

"No, no. I'm tellin' the truth. Promise."

"All right then, Raven, I was never more serious than I am right now. I don't know how in the world a cutie like you got hooked up with these cats, but trust me when I tell you, it's game over. You need to get whatever's yours—whatever is in arm's reach, and find yourself a place to hide. 'Cuz it's about to get ugly around here. In the meantime, consider some other options for a place to work."

Mason redirected his attention to the stairway. He checked his rifle to confirm it was fully loaded as he eased up each step. Up until now was the easy part. Now that he'd reached the top landing, his every body part seemed to throb like his swollen eye.

To be sure that there were no other threats to creep up on him from behind, Mason bypassed the master bedroom for now. The shower was running and he could picture Trixx in there tending to that pretty, shapely body of hers. The door was locked, so he was left to assume she was in there, unaware of Mason's fight to regain possession of his house and his wife. Almost adjacent to the bathroom was another bedroom—the house had a total of five on the second floor. Mason knew this was where Trixx was with a guest, so he poked his head in the doorway, giving the room a brief examination before moving on down the hall. He was looking for Ace, Bones, and two other girls.

With his rifle, Mason pushed the next door open. Two of the girls were in there—Bones and Stormy. Both of them squealing once they saw the gun. Mason put his forefinger to his lips. "Shhhh," and he further assured he wouldn't harm them by his hand gesture and wagging his head. "Get up out of the corner," he told her. And again with the finger to his lips.

The two other bedrooms were empty, leaving Mason with a sense of relief and worry. Three girls and two goons were accounted for. Trixx was in the shower. So there were a handful of Juggler's followers to be on the lookout for. Mason wasn't so concerned about the women, though; it was mainly Juggler and his enforcers and, of course, Wheelchair Sid.

However, Mason was assured that nobody else was on the second floor. Nobody but this target behind the door of the master bedroom. Without hesitation, he used the length of the hallway to get a running start before he charged the door.

D elirious with fear, Adena wondered why and how she got this far. She couldn't save herself, but no doubt it was all out of control now. The final verdict was in: The pleasure wasn't worth it. Yes, the sex was exciting while it lasted, but in the end, if she couldn't hold the man she was with and still feel secure and wanted within his embrace—then what was the point.

All she had now were the raunchy memories, these images that might never leave her mind. The sucking and fucking and following orders might have been titillation to be a willing participant in; however, now that it was all over, Adena could tell how temporary it all was. Now that she thought about it, why the hell was he laying his dick on her face. Did he think that was cute? Did he get off on that?

Assuming that Juggler got a thrill and a high if humiliating her, Adena then had to get past the next task of the night—cleaning his nasty ejaculate from her face and body. The way her face looked, Adena could have been a cake with all the icing.

Juggler's laughing was interrupted by his spasm, but he was sure to inform Adena that the money on the bed was in fact his. "And don't you touch not one greenback," said Juggler while he wiped himself in front of her. Adena added up all the torment, the demands, and the abuse; all of the emotions swirling around her numb thought process, until she was red-eyed and teary. She was at that stage where helpless felt okay—like that dog lying on that nail for so long that it didn't matter anymore. Even in light of what Juggler had said about the money, Adena couldn't say that she wasn't entirely humiliated by this man's actions, since it was always such an invigorating feeling to be used so thoroughly. To have that specific cavity filled and even punished until it was somewhat useless. Adena realized now what her passion was and she had to chuckle to herself about the revelation: *Whether it's Mason or Juggler or any man before them, I actually enjoy this.*

She began to think on those Hallmark moments of her sexual history, the highlights easily came to mind one breathless moment after the next. It got so crazy that she was hot again and shivers began to overcome her. She was actually about to come again.

A gunshot went off upstairs and it stopped all bullshit. Adena's hot flashes; Juggler's passing in the mirror, starring at his tattoos. The energy that came from the blast seemed to be the "reality switch" from both parties.

"What's that?" Juggler made a statement more than he asked a question. And then, as if he had a window to all things threatening, he said, "That's a fucking gunshot! That nigga!" Juggler worked up such an immediate rage and he no sooner took it out on Adena, the scapegoat. He smacked Adena so hard across the face so that she bounced back onto the bed.

"I know this is some Mason shit," Juggler said. "I just know it."

Adena was dazed past the point of pain and cries but just short of blacking out. Although she was dizzy, she could still make out Juggler's image and how he was acting erratic and out of control. He was zipping around the bedroom like some fast-forward button was pushed, looking out the window, checking his pistol, and snatching up his money.

Somewhere in her mind, way behind the current state of dementia, Adena figured his giving her so much money that easily was way too good to be true. And before her eyes, surrendered to her own inner valley of dreams. The last thing she witnessed was Juggler opening the bedroom door, then closing it behind him.

What seemed like hours was really minutes later when Adena's eyes opened again, and now it was Mason coming through the same door—only Mason crashed through, rifle in hand. "Where is that muthafucka?" There was a tone and intensity in Mason's voice and attitude unlike any Adena had ever seen before, or at least there were traces of it in the old Mason—the presuccessful Mason. Still Adena knew that this was uncharacteristic of her husband: the gun, the aggression, and the yelling?

It was all movie acting to her. All smoke and mirrors, until she noticed Juggler's hulking body behind him.

"Mason." Adena's warning was but a weak sigh; even if Mason heard it as a sigh of her relief, he was sadly mistaken.

Juggler had enough of his wrench in his palms. He had quickly slipped into the bathroom where Trixx was still showering. When she felt the draft she poked her head out of the curtains. "Oh, it's you, Juggler. I just came back from a trick. Don't play horny with me tonight, all right?"

Trixx had gone back behind the curtains and was about to say more, but Juggler reached in and cupped her face with his huge hand. Then, through his clenched teeth, he said, "Shut the fuck up and don't say a goddamn word." And that was right before he checked to make sure that the door was locked behind him; before he stepped into the shower with Trixx, clothes and gun included. Once he took his hand from her mouth, Juggler warned Trixx in a whisper, "We've got trouble, just keep showering. Act normal," he told her. And he crouched down with his clothes soaking and his gun aiming.

Inevitably, the two heard the try at the bathroom doorknob. Juggler said act normal so Trixx began singing, *"We just might be breaking up, but y'all know we'll be back this week. This love is unbreakable."*

Juggler made a twisted face at Trixx, and she shrugged and kept on singing, *"No money, no thing, no sin, no temptation. I'm talkin' 'bout nothing . . ."*

Meanwhile, he was listening carefully for another try at the doorknob. Nothing. Nothing at all for almost a minute. Then a crash. And Juggler was quick to shoot out of the bathroom door, and seconds passed before he pistol-whipped Mason unconscious.

# twenty-two

Mason had said to Raven, "I don't know how in the world a cutie like you hooked up with these cats," and, "It's game over," and, "Find a place to hide."

Well, Raven knew only one place to hide once she realized things were much worse than they seemed. She also heard the gunshot from the garage and was curious enough to see what was what. Once she eased the door open, the valley girl came out of her.

"Ohmigod, ohmigod!" And although there was still one conscious goon in there, apparently writhing on the floor, still trying to loosen the duct tape, Raven was glad he couldn't see her from the way he was positioned on the floor. It was crystal clear that she had to get to safe ground. Anywhere was safe outside of this house. She eventually found herself outside, strutting down the road, trying to call one of her capable clients via cell phone. Except cell phones were near impossible to operate on Blue Mountain, so she was out there in the December freeze with a skirt, flat slippers, and a sweater.

It was of little consequence, but Raven was spotted by Martha out on that same road, both of them trying to make their cell phones work. It was no use. The batteries could have been dead for all it mattered—and indeed they were dying with every unfounded attempt.

"What happened in there?" asked Martha.

"Where were you?" asked Raven after the girls hugged each other.

"You didn't hear that gunshot? The screams?"

"Did I? Child, I left that house so fast I think I left tire burns on the grass." Her teeth clicking rapidly, and hugging herself, Raven wagged her head in place of a laugh. It was of little concern to hear Martha go on to say, ". . . I even left food cooking on the stove."

Not only did Martha leave the food cooking, but she left so fast that a dish towel that she used to wipe her hands with was dropped too close to the burners on the stove. By the time the girls met down the road, by the time Mason climbed up the stairs, and by the time Juggler pistol-whipped his pain in the ass, a blaze had already kicked up. Flames in the kitchen had crept up the wall, caught in the cabinets, and begun to engulf the ceiling as if it were flammable. The second floor was about to be hotter than six people could imagine.

The Fickle home was five miles from Route 402, and there were two more miles between Routes 409 and 207, where the nearest firehouse was. By the time engine 37 arrived, members of the block-watch patrol were already pulling up well water in buckets and forming a human chain in an effort to salvage whatever they could of the colonial house that Mason built.

All was dark outside, but for the bright orange glow that the fire cast across the atmosphere.

"The Whale," the area's emergency mobile unit, was parked right in the middle of the flower bed, while the half-dozen other vehicles, all belonging to block-watch members, were scattered along the driveway and roadside. To say that this was a big mess would be an understatement; but to say that this was one of the Pocono's worst tragedies would hit sho' 'nuf dead on the head.

Certain block-watch members like Ms. Kapenski (too elderly to help with the ongoing physical labor) and Barbara Clemons (now three months pregnant) were doing some initial investigating with clipboards and survivors. So far, these survivors included the nicknames Trixx, Yap, and Raven, as well as Martha and Adena. Rescuers were also able to drag Mason from the flames, even though he had been overcome by smoke. He was now on a respirator and expected to soon regain consciousness. However, set aside the whos and the hows of the rescue effort, somebody, somewhere, had some explaining to do.

There were two dead bodies on the second floor, which, based on Raven's account, left Barbara Clemmons to assume were Bones and Stormy. But there was another dead man in the garage with a chunk of his face missing, and yet he was lying in a pool of blood, and yet he didn't show so much as a sunburn.

And then, Barbara told the first sheriff who arrived on the scene, "There is still another guy who was found in the garage trying to wiggle out of a pond of duct tape!"

The officer was doing his own calculating as he took notes in his head. There was some obvious foul play here.

"And so I understand you right when you say that a man was seen jumping out of a second-story window?"

"With clothes on fire," Barbara added.

"And this you witnessed?"

"Oh no. I got here a little later than a few others. I believe it was June Studemeir who saw that."

"So, where is this fella? I counted only four and a possible five who are being treated."

Barbara shrugged as she looked around at all of the activities, how the half dozen block-watch members were passing water from the well to the still-burning house.

"Beats me," she replied. Then came the loud noise, flames, and a part of the house caved in. In the nick of time the sheriff reached out and grabbed Barbara since the flames swelled real fast, caught by the winds that were helping to fuel the fire.

In his Irish accent he said, "Careful there, lassie. Ya got a new family member on the way, I hear."

"Thanks, sheriff," Barbara answered, although her mind was clearly someplace else. There was so much more that Barbara knew about; so much more that she could have spoken on, like where did all of these people come from. She was surely thinking about the girls in the slinky outfits. Were her friends operating a rooming house? Or maybe what Mason had told Bill had gone completely out of control; were the Fickles having orgies at home? Either way, Barbara was somewhat determined to quench her curiosity and get to the bottom of all this.

When the Irish sheriff stepped away, Barbara could overhear him chewing someone out on the cell phone. "You guys gonna make it before next Christmas?" he asked. And she was sure that he was referring to some backup.

"All righty, folks. We're gonna need you to back up some. We appreciate all your hard work, but now it's time for old red to do her job." A fireman had made the announcement while the block watchers scurried away from the danger. But, even with half a house left, the crew of firemen went to work as if the fire had just started.

Barbara stood by and listened to the sheriff question Raven and Martha, wishing that she had beaten him to the punch. Both of Juggler's pros were wrapped in blankets now, perched on seats up inside The Whale—that big useless mobile unit that was suddenly getting more usage than ever before.

"I understand you-know-who was in the house when the fire started?"

Raven said, "I was in the house, but I don't know exactly who was home, what they were doing or whateva."

Raven looked back over her shoulder, back where Martha was shivering, also wrapped in a blanket. Their eyes told a bigger story. Martha spoke up as if on cue. "It's me I think you're lookin' for. I was in the kitchen. But, I left before the fire broke out. I was down the road some with Raven when that nice lady—wha's 'er name?" Martha pointed toward Ms. Kapenski.

"We call her Ms. K."

Barbara conveniently intervened.

"Okay. Well, Ms. K was the one nice enough to scoop us up from the road 'cuz we were cold out there."

"I got that much," the sheriff said, "But, I'm trying to find out who was in the house. Who are the dead girls?"

There was a silence that followed the sheriff's latest question. But Raven decided to break it in an effort to expose some truth. That, and she seemed intimidated by their questions.

"Sheriff, you ready for this?"

The sheriff seemed to brace himself.

"Bones and Stormy were probably up in the bedroom hiding like the rest of us. Only, Raven and I did more than hide," added Martha.

"Hiding? Why would they be hiding?"

"Um . . . the gunshots?" Raven spoke up as if by an uncontrollable reflex. "We were a little scared maybe?"

The face Raven showed may have been a little more sarcastic then she intended, but she made her point.

"And I suppose you don't know what that was all about," suggested the sheriff. The question provoked head wagging from both women.

The sheriff went on with his line of questioning.

"All right . . . maybe you can tell me this: Was there a party here today? 'Cuz I don't know a household that has so many folks under one roof, and nobody seems to know what, who, or how."

"You can say it was a party, sheriff. Just some friends getting together."

"Is that so? Just a party?"

Martha seemed calm when she replied, "Yes, sheriff. Just a party."

"And the guns, the duct tape, and the fire? That part of the party, too?"

Martha and Raven looked at each other to maintain that sense of solidarity. Barbara could feel that woman-to-woman signal. And in her mind she was hoping that the sheriff would find something else to do; something else to investigate. But that was a dead issue when he told the girls, "I'm gonna need to see you two down the road when I finish here."

"Down the road?'

"Yes, at my office."

Barbara had seen enough TV to know that the sheriff was being nice about it, but that he was saying that he wanted them to come in for questioning. And that's when Barbara stepped away to find Adena.

While the house was bearing all of the burdens of various impulsive actions, Juggler was at least a mile away, where he found refuge in someone's rusty pickup truck. To get to this point was bananas; sprinting through flames in the house and practically tossing himself through the second-floor bedroom window, then to find his way through the forest, in the dark; and not having any idea where he was going, Juggler could have just as well been a blind man— blind and desperate to stay out of jail.

It was a long story, but the short end was that he might have left an outstanding warrant down in New Orleans—which he wasn't that worried about, with all of the confusion that was still going on in the aftermath of Katrina. And even if that wasn't threatening enough, he was extra sure that there was an outstanding warrant in Harlem, New York, where he beat down a cat and fought with a few others for clowning him over his name.

All told, with the fire drawing a crowd of neighbors, firemen, and police, a whole lot of worms were going to escape from the can. And not just the operation would be unveiled—that was easy to handle; a cinch to set up since the money was flowing again. *But,* he wondered, *how the hell did Mason get loose? Did he hurt my boys? Did he set a fire to his own house?* Juggler had so many questions of his own as he ventured off alone, through the forest, trying to use his cell phone along the way.

"These fuckin' mountains!" he grunted.

And now that he'd found the rusty truck, it was his chance to relax some after so much running. He kept pressing the redial, trying to catch Sid or Ace, who he recalled were out handling escorts and clients.

When Juggler finally did get through, it was only momentary, enough to hear Sid's voice. There wasn't even enough opportunity to give details regarding where he was. For now, Juggler was stuck in this truck like one big fuck.

# twenty-three

Adena was shivering, crouched in the ambulance that shot down 402 toward the township of Marshalls Creek. Of course, Mason was there on the stretcher with a mask over his face and an IV in his arm She couldn't recall ever seeing him this blue. It was an eerie thing to watch, even with the medical technicians on hand to assure her that everything was going to be fine. Things were definitely not fine with her husband lying unconscious in a speeding ambulance.

In the meantime, Adena held her husband's hand while also grabbing a hold of the handle in the ambulance while it rocked from side to side. It was only now as she looked close at his eyelids and felt his pulse that she realized the worst. Their dream home was gone, along with everything in it. All their mementos, clothes, photos, and furnishings were history. She was sure of it. And now it was clear as day that none of that other stuff mattered, and all she had was her husband. As a matter of desperation *and* dire need, she'd have to lean on him as well as she'd have to be his crutch, regardless of the outcome. Everything in their past—Adena was thinking about her foregone choices back at the house—had to stay there, and as a couple they had to move on, no matter what the future held. She didn't think about the dead body behind the house, nor did she wonder about all of the neighbors and emergency responders in the yard. Would they get down to the heart of the matter? Those things weren't an issue right now. What mattered most was Mason. Mason had to survive this. The two of them had to start over, and they had to live out whatever destiny had in store for them.

Tears filled up Adena's eyelids, but she wouldn't let them fall. Weakness wasn't what she needed now; she had to be strong for two.

Y ou okay, Adena?"

Adena nodded but then she looked up and was immediately startled. Since the ambulance arrived she hadn't gotten a good look at either of the EMS workers. Only now did she realize that this was an old fling that she had; the cop who— "You're driving ambulances now?"

"Oh. Hi. Sorry, I . . . with all that as goin' on, I—"

"Please. Don't mention it. You've got other things on your mind, I'm sure. I just wanted to make sure that you were holding it together. He needs you now more than ever."

A tear finally slipped out and down Adena's cheek. It was that someone else brought attention to what she only now realized: that she had something good here, so hold on to it. It may be that keeping something this good in her life was worth all the sacrifice and the discipline; maybe a raunchy romp in the bed, or impulsive rendezvous in a hotel room, or sudden threesome, or the other nasty shit that the couple indulged in, wasn't all that it was cut out to be. The instant thrills that she was seeking, that she sought out for the both of them, were too superficial and too short-lived. A thrill (in a nutshell) was what sugar water was to a nutritious fruit drink.

T he ex-boyfriend handed Adena a tissue and indicated that they'd reached their destination. The moment the vehicle came to a halt at Pocono Hospital, things began to flash by as if someone had pressed the Fast Forward button. She tailed the gurney as far as the hospital staff would allow before she was redirected to the counter where she was presented with questions and paperwork to sign. Then came the waiting. In the hospital lobby, Adena found an isolated corner to be alone and concentrate on her concerns. She fell asleep for a time; she awoke to a local news broadcast on the TV monitor just above her. The timing couldn't have been more coincidental.

". . . Details bare and sketchy at this time, but firefighters have so far pulled two unidentified bodies from the blaze, and another body, a man in his late thirties, found with a gunshot wound to the face, was pronounced dead at the scene. Naturally, officials are investigating foul play here and how it relates to this four-alarm blaze that has mostly destroyed the home owned by real estate mortgage broker Mason Fickle. . . ."

Adena starred up at the images of her home engulfed in flames. Emergency workers and firefighters were on hand, stepping lively in one direction or another. And now came the neighbors she knew all too well from various block-watch meetings.

"I've known the Fickles for a long time now. The husband had been an anchor in our township and all, and the wife is just so sweet. . . ."

"I've noticed a lot of strange things over the past months. I can't really say what was going on in the house, except that there were a lot of people always going in and out—people I've never seen before; cars I've never seen before. I was even becoming nervous."

"I can't imagine how a dead body wound up in the house. Maybe a hunting accident? I mean someone's always breaking the hunting rules and coming closer than five hundred feet. . . ."

"Whatever was going on in the household, this has got to be one of the worst tragedies in this community since the dynamite explosion some forty years ago. . . ."

That last interview was followed by pictures from that event, as well as images from the memorial service just six months earlier.

To Adena, however, this all made no sense. What did the forty-year-old dynamite accident have to do with her home? And why were these neighbors coming out of nowhere with these comments? Like they were earning their fifteen minutes of fame from the Fickles' loss?

"Officials tell us at News Twelve that this will be investigated for foul play and possible murder charges. The question is, who would be charged? Were Mason or Adena Fickle involved? Or maybe one of their many houseguests? Only time will tell. Warren Dash. News Twelve, on Blue Mountain."

On the heals of the newscast, Adena's senses blurred some. Someone was approaching her—a woman. The closer she came, Adena realized it was her neighbor Barbara Clemons. Meanwhile, over by the security desk, two deputies were just coming through the door. Soon thereafter, the hospital security guard was pointing in Adena's direction.

"Adena? You okay?"

Even as Barbara's compassionate voice was heard, and while the two deputies strutted through the hospital's waiting area, the doctor was also coming to Adena, likely with news about Mason.

The TV, Barbara, the deputies, the doctor. The voices followed the images, those implications from the neighbors, Barbara's concern, and now the deputies.

"Mrs. Fickle?"

The doctor now: "Mrs. Fickle, I'm Dr. Felton."

All of these sights and sounds were enough pressure for a heart attack. But for Adena, they were enough to have her faint right there in her seat.

Not until Sid approached the scene with the emergency vehicles and people scattered on and off the Fickle property did he realize the bigger story. He was directed, along with other passing vehicles, to keep it moving. But there was enough of an opportunity for Sid to know that this was a problem that had obviously gotten out of hand. Something even his boss had no control over.

For years now, Sid had been putting up with Juggler's condescending ways. He'd been disrespected, humiliated, and now, all of a sudden, when the chips were down, Juggler needed him? This was hilarious to Sid—the legless, disabled, handicapped woadie that he was. For Juggler to be in a state of distress, something that all the money in the worked couldn't change. And now that it was clear that Juggler was helpless, somewhere hidden in a pickup truck, trespassing, and wanted by the law, Sid had a plan up his sleeve that would "outdo Katrina."

Juggler had said enough on their interrupted cell phone call for Sid to get an idea where he might be. Thing was, it was so dark out; even a green pickup truck would appear to be black. And the only knowledge Sid had of the miles of forestry and the homes that were scattered about was really coincidental to his coming and going up and down 409.

*Where the hell am I going to find a green pickup at this time of the night?* But even as Sid was discouraged by the elements and circumstances, he continued to drive in circles around the vicinity of Blue Mountain until he identified the pickup truck, and it wasn't even a certainty that this was the one; he just had that itch that told him yes. Now for the tough part.

In order to carry out his plan, Sid had to sneak onto the property in his wheelchair undetected in his wheelchair, and after he'd made contact with Juggler he'd have to— *Well, no sense in thinking about it. Just get it over with. Embrace your courage. Walk the walk.*

Sid was kidding himself really. Repeating some ideas he'd heard on the TV recently—a pastor and motivational speaker trying to inspire viewers. Sometimes that's how Sid spent so much of his idle time; when he wasn't playing gofer, or taxiing girls here and there, the TV was his friend. Over the past two months he must have seen all of *The Honeymooners* episodes, just about an entire season of *Cops*, and too many repeat music videos with soft porn to count.

There came a moment when Sid wondered what more he could expect out of his life. The lower half of his body was gone; but did that mean that the upper half would be totally useless except for chasing after Juggler's every whim and getting little more than five hundred dollars a week, was this it?

All of this weighed on Sid's mind as he nixed the headlights on his truck and rolled the vehicle onto the driveway of an adjacent property. He did so at the slowest possible pace, hoping not to trigger any motion detectors or floodlights in the yard. So far so good. And once the motor died, he marked a cross over his chest and reached in the backseat for his wheelchair. Once he maneuvered the chair between his body and the steering wheel, and after he set it on the ground outside the driver's-side door, Sid reached into the back again, where his new oil-finished, hardwood-stock, single-shot rifle was hidden beneath the seat. The weapon may not have been the fancy model with a scope and a sling, but was (so far) "able to take down six deer," explained the gun seller.

Encouraged by that idea, the six dead deer, Sid made his move quietly and strategically. His biggest conflict right now was trespassing onto yet another property, as slowly as possible, with his wheelchair making it over gravel, branches, and other small obstacles. But Sid had become a pro at this, to the degree that he could do wheelies, whip-around curves, and he had even arranged for a "wheelchair jump" back in New Orleans, trying to be the Evel Knievel of handicaps.

Rifle across his lap, Sid made his move onto the property. It never occurred to Sid that this small, one-bedroom house might belong to one of the township's deputies, or even a hunter who could turn Sid into the hunted. However, he maintained that leap of faith and wheeled his chair across the rough wooded grounds. He kept it as quiet as he could, still with his eye on the cottage home and the window where a dim light glowed inside.

The pickup truck still appeared to be a dark color from fifty feet away, and the closer Sid got to it, the more caution he exercised. Once he was within ten feet, he wedged the rifle under his arm so that he'd be prepared to carry out his mission.

"You lookin' for me?" The voice came from behind Sid, when all the while his attention had been directed ahead where the truck was parked.

"Shit—you scared the fuck outta me, Juggler!"

"Scared you? What's all this creepin' for? I told you to flash your headlights and I'd see you. . . ."

Sid didn't answer. He just worked at redirecting his wheelchair.

"Here I am ready to jump in the truck, and where are you? Creepin' up with—"

Juggler twisted his face. "What's the gun for?"

Sid stuttered when he said, "I—well—ya know, goin' on someone's property in and ah . . . You never can know."

"Ya neva can know? Is that right. I'll tell you what I think."

Now Juggler lunged for the rifle before Sid could face him.

"I think—muthafuck! You'se tryin' to kill me, wasn't you?"

Sid sucked his teeth. "Please, boss, what the fuck you talkin' 'bout?"

Juggler had already made up his mind, and now he leveled the rifle so that it pointed at his homey's head.

"Look at me, straight in the face and tell me that you weren't just sneaking up on me . . . that this rifle ain't for me . . . that you ain't thought about takin' shit over. . . ."

"You weird, man. Wasn't nobody doin' all a that."

Juggler just stood there and stared at Sid, assessing whatever he could in the dim of the night. But his not saying anything, instead, said a whole lot of things. Sid was encouraged to defend himself.

"Juggler, you're buggin fo' real. Why would I—your right-hand man, your ace boon—do somethin' that stupid? Where would that leave me, after all we been through?"

Juggler still said nothing. And to turn things up few notches, he pressed the base of the rifle into Sid's chest.

"I don't believe you," Juggler finally said. "You lyin'."

"Aw, jeez, Juggler! I'm tellin' you! That shit is so far from the truth, homey-woadie."

"Nah, fuck that homey-woadie shit, now. I gotta call it like I see it, Sid. You probably tryin' to knock me off; tryin' a take over."

"Nah, Juggler."

"You figure I'm fucked. Authorities looking for me. A couple of bodies lying around, and all kinds a questions. And you the only other one, besides Ace, who got access to-oh . . . so it's you and Ace in this together."

"Jeezus, fuck, Juggler. Ask Ace. Ask anybody. It just ain't goin' down like that."

Juggler cocked the rifle slide now to prepare it for firing.

"Juggler, what you—"

"Shut the fuck up, Sid. I'm goin' wit' my heart. And my heart says you fucked up."

"Juggler, no. No, no, no." Sid begged for his life. Juggler pressed the rifle's back into Sid's chest.

"After all I've done for you. Got you back on your feet after the accident. Gave you money whenever I could. Got you a new wheelchair, your truck, your dead pop's gravestone. After all that? Treated you like a brother, Sid. Put up with your mouth for almost ten years and—"

"Please, Juggler. Please."

"—This is the thanks I get? This is how you treat me?"

"Boss, no! No! No!"

"No, Sid. Yes, yes, yes. And good night."

Sid braced himself and squeezed his eyes close. A tear glistened under the moonlight. "Say Good night, Sid! Say it!"

All Sid did was pant and whine.

"I said, say it! Good night, Sid."

Sid's lips quivers and he trembled like a wet cat.

"You ain't gonna say it?"

Juggler poked the rifle at one pec and then the other, emphasizing his words. His lips curled up and pursed themselves in some final judgment.

There was an instant of dread on Sid's face, how he was hanging on to every last breath and ready to swallow the worst yet to come. But Juggler apparently had something else in mind. He lowered his head so that what he had to say was taken seriously.

"That's it, Sid, You're over. Finished, Through."

Juggler was close to Sid's ear now. "Bang, you're dead."

But Juggler hadn't squeezed the trigger. Her was, however, holding back a laugh. Just when Sid accepted his doom, Juggler had flipped the switch and tricked him.

"I ain't gonna kill you, woadie. . . ."

Juggler now lifted his foot and put it against Sid's chest. "But I am gonna fuck you up." And he thrust Sid so that he fell backward, out of his wheelchair and into a helpless heap on the ground. To add misery to Sid's pain, Juggler went for the abandoned wheelchair, and he swung it around and around until there was enough motion and velocity to send the wheelchair flying through the air. It eventually caused a crashing sound when it hit a tool shed.

"Now, that's what I call fucked up."

Sid was moaning, trying to work his body back into some state of normalcy, when he realized what was happening. The house lights came on. Juggler was laughing, and that laugh was becoming more distant. The truck was started, there was an engine's roar, and he swore he heard Juggler shout, *"Holla atcha boy!"*

His body was feeling less pain than it was feeling useless. What could he do now? And what explanation would he give these people who were looking out of their window? How could he explain trespassing? A floodlight came on and Sid knew what Juggler said was right: He was truly fucked up.

The phone conversation that Barbara Clemons had with her husband, Bill, was not brief and to the point. Yes, their friends, the Fickles, had been acting strange for a while now, but if you're a friend, do you abandon someone like Mason or Adena when the chips are down? Is there anything so bad that would encourage a real friend to turn his back? *"And,"* Barbara argued, "what if certain things got out of control?"

"Things like what, Barbara? Those two are grown-ass people. They know the consequences of their actions. Plus, and I hate to rub this in, but I can't say that I didn't tell him so. 'Too much of anything can kill you.' I told him that, Barbara."

"Okay, okay. But people make mistakes, honey. None of us are perfect."

"Don't you give me that horseshit that I hear every day. At least once a day say, 'I'm only human.' And, 'People make mistakes.' "

"You don't have to raise your voice at me, Bill. Remember me? Your wife? I'm not the one who's in hot water—"

"Okay, baby. My bad. But, don't you understand? Somewhere, somehow, there's gotta be a line drawn. Like in that book we read together."

"Which book?"

"Remember *Standing at the Scratch Line*? Maya Angelou's son?"

"His name is Guy Johnson, Bill. He *does* have a name."

"Okay. Whatever. But my point is, the scratch line is drawn, and you dare the person to cross it, and if they do they're in violation. And the fight begins."

"So?"

"So? Barbara, life is always drawing scratch lines for us. Actually, that's life forcing us to make decisions. That's life daring us to cross the scratch line—whatever it is. And the only thing stopping us human beings from our animal natures is the choice to make conscious decisions. We're not so stupid that we don't know the difference between right and wrong, baby. We have the option of reasoning."

"But, what I was saying is, what if there were circumstances beyond their control? Like, what if a gun was put to their heads?"

"Like how?" asked Bill. And the phone call took another turn.

Barbara repeated all that Adena had said, how the Fickles had Cynthia, aka Loween, the underage southern girl, over for one of their "encounters." (Barbara chose to call those sexual indulgences "encounters" since there were so many of them and that they were, for the most part, too raunchy for words.) She told Bill about the A.M. visit from some guy the Fickles came to know as Wheelchair Sid, and there was the crew that came behind Sid, and all the happenings with Loween's body, and—

"What did you say they did with the body?"

"I said—and you heard me, Bill."

"I know, I know. I just wanted to make sure I heard you correct, that's all." He chuckled.

"They buried her body in the forest, Bill. Behind their home."

"That's what I thought you said," said Bill.

"And you know what that means?"

"What?" Barbara asked.

"It means the courtroom, Barbara. The Fickles will be in court before the week is out. I promise you that. Whether it's criminal or civil, there's gonna be a trial. People don't end up dead, and there's nobody to get the blame. Oh, no. Those two are in *way* over their heads. And that means somebody's gonna want their heads. Push is eventually gonna come to shove, Barbara— Shit!"

"What, Bill?"

"Barbara, we're gonna have to take the stand. We're gonna have to tell what we saw, what we know about the Fickles . . . hell, they'll have the whole block-watch team testifying. See that crazy shit? We didn't have a thing to do with the events in that house, and yet we're already knee deep in this twisted mess."

Barbara was still in the lobby of the hospital while Bill explained the full extent of things over the cell phone call. At the same time, her eyes recorded everything in the distance: the Marshalls Creek deputies questioning Adena, the nosy reporter from the local paper, a camera crew was charging through the double doors in search of a story, and the florist had another flower delivery.

"Okay, Bill. Hate to cut you off but . . . we gotta decide, and we gotta decide *now*. Do we get behind the Fickles one hundred percent, or play it safe and—"

On the phone, Bill said, "We have no choice, Barbara. Just like the Fickles chose to be with that girl, we chose the Fickles as our friends. We have to play the hand dealt us. We can't pretend we don't know 'em. 'Cuz everybody we know is gonna swear otherwise. They're good people. I really do believe that."

"Then it's done. One hundred percent support. All right, hun. Gotta go. The news people are here."

"What news people?"

"You have a TV at work?"

"Yesss."

"Well, put it on channel six. Your sweet peach is about to make her world debut."

Barbara didn't wait for a response. She snapped her phone closed and headed for the reporter.

# twenty-four

The following day was one that was uncharacteristic of a Christmas Eve. It was fifty-two degrees outside, the sun was beaming, and you could safely venture outdoors with a thin jacket on without catching a cold or a flu. But, while everything seemed backward with the weather, things were just as backward on Blue Mountain and around the township of Marshalls Creek.

Everyone was buzzing about the closet freaks who accidentally killed a girl. And Mason Fickle had a big enough name in the township that this "accident" was looked at as peculiar activity instead of murder.

"Okay. So the guy is into the threesomes. But if his wife was in agreement, could you blame 'im? I'da done the same!"

"Who woulda thunk it? Those two seemed like the quietest couple on the mountain. He's a man of great distinction," said a neighbor. "Into the real estate financing 'n' all. He deserves the life he was livin'. But I don't agree with the young girl—except the way these young ones look nowadays, you'd swear they were built to look older 'n' they are."

"Seventeen? That's how old the girl was? Poor girl. Probably wore the pants of a twenty-something. You know how the younger folks do today, always biting off more than they can chew."

"I don't condone a bit of it. I say if it don't come out in the wash it'll come out in the rinse. And Mason Fickle has played his last trick. Now he's all washed up."

"I heard there was some kinda home invasion goin' on—holdin' the Fickles hostage and whatnot. What's that about? I remember way back in the day how they did that Patty Hearst girl. Was it something like that? Sounds intriguing. I'd like to see the story on Lifetime."

"Okay, I understand that them Fickles mighta got scared, but I feel for the girl. So what she was a freak. We all freaks. Thing is, ain't the girl got a family? I'm sure somebody loved her in this world. And then, add the part about New Orleans. I'm just sympathetic, I s'pose. Still wish she coulda lived to tell her side a all this."

"The whole thing is strange if you ask me. First, there's the freaky sex. Okay. We understand all that. But was this guy trying to kill her with his . . . I mean, how blind, deaf, and dumb do you hafta be to see a girl is choking on yer thing? That speculation about involuntary manslaughter—I think that should play out in the courtroom. 'Cuz none of us can really say what happened up on Blue Mountain. I s'pose ya had to be there."

"I've known Adena Fickle for a few years now where we work at the same job, and all I ever seen was a hardworkin' girl. She always seemed to have her mind somewhere else, but she got the job done every time. It's a shame all a this is happenin'. I still wanna know exactly how the girl died. I do!"

"This is the sort of sick and perverted activity that moving to the mountains is supposed to leave behind. All the smog, the noise, and the people—problems are for them city folk. And now that these two are done brought the whole wide world to our doorstep . . . Now that these two make it appear as though this is the sort of thing that you can get away with when you move up into these parts, well . . . I only got one thing to say: There goes the neighborhood."

"I disagree with those people who say Mason is guilty. Let the courts decide that. Why are people so full of hate? Just because the man likes to get freaky doesn't mean he deserves persecution for his tastes. We need to separate the business and the pleasure. The business is the legal side. Exactly what happened in that house that caused the girl's death, but anything else is a private affair. Don't just lump it all together, because one thing has nothing to do with the other."

Once Adena finished with the deputies, they began radioing their comrades about the burial. The news that originally earned its own legs now took on wings. And before long, the buzz about Mason and Adena turned into the talk of the town and the one question that everyone was asking: "Where's the body?" Mason asked his wife; it was one of the first questions that came to mind right after the ones about the house and the truck.

"Mason, since the fire I've been with you, by your side. This is the first I'm hearing about a missing body. And that came from a reporter, not the deputies. So either they're looking in the wrong place, or somebody . . ." Adena didn't finish her sentence.

"Or somebody *what?*"

"Or somebody moved it," Adena said. "But listen, that's not important right now. Your health is what's important."

"I don't know what good my health is if I don't have a life. No house, no car . . . Did your car make it?"

"I was parked outside—close enough for the ashes, but it should be okay. Your truck has insurance, and so does our house. So it's not as bad as it seems, Mason. Remember, we gotta stop sellin' ourselves on hard times, otherwise that's all were gonna see. Isn't that what you tell me, Mason?"

Mason made a face; acceptance of Adena dishing him his own serving of advice.

The doctor entered the room, and Mason swore he knew the guy from somewhere.

"The local deputies still want to speak with him, ma'am. Oh, hey there, Mr. Fickle. I see you're fully alert again. Good. How are we feeling?"

"My body is good, even if my mind isn't."

"Well, you just take all the time you need you to, I'll keep the dogs off until you give the word."

Adena said, "Thanks, doc."

"Buzz me if you need me," he said on his way through the door.

Mason thought for a moment before he asked, "Baby, why does he look so familiar?"

But Adena swept Mason's curiosity aside and went to fluff his pillow some.

"Mason, you need to relax your mind. I need you to get better and help me sort things out. Remember, we don't have a place to live right now."

"We will in a minute," Mason said. "You said you told the deputies everything?"

"Everything, Mason. And it just wasn't as bad as it seemed. They realized it was an accident and they just wanted to see the body to determine the cause of death."

"And you told 'em we buried the body?"

"Not exactly. I told 'em our guests buried the body—which they did. I just left your name out of that part."

Mason thought about it. Then he grew a smile.

"And they bought it?"

"All ten yards."

"Come here and gimme a hug."

Adena did. And even while they were snuggled together on the hospital bed, Mason shared his deepest sentiments.

"Just when I thought the worst, you came and turned it all around, baby. You did the most unlikeliest thing, Adena. And I know it took a lot of heart." Mason squeezed her tighter. "Thank you so much for stickin' by me."

"What else would a good woman do, Mason?"

"You're right. And you're *such* a good woman."

There, in her husband's arms, Adena wondered about so many things. First, she was relieved that Mason didn't altogether recognize the doctor—the same doctor who was a client of Juggler's and who had sat in the bedroom while she and Stormy performed. And on that subject Adena wondered as well, recalling how Juggler and his goons had beaten Mason, if Mason would remember what he'd seen. After all, it wasn't like he'd caught them in the act; they were merely on the bed together. And even so, wouldn't Stormy's death sweep all of those images aside? Weren't there more important things than infidelity? Infidelity, that was another thing Adena concluded in her mind that the episode with Juggler never happened. And if Mason asked about that, then Adena would just have to—

"Adena?"

"Yes, baby?" Adena was still holding her husband, with her body half on and half off the bed.

"I've been meaning to ask you . . . lot of things were goin' through my mind, some that I'm not too clear about."

"Yes, honey?" Adena said, not sure she wanted to hear this.

"In our bedroom . . . was I dreaming? Or were you on the bed with another woman?"

"Well . . . we've had a number of women on the bed, Mason. Maybe you weren't dreaming. Maybe you were fantasizing."

"I guess," Mason replied. "But then when I was . . . when you and Juggler . . . I mean, did . . . "

"Mason, you really need some rest. All sorts of things must be goin' through your mind, and the best answer the doctor gave was rest."

Adena kissed Mason's forehead and caressed his cheeks.

"Right. The doctor. The doctor. Real familiar, that doctor."

When Mason finally closed his eyes, Adena went to see the doctor. On one hand, she wanted to know how much longer before he'd be released. On the other hand, she had to say, "I don't think he recognizes you. Remember, those guys lumped him up some, so no tellin' what's goin' through his mind."

Relief filled Dr. Joel's face. He said, "Thank God. I know how I'd feel if I were in his shoes and I saw my wife—"

"Uh . . . Dr. Joel? We don't hafta relive the occasion, do we?"

"You're right, you're right," he said, nodding. "Let's just get him better and get him home."

"By the way, your other friend is about to be released as well."

"Other friend?"

"Why, yes. She says to call her Trixx, but her birth name is—"

"*Trixx is here?* You mean she's *alive?* Oh my God, please take me to her," Adena demanded.

Just a few doors away, Adena was led into a room that was filled with flowers. She and Trixx immediately turned joyful and shared a big hug.

"I'm so glad to see you made it out alive," Adena said.

"Barely," Trixx said. "My arm isn't gonna look too pretty, but then, that's one of my valuable assets." She smiled up at Adena, but there were tears in her eyes.

"What's up, girl? Why the tears?" Adena took a corner of a bedsheet to dry Trixx's eyes.

"My friend, Stormy."

"I know, I know. I'm sorry. I'm really sorry."

"Everything seemed fine yesterday, like the world was ours.

I didn't have a care in the world for the first Christmas holiday in my life. I mean, it just seemed like the clouds parted and the sky opened up to some light. Then all a sudden, this."

Adena didn't linger on the thought too much, but in the back of her mind she was saying, *What sunlight? You're a hooker. You sell your body and you need to get a real job.* But, of course she didn't say any of that. Instead, Adena had compassion for Trixx. She tried to imagine what it would be like to have no other choices in life but to sell her body. And in that event, maybe that certain instance with the clouds parting and the sunlight shinning wasn't such a lame concept after all.

"I think life is gonna always do that to us, Trixx."

Wiping away one more tear, Trixx asked, "What's that?"

"I mean, it's gonna tease us and tempt us and make us think it's all peaches and cream, right before we get smacked in the face with another challenge."

"I know, right? I hate when that happens. You think you got it goin' on, then it's one thing or another that turns it all around. I'm startin' to think that we're not supposed to make it in life. At least, not people like me."

"Don't say that, Trixx. Mason and I are always tellin' each other to stop selling fear. We always say it, but then we still do it. I don't know. Maybe we were born with that fear factor locked in and we can't help ourselves. When we wake up in the morning it's with a pound of worry and an ounce of hope."

"But what other choices does a girl like me have? I find myself banking on my looks every day. I can't help but to think that's what makes a difference in life—in my life anyway. Good looks gets you places. I see it all the time, ever since I was a teenager. I always got more food on my plate or that extra present. And now that I'm older, that's the only thing I know, using what I got to get what I want."

Adena showed a proud grin before she said, "You know something? I've been watching you guys, and I've been getting to know you better during the past two months. At first, I'll be honest, I kind of frowned

on what you do for a living. I did. But now I see something more. I'm
no different from you, Trixx. I remember when I first met my husband,
I thought I was the shit. I thought I was unstoppable and that nothin'
could bring me down to earth. Well, maybe I lucked up, because damn
if my husband didn't stop my ass. I fell head over heals for that man,
and just hours before I met him I could swear on anything that I was
gonna stay single and pimp the world. I was lookin' good, I had that
hood background, and men were throwin' gifts at me for just *breathin'*
their way. But, you're right . . . it had a lot to do with my *looks*, Trixx. As
long as I looked the part and switched my ass like Momma did—"

Both Trixx and Adena laughed at her testimony.

"I could get what I want. I could go where I want and I was
happy. Only after I wound up with *this* man . . . the *right* man, did I
see that there was other things in life besides getting over temporar-
ily. Things like real estate and banks offerin' lines of credit, and being
asked to be part of this group and that—the Masons and the Stars.
Shit, girl, where I came from, the only groups to get with were the
gangs or the hustlers. And I bypassed that stuff, luckily. I just wanna
see you get more out of life, like I did. And if I have anything to do
with it, you *will*, Trixx."

There was a silence that was worthy of a good cry, but it was interrupted by another presence in the room.

"Surprise! I thought you two could use some friends," said Dr.
Joel. But the ladies were already throwing hugs and kisses at one another. Martha, Raven, and Neva (who was on an escort date when
the fire erupted) practically stampeded the room.

"Oh my God, I thought I'd never see you guys again!"

Martha made a face, and Raven said, "Us? What about *you*? We
never saw you come out the house!"

"Girl, when those gunshots started blastin' off, I was O-U-T, out,"
Martha said.

"And all this time we've been answering questions from those
two deputies. I thought they were gonna go on forever."

"I feel your pain," Adena said. "They came to me, too."

"And me," Trixx added.

"Why ya'll lookin' all somber in here? All teary-eyed?"

"Oh, nothin'. Just a happy moment," Trixx said.

"And some deep conversation," Adena said.

"Well, don't leave us out," Martha said.

Adena was quick to brush off her interest, so she said, "It's money talk. I'm sure you girls wouldn't be interested."

"Are you kidding?" Raven snapped. "That Juggler is nowhere to be found. He's got all of my money tied up in his venture, and I'm *hot.*"

"Oh *shit.* You too? He hit me up for two grand, said it was to help the empire grow and that I'd get stock or whateva."

Raven shook her head. "Ladies, ladies, ladies . . . I might be the quiet one in the bunch, but if there's one thing Granny taught me before she passed is never give away more than you can afford. And never give it to a man who hasn't been in business for more than two or three years."

Adena said, "And never give it to a man who mixes business and pleasure."

"Oooh, I got one," Martha said. "How about never give it to a man who's full of promises."

"Well, shit, ladies . . . I say, just never give it to a man, *period!*" Trixx's comment caused a riotous laughter in the room.

Adena took a seat on the edge of the hospital bed and sought the attention of everyone.

"I have a proposition for all of you. I know a friend who's involved with that iPod. The Video iPod?"

"Yeah, girl. I got one of those comin' for Christmas."

"Okay, well, my friend and I were talkin' and she says—"

"Your friend is a she? I like this proposal already."

"Okay, but listen. She wants to develop a little thirty-minute show called *The Slumber Party.* Her idea was pull together a group of sexy women, put them in sexy nightwear, and have them lounge around and talk about *whatever.* Easy."

"Whatever, *meaning?*"

"I mean what-*ever.* She suggested that there be themes that are sexually motivated, but also she mentioned music, movies, just anything you can think of. But here's where you win. . . ." Everybody got real quiet.

"The Video iPod has tens of millions of owners all around the world. It's a gadget that they say can catch up to the cell phone and the television. But, even if it doesn't, tens of millions is a lot of people to reach."

"You got that," Martha said. "So we sit around, kick it about, *whatever.* We keep it sexy . . . and what, we get a million dollars?"

"Be realistic, Martha. We can get someone to videotape us, get it put on the whole Internet craze—I been thinkin' about this for a minute now, and people will pay to visit *The Slumber Party* as often as we make episodes."

"And if you multiply that by—oh, shit, count me in!" Trixx said.

"Adena, how long you been holdin' back on us?"

Adena chuckled. "It's just . . . It was only a thought a week ago. And I was gonna bring it to Juggler's attention. . . ."

"Oh, *hell* no! I'm done with that fool."

"I'm with you, Trixx. Who wants to be around shootouts and fires," said Raven. "I don't care *how* much money he owes. My life is worth more than all the money in the world."

"High-five on that one."

"So, Adena. What do we do to get started? I mean, if that's all that it takes, and I don't have to have another man in my face, or with his hands on me?"

Martha's face dropped in her hands and she let out a bellowing sob. They consoled her as best they could, but she went on a tantrum, crying about strangers touching her, and how she wasn't raised to be a hooker, and how all her dreams were slipping past day by day. These were words that all of the women in the room could sympathize with. They could all feel her pain in some way, if not more.

Then that settles it. I'm no longer Adena the housekeeper. I'm Adena the entrepreneur from here on."

"You mean, you're quitting work?" Neva asked.

"Well, I'm not *that* crazy. But, I will say my days at the Days Inn are numbered."

"I heard that. But what do *we* need to do to get started?"

"For starters, we *all* need a place to stay right now," Adena said. "My guess is that I can talk to one of the managers at the job, explain my emergency, and I'm sure we can get three rooms, at least."

"And if we need it, I have a few thousand dollars stashed away," said Raven.

"Your money wasn't at the house, under the mattress? *Shoot,* mine was," Neva said.

"I got you, Neva. I got all of us," Raven said. "Even if it's down to my last penny."

"See? And all the while I'm thinkin' Raven was one of those pretty-faced, stuck-up chicks. Boy, was I all wrong."

"Trixx, there's a lot you can learn about me, and one of those things is that I'm one of the most down-to-earth women you could ever know. I'm sweet and quiet, and I'm a workaholic, but I'm all of that and *still* down-to-earth."

"Ladies, there's a reporter outside in the lobby. Any takers?" It was Dr. Joel with the news, and it seemed like everybody wanted an interview with Mason Fickle's houseguests.

"Let 'em speak with our new agent," suggested Martha, finally recuperating from her sorrow. And a couple of girls playfully lifted Adena from her seat and directed her toward the door.

"Oh, and don't forget to tell the press about our new venture," Trixx said.

# twenty-five

If ever Juggler was in a bind, it was now. He had Ace with him, the last of his hired help by his side. They still had a hotel room to work with, so a place to sleep wasn't the biggest issue. What mattered more was that his clients were calling and waiting on the very resource that Juggler provided: that same resource that he was now missing. This was almost the same shit he'd found himself in just days after the storm: no girls, no product, and no business. He slammed the phone down after his latest call, a client who was staying up at Caesars Casino, farther up on Route 207. The client was definitely *big money*, but he had to catch a plane soon, and now was the opportunity (while his wife was away shopping) for that client to get his nut off.

*"If you can't get her here now, then forget it. And don't count on me calling you the next time I come to town."*

What happened?" Ace asked with no emotion in his voice.

"Fuckin' guy is impatient. Says he wants it now."

"Doesn't everyone?"

"Thing is, what's stoppin' our cash flow is our missin' cash cows."

"Then that's it. We just get new cows . . . I mean, girls," Ace said.

"Easier said than done, Ace. Plus, I used to have Sid to do all that. Fuckin' paraplegic."

Ace didn't respond since he knew how upset Juggler was at Sid. No sense in making him *more* upset with nobody left to bitch at.

"Then we're just gonna hafta pick up where Sid left off. It don't take too much talent to do what Sid was doing. I can do the scouting. At least, next time a client calls we'll be ready."

"Agreed," Juggler answered, somewhat doubtful of Ace's capabilities. But still, Juggler lied when he went on to say, "And I have a hundred percent faith in you. Just remember, we also have the *other* problem."

"You're talkin' about the body."

"No shit."

"Juggler, I been thinkin' about that body and I think we should part with it. Anywhere else but in here, in the tub. Before you know it, the whole hotel's gonna smell like dead cat."

"Okay, Einstein. Whadda you suggest we do with her? 'Cuz that's our insurance."

"What insurance, Juggler? When we originally moved the body, it was to get it away from Mason. But now, everybody knows there's a body, woadie. The whole town is lookin' for this chick."

Ace was making good sense. Before the fire, the leverage was, *Work with us, let us use your house, and we'll keep a secret. We won't drop dime on you.* And Mason had no choice but to comply. The secret would be buried and nobody would know. But now, on Christmas day, turn on the TV and that's all you heard, about the sex-craved couple who had a freak accident with a girl who lied about her age. Mason was getting away with murder, in Juggler's eyes, and the only thing the authorities needed was the body, so they could confirm the asthma, and that (as it had been reported on the news) Loween had choked to death.

So that "insurance" that Juggler was looking for was unfounded since the world now knew the truth. Or, at least, the truth that Mason

Fickle wanted the world to know. And besides that, the whole "insurance" bit aside, Juggler was holding Fickle accountable for this latest interruption of his business. Furthermore, that twerp had killed his homeboy, Pooh.

*I bet he didn't tell 'em that,* Juggler presumed. And he turned the TV back on to find out more.

Channel Six, Action News, here are the latest developments in the Blue Mountain tragedy, with our local news reporter Melodie Daniels. Melodie?"

"Thank you, Joy. I'm standing outside of what is left of the Fickle home, the scene that found two dead by fire, one dead by a gunshot wound to the face, and a whole lot of unanswered questions. But further investigation has revealed that there is much more that took place here on Blue mountain than meets the eye. . . ."

Some graphics skated across the screen with the Channel 6 News logo and a small title that read: BLUE MOUNTAIN MURDER.

And now the reporter's voice again over some preproduced video footage:

"On or about October twentieth of this year, just two months ago, it is alleged that Adena Fickle had a surprise in store for her husband, Mason. Mason had been on a business trip in Chicago, and he came home to find not his wife, but another woman who answered his door. That other woman, who Adena befriended down at her housekeeping job, turned out to be a very different woman, the Fickles later learned. . . ."

A remorseful Adena Fickle appeared on the screen. "She told me her name was Loween. We knew her as Loween on the job, and that she was turning twenty this coming year. . . ." Adena's expression for the camera was a helpless one, showing the world that she knew only what she'd been told. "I mean. . . . I believed her; had no reason not to. And I didn't see why she had to lie about it."

"Loween was none other than Cynthia Brewster, age seventeen, from New Orleans, Louisiana," the reporter said. "She had escaped the great Hurricane Katrina and apparently took on a new identity here in East Stroudsburg, where she had been working as a house-keeper. . . ." The news reporter was telling the story out in front of the hotel now, and more background footage flashed across the screen while she walked, television viewers through the ABCs of the story. "But Adena Fickle knew Loween the nineteen-year-old and in-vited her over to the house for a drink. That drink, however, turned into so much more . . . a night of what Adena says was *kinky sex.*"

"We were just havin' fun," Adena said with some embarrass-ment. "I wanted to surprise my husband, he went for it, and the rest . . . well, the rest is the stuff that happens behind closed doors,"

"When we spoke to authorities this afternoon, the Marshalls Creek Sheriff had another perspective."

A woman said, "We're puttin' the pieces together now. But, so far it looks like an innocent accident. It's just a *different* kind of accident than what the world is used to hearing about. A little *outside* of the norm."

The reporter again: "That was a statement from the sheriff not more than an hour ago. However, the latest developments have re-vealed that in this same house, now reduced to some charred wood, rubbish, soot, and ash, another man was found dead from a gunshot wound to the face. There has been no press conference from the sheriff's office since this latest news; however, emergency medical workers say that the victim probably lived despite the trauma, but then bled to death. Not only that, it seems *another* man was alone with the victim in the garage of this property, and that man was found duct taped from the shoulders on down."

A title flashed onto the screen: BLUE MOUNTAIN RESIDENTS SPEAK OUT.

"I spoke with both Adena and Mason over the past week," said Barbara Clemons. Barbara's name showed up on the lower portion of the TV screen, noting that she was both a NEIGHBOR AND FRIEND. "I realized that *something* was fishy at the house because there were these strangers all of a sudden. But, now I put the pieces to the puzzle together once I found out that some hoodlums forced their way in, more or less invading the home, with guns 'n' all? I'm just so grateful that our friends lived through this ordeal."

"Details are still falling into place, even at this moment," the reporter noted. "Identities are uncertain, as well as the accounts within the past two months as to how it all came down to this. But we can rest assured that amidst the soot and ashes there are answers. And as the day progresses there will likely be breaking developments in this story as well as a follow-up press conference at the sheriff's office. Mélodie Daniels. Channel Six, Action News."

"Thank you, Melodie. We turn now to that very press conference, already in progress at the Marshalls Creek Sheriff's Department."

". . . However, the one thing that is clear is there are four dead bodies that must be accounted for. One of those bodies is an underage girl of seventeen. That's the body that is currently missing. Insofar as the others in the house . . ." The sheriff was handed a page of notes. "There were two other women who are said to be in their twenties, and we're still awaiting the full reports from the coroner's office. And finally, there was one man, thirty-five years of age, known as Travis Washington, Louisiana resident. Now, while the report is showing four bodies, our priority is to find that missing body. Somewhere on Blue Mountain, or in the Marshalls Creek vicinity, there's a dead body being hidden. By now the body should be badly decomposed, and there should be a horrible odor to go with it. Any suspicious activities need to be reported to the Marshalls Creek Sheriff's Department. And I'd put our neighboring towns on notice, as well. Let it be said at this time that the township office, as well as the Blue Mountain community, is devastated by this tragedy and the associated homicide. But, at the same time, y'all should know that no charges are being pressed until the story is straight and the

suspects are identified. I'll be glad to take any questions at this
time."

"Sheriff!"

"Over here, sheriff! Why isn't Mason Fickle being charged?"

"I'll take your question first. On the Mason Fickle issue, there is
nothing so far that leads us to believe that the Fickle couple—that
goes for Mason *and* Adena—was involved in anything more than a
consensual, uh, association with the victim. Not only that; so far, despite all the talk and rumors and reports, we still don't have a body to
confirm anything, whether it's a homicide or an accident. When I
have a body, the coroner's office is highly equipped . . . they'll do
their job and I'll have, I'm sure, the why and the how questions answered. Until then, all we have is speculation. And we shouldn't per-
secute, prosecute, or hang our neighbors based on speculation.
Gotta have much more than that, especially where it regards Mason
Fickle. These are upstanding citizens of our fine township, and . . . I
believe time will heal all wounds . . . the truth will come out within
the next twenty-four to forty-eight hours, I'm sure. Next question?"

"Sheriff, do we have any further details about this gang that al-
legedly forced entry into the home and held the Fickles hostage; and
if that's the case, are they in custody? Or should we—"

"We're still investigating that allegation. We are questioning suspects of all alleged crimes in this matter, but what I can say for sure
is that the Fickle home *was* occupied by more than just the owners.
There was a group of people living there for close to two months
now. We're currently identifying those individuals as well as inter-
viewing them." The sheriff pointed to another reporter.

"Yes, sheriff. Shawn Gary, Channel Twelve News . . . Do you
have any information about a possible prostitution ring that might've
been operating out of the Fickle home?"

The question raised a series of conversations in the crowd that
became unruly.

"Please, folks! Let's have some order!" a deputy shouted.

"No such information about that. As far as we know, so far, there was a party ongoing. However, let's be clear that my office and this community will not tolerate illegal activities, whether inside or outside of the home. *Yes.* You in the green shirt."

"Sheriff, by all accounts, there hasn't been a murder in this community in more than twenty-five years. How equipped is your office in handling a case like this, and should we be calling for assistance from the state or federal government?"

The Marshalls Creek crossing had always been due for a bypass, a redevelopment that was on the table for years. Board meetings, town discussions, and researchers' statistics were, for the most part, in favor of the bypass, a road that would be built to help alleviate the daily traffic jams along the road where Routes 209 and 402 crossed paths. It was much worse in bad weather.

To add to the congestion, there were now roadblocks set up to help locate the missing body. The result was nothing more than a massive parking lot along these routes, all day and past dinner. The town and everyone in it was being punished, unable to get around these single-lane roads, late for Christmas-this and Christmas-that. The locals and vacationers alike were being tortured, and whether they knew it or not, it was all because of Mason Fickle's deadly dick.

Up until now, mason hadn't said a word to the authorities, reporters, or so many others who were desperate to speak with him. Up until now, they only had past, inspiring articles to dwell on; articles that had been written about Mason and that painted him as a fine, upstanding entrepreneur in the community. On television there was video footage repeated over and over again, on the hour, showing Mason attending various community event and fund-raisers, some of which he also spoke at. All this history, and how he helped so many people to acquire their first homes, helped out tremendously when it came to the public's perception of him. It was as if he had prepared for this. As if the damage control had already been in place for the media machines to devour and feed to the world. Someone even had the nerve to compare mason Fickle to OJ Simpson, with the only difference being the use of a gun, versus the muscle between Mason's legs. And oh what a muscle it was! Even in the bar rooms, the walls were talking!

A re you serious You mean, he killed her with his dick? I thought I heard it all, but whooo-eee!"

"A man has got to know his limitations. For real. Can you imagine what he had to be doin' to that girl. To kill her like that? I'd pay a couple hundred to see that. A course, my wallet can't handle that, but my heart sure enough could."

"I say we make a golden cast outta this Mason Fickle's dick. Make a new statue for the middle of town. We'd be world famous for the man with the golden dick! I can see the new Sprint commercial now: Come to Marshalls Creek: Hell, your cellphone might not get a signal, but the action here can make you gag!"

"Wish I had a man with a dick like Mason's. I could die a happy woman, and leave my dead-dick husband with somethin' to think about after I'm long gone."

T he conversations seemed never to end. And some of those comments and jokes got past the hospital doors, with the nurses giggling about the same. Mason, however, was not in any laughing mood. He realized his dilemma here, and that one false more—any shift of the wind—could sway public sympathy until it turned into sour milk. He'd seen it happen plenty of times before, and he'd be damned to be the next possum. Already, his private business was everybody's business. And there was no way he wanted to take it to the next level.

"Adena, did you hafta give up details? Jeez . . . it's like the world has a window into our bedroom now. And it wouldn't matter if we were the simple ones with straight-up missionary sex; but *damn*. You mean, you don't feel some type of way about everybody knowing?"

"Mason, I'm *waaay* past that. Do you know I got another Western Union telegram this morning?"

"Another? I never knew you even got one."

"Here. Read."

to mrs. adena fickle
days inn hotel
e. stroudsburgh, pa

The following is a message to Mrs. Adena Fickle & husband, Mason Fickle. We have been seeing the news stories over the wire and we wish to have you and your husband as guests on the Larry King show. A car and air transportation to Washington, DC is available at your convenience. Please contact our show's producer when you receive this telegram.

"Wow," Mason said. "The direct phone number and *everything*. Did you call them?"

"Mason, that's just one request. There's five more like that for TV shows, and about two dozen radio shows around the country that want us to call in. It's madness, Mason. Like they wanna interview the man—they're actually calling you Killer Dick."

Mason lifted himself from the bed.

"All right, all right. I gotta get up and outta here," he said. "I told them doctors I was good."

"Mason, you've *been* good for a few hours now. You were only treated for smoke inhalation, not a hysterectomy."

"Perish the *thought!*"

"Truth is, I have a friend here at the hospital and he's been hold-ing everyone back, deputies included. He's been telling them you can't be seen and that you were under heavy sedation."

"But why?" asked Mason.

"Just room for you to breathe, I guess. Time for us to think and plan. With all that's goin' on, we just needed to slow things down some."

Mason took a minute to study his wife before he said, "I like this side of you, when you're in control. Only other time I've seen that was in the bed."

"Don't remind me; isn't that how all of this got started?"

Mason rolled his eyes in agreement.

"So, you think you're ready for the mess outside?"

"Ahh . . . maybe after I'm dressed, but yeah, I can handle it."

"One other thing, Mason. I just couldn't bring myself to tell any-one that you shot that man in our garage. I played dumb on that question, plus there was all kinds of confusion in the house, anyway. So, nothing is all that clear about who the shooter was."

After a deep breath, Mason said, "Well, since we told 'em every-thing else, let's go the whole hundred yards. *Why not?* They attacked me, Adena. Three guys attacked me, not one or two guys—three of them. They're a bunch of coward-punks. And if I could've shot all of 'em, I would've. And I wouldn't lose a night's sleep, either."

A sense of fear filled Adena's eyes, and she trembled some. Just the thought of her husband killing someone gave her the willies. But there wasn't time to dwell on what already happened, or what might soon happen. It was only time to deal with the present. Both Adena and Mason had to maintain their focus and momentum in order to overcome this challenge.

D r. Joel was informed that Mason would see the deputies now, and they came into the room with their earth-green uniforms and all the utilities to accommodate their public service and (were they?) those high-tech investigative techniques. The one deputy who was a woman had a colorless, pale skin tone and the giddiest smile you ever saw, as if she were on a picnic and not a homicide investigation. The man with her was older, with that same pale skin, only reddened with wrinkles, and his hair was yellowing at the edges. In a peculiar way, his jaundiced ends matched his partner's blond tresses. Still, the elder deputy appeared to be more discerning, with eyes that held a somewhat crisp and cold gaze.

**H**ow are you feeling, Mr. Fickle?" asked the blonde.

"I'm making it. It's been rough, but at least I'm off the oxygen machine. I can breathe by myself again."

"All righty then, let's cut to the chase, if you don't mind. There are quite a few questions that we need answers to, the most important being—" The deputy flipped a couple of pages into his pad. "There was a man shot in the face in your garage, his name was Travis Washington. Did you know him?"

"I knew *of* him. But I didn't know him personally. I think they called him Pooh."

"Pooh."

"Yeah. That was his nickname. Pooh."

"All righty then, did you happen to know anything about this shooting? He was shot in the face. Right here in your house. I would imagine that . . ."

Adena whispered something into Mason's ear, and he seemed to take a minute to digest it. But, before he answered, the deputy butted in.

"Uh, *excuse me?* We're conducting a homicide investigation, ma'am. Could you share what you said with the rest of the class?"

Without hesitation, Adena said, "I told him to tell the truth, and that he shouldn't worry, because God is on our side."

"Oh. I don't see why we all couldn't hear that. Seems innocent enough to me."

"I just . . . there are things that Mason and I share, totally apart from the outside world. Just our faith, ya know?" Adena felt her heart skip as she talked her way through the lie.

"O-kay. From now on, please don't do that, if you don't mind."

"To answer your question, deputy—not to butt in, but, honestly? I didn't see or hear a shooting. On the news today was the first I heard of it. I couldn't even believe that happened in *my* house . . . on *my* property?"

"I see. How about the gun? Do you even own a gun, Mason?"

Mason felt that; how the mention of his name threw the conversation a few levels deeper, as if the deputy knew him personally, or wanted to, or was pretending to.

"I think . . . somewhere in the house might be a hunting rifle. There, or at the traveling rifle club I use to be with?"

"Traveling rifle club? Why there?"

"I had retired that old thing so long ago. Even tried to sell it. But so much has happened between then and now. The club closed down. And I hear my trophies and my rifle were misplaced. Just a big mess that I never thought twice about. So busy with more important things, I guess." Mason was proud of himself for the cockamamie story he was spilling out, like he was a born-again liar . . . *like Adena?* He only hoped his story was believable and that these deputies were as slow and lame as they appeared, and that . . .

Interrupting Mason's thoughts and explanations to the deputies was a disturbance just beyond the doors. A man's loud voice seemed to be approaching the room. Mason felt it was a familiar voice.

"I'm tellin' ya, this is *real* important, and it can't wait. Now, please, don't get in the way of progress here!"

And now the loud bang as the door swung open. The group that included the two deputies, Mason, and Adena all looked toward the door. Yet, Mason and Adena were the most shocked and amazed when they saw it was Wheelchair Sid.

" 'Sup, y'all? Whassup, Fickle? Heard you were down the hall from me and I couldn't wait another minute to get atcha."

Sid's presence could as well have been the restart of the nightmare, that fateful day when Loween died and when this guy came knocking at Mason's door; one of the great interruptions of his life. First, the accident, then the knock at the door, then the band of cronies that eventually followed . . . not to mention everything else mixed in. But then again—*Maybe this couldn't have better timing,* thought Mason.

"I was straight-up worried about you, Fickle. How ya' doin', Adena? Deputies." Sid rolled his way in on the hospital wheelchair, not that powered wheelchair that Mason recalled him doing the wheelie in, even dancing in place once he became an unwanted houseguest.

"I saw the news just a few minutes ago and I had to come and tell *somebody* what *really* happened in that house," Sid said. "Before this poor man gets the death penalty for somethin' he didn't do."

Mason and Adena shared a look; that strange look when you don't have any idea what's going on.

"Oh yeah? And what's your name?" asked the older deputy with the yellowing ends.

"I'm Sid. Sid Oaks, from N'awlins, Louisiana. I came up here lookin' for Loween—her *real* name is Cynthia, by the way. But then, my partner—my *old* partner, that is—started wildin' out, takin' these poor folks hostage and extortin' them outta their home 'n' whatnot. And then—"

Adena and Mason shared that look again, both of them knowing how Sid could talk his ass off when he got rolling. Thing is, this time they *wanted* him to keep running his mouth!

"—My man gonna shoot our *other* homey, and set a fire, *too?*"

"Hold on, hold on. Slow down, please. Oaks, did you say?"

"Yeah. *Sid* Oaks."

"Okay, *Sid* Oaks. Slow down, you're speedin' here. Now, back up some, to the part about your man. Who's *your man?*"

"He ain't my man no more," Sid said. "Not after he done shot my homey . . . not after he done took me out to the woods and tried to kill me."

"Whoa-whoa-whoa. You're speeding again, son. Slow down and catch your breath. I feel your anger and we realize you wanna get the story out, but take it easy. Get some oxygen in between those words."

There was that instant when Sid and Manson made visual contact. On one hand, Mason wanted to laugh his ass off; on the other, he really didn't know *himself* what to believe or not to believe. However, with Adena, Mason could cast her a look and say a million things in that one glance. And presently, the two of them couldn't have been more amused by this latest development. It was a godsend; it was relief; it was unbelievable. But, at the same time, they were sucking up every word.

"Now, who are you talking about? Who tried to kill you?"

"Juggler. He go by the name Juggler, but I know his gov'ment."

"Gov'ment?" The deputy looked this way and that for some interpretation. No sense in looking at the doctor, since he merely shrugged.

Mason, however, was quick to add his two cents. "He means, *birth name,*" Mason explained. "The name in government records." Mason, the ebonics theoretician.

"Okay, so what's this Juggler's real . . . *ahem* . . . government name?"

"Bernard. I seen his license, and it says Bernard Torry. Can you believe in all these years I never knew the truth? All the risks he took with me by his side, and I coulda took a fall a looong time ago."

While one deputy wrote in his pad feverishly, the other pulled out her pad as well.

"Now, which part of this you want first?" asked Sid. "The shooting? How he started the fire? Or how that sorry, no-good nigga threw me to the bears?"

The deputies looked at each other in light of what were obviously the most exclusive and the newest developments in the past day or so. And all of it about to drop right in their laps.

**M**ason and Adena couldn't believe their ears as Sid magically turned every bit of the deputies' attention onto himself, lying in terms of just about everything (and so seamlessly!) so that all of the blame fell on Juggler's shoulders. It all sounded so justified and so righteous with Juggler as the scapegoat for everything. However, it couldn't be helped, that uneasy feeling, the chills that came about in light of the lies and deception. It all made for such an unnecessary spin on things; a chain of events that Sid was suddenly entirely responsible for and that he had to be clear about regarding every detail, both real and fabricated. Any slip of the lip, and the whole stack of cards would fall, and they'd fall right on top of the Fickles since they went along with Sid's every word. And there was no turning back now, not since the story was already growing legs, and that (likely within the hour) the whole mess would hit the newswire, televisions, and radios all over the country. That's just how it went nowadays: One news source would tell another, and before you knew it, even speculation could be labeled as news. The bare reality was that everybody who liked to stay up on current events was surely waiting for the next development in the story about "the man with the killer dick."

On and on Sid went with his story, most of it unimportant to the Fickles since it was all news to them. And yet, if there was any issue or statement that they could help confirm, they'd simply nod to affirm what they'd heard.

Marshalls Creek's rendition of a posse was two deputies and a sheriff who had just finished her weekly spa treatment, and the visit
to the hair and nail salon. There were also two auxiliary deputies
who joined in on the hunt for Bernard Torry, aka Juggler. The tip-off
was a cinch, where (Sid said) Juggler had a couple of rooms rented
out at the Days Inn.

*He shoots videos in one of them, and he so-called sleeps in the other,* Sid
had told the deputies. *Except, Juggler had been doin' a lotta hangin' at these
folks' place. He told me that eventually he was gonna destroy these folks' world.*

*Why would he wanna do a thing like that when he needed their help to
get his business off the ground?* asked the deputy.

Sid's answer was, *I don't think Juggler likes folks who got there own;
ya know, well-to-do 'n' all. That's sump'm Juggler always been jealous
about: other people's success.*

While the deputies were off on their Juggler hunt, Mason and
Adena went to have a celebratory visit to the insurance company
down on Main Street in Stroudsburg. There were some immediate
concerns they had about the home and vehicle they lost to the fire,
and (most important) they wanted to get an idea of how soon they'd
get some money in their hands to start this thing over again. It was
only when they arrived and found most of Main Street deserted that
they realized, isn't this Christmas?

"With so much happening, Christmas didn't much matter,"
Adena said. "At least we have the one car."

"No, Adena . . . I can walk, if need be. What I'm thinkin' is, at
least we have *each other.*"

"Awww, pookie . . . you know how to say the sweetest things,"
Adena cooed as she took Mason's cheeks between her hands and pulled
him in for a kiss. "Merry Christmas, my love. I'm glad you're back."

"Back? Back where? We ain't got no place to live!" The way Mason said that was to provoke a laugh, and maybe it was time to do that, to laugh away the issues, the challenges ahead and the struggle that they faced at present.

Before they got too involved with the romantic moment: "Oh, look . . . isn't this poetic? Remember the first time we sat down together to eat? Sort of our first date?"

"Oh yeah, Brownie's. How could I forget that? You had me chasin' after your pretty ass."

"Ahem, *excuse* me?"

"Well, you know. I know you ain't takin' *that* personal, as raunchy as—"

"Silly, I was just sayin' you got it twisted. I had a pretty *young* ass. Let's get that straight!"

Mason chuckled and Adena eventually tossed the acting aside to laugh along with him.

"Oh my God, look! They're open, Mason! On Christmas, they're open?"

"Sign of the times, boo. Business people ain't stupid. They know there's gonna be people out here with no place to go . . . people are off work and out here lookin' to spend that leftover Christmas money. So, the smart businessman is gonna look at that and think, *Hey, I can take a slow day off. But today? Christmas money is waitin' to be grabbed up.* At least, that's my philosophy," Mason said.

"Well, my smoke-inhalin', knowledge-droppin', hospital-leavin' philosopher. I'm hungry! Let's eat."

In the restaurant, although their lives had changed (virtually overnight) Mason and Adena were the same ol', same ol'—Mason with the Caesar salad and Cheddar shavings, Adena with the strawberry shortcake and the thick shake.

"This is funny; feels like our first date here."

"It sure wasn't no date," Mason recalled.

"Are you talkin' about when I had you chasin' me out of the restaurant?"

"That. But, I can almost recall everything. The words I'll *never* forget are when I mistook you for having a child. I said, 'Oh, you're a mother?' And that's when *you* said, 'No, I'm not a mother. I lost the baby, I got my tubes tied, and now I'm a motherFUCKER.' Wow. That was the sickest combination of words I ever heard from a woman's mouth. And I think, well—*I know*—I was head over heels for you from that minute."

"Yeah, but I don't think you *loved* me, Mason. I think you were more, like, *infatuated* with me. I think you wanted to get into my panties, not necessarily my life.

"Shit. What does a man *really* know around that age? I was . . . you heard the saying, *young, dumb, and*—"

Adena completed the sentence for him: "And *damn* you were one *well*-hung buck, Mason. I ain't gonna lie. That first night we slept together you had my ass strung out. I mean, *strung-the-fuck-out.* I was in the bed the next *few* days like a crackhead goin' through withdrawal. *Man,* I remember them days. And every day you didn't call me back I felt my life was coming closer and closer to an end. For *real,* don't laugh! That shit ain't funny, Mason. You had a sista *touchin'* herself and the whole nine!"

Mason was cracking up, but was still aware they were in a public restaurant with a few customers scattered about. "Shhhh," he implored. And then he said, "All I can say is, you were *straight trippin, boo.*"

"You always say that, ever since we saw that Queen Latifah movie."


The food came, and the two ate like castaways; the evidence of Mason having been on a twelve-hour oxygen diet, and Adena eating hardly anything at all while she awaited his respiratory checks and balances.

After the meal, the two had a few more laughs and left for the streets once again.

It was Mason who said, "You know, the funny thing about it is, I don't really *feel* homeless, but I *am*! I mean, after having my life threatened and almost dying in a fire; after having my liberty threatened? I feel so full of life right now, like nothing in the world matters. And add to that, I'm with the woman of my dreams? What more could a man want? Sure, I'll be laying on some hot manhole cover come nighttime, but . . ."

Giggling, Adena said, "You stupid, Mason."

"No, but check it! I'm like, floating right now. I'm feeling like a kite, and I ain't even had a drink, a drug, or—"

"It's the oxygen, Mason. Trust me, there was somethin' in that tank that got you buggin'!"

Adena and Mason were strolling along Main Street when they approached an electronics store. The store was closed, but in the window the TV was on, and a video camera was positioned so that it captured everything that was on the sidewalk. At the moment, that was these two lovebirds. They were eventually making faces for the camera while watching it on one of the monitors.

Still another monitor was programmed to Channel 6. And as irony would have it—

"*Ohmigod.* Look, Mason." And as Adena pointed to the monitor, the screen flashed pictures of the now-toasted house that Mason built. However, this wasn't just a repeat of what people had been exposed to over the past twenty-four hours. What was being shown was an account of the events leading up to where reporters were now, outside the Days Inn Hotel. It never crossed their minds, but these two happy campers were just blocks away from an unfolding drama. On the screen, there were police cruisers from East Stroudsburg, Marshalls Creek, and two other surrounding counties.

"Wow!" exclaimed Adena. "Whaddya think is goin' on?" She was more curious than anything else.

"Looks like some kind of standoff, baby," Mason said with a heightened interest.

Now, a couple of mug shots were positioned on the screen.

"Get the fuck outta here!" Mason gasped when he recognized Juggler's picture, even with the unruly hair. The photos were obviously outdated, but Juggler's sharp facial features were right there for the world to see. After that picture, the screen showed a second mugshot.

Adena just breathed Ace's name as an unconscious response. Not that she endeared that man, just that it all played out so surreal there on the TV monitor.

"You know what? This *is* a standoff. We can't hear what's going on, but I guarantee there's some kind of hostage thing happening," Mason said.

"Oh *damn*. What's Bill Clemons doin' on the TV?" asked Adena.

"And he's cryin'? What the—" Mason froze when the screen spelled out more drama.

"OH MY GOD. Mason, *nooooooo. Noooooo*. This can't be happening. It . . . can't . . . it can't be?"

The images were self-explanatory. And Mason realized that he and Adena were just ten or so blocks from the Days Inn. Not that they had any more wherewithal to handle the crisis than the local authorities. It was just that the Clemons couple were their friends. Those two stuck their necks out to help them when they didn't have to. So it was only right that the Fickles do the same, no matter what.

Sprinting through the streets of East Stroudsburg, Mason and Adena tried to make sense out of it all. Huffing and puffing and crossing against traffic lights. Fact is, they weren't making sense at all. They were acting with their hearts.

"What are we gonna do when we get there, Mason? What *can* we do?" Adena cried.

"I don't know what we can do, but we gotta do what we *can*. That fool has Barbara, Adena! And she woulda never been in that position if it wasn't for us!"


Those images on the screen were enough to force a reality check on Mason and Adena's whole spell, how they were floating in the clouds, and talking about love, and liberty and happiness despite homelessness. . . .

Adena was running just as fast as Mason, and she suddenly grabbed him, and struggled to get the words out as she panted and puffed.

"Mase—Mase—*Mason*, ohmigod," Adena cried, tears running and all. "I feel something had about to happen. I feel it right here." Adena held her hand to her heart as she buckled over and hurt for air. "Oh, *man* . . . it's all catching up to us now, Mason. It's backfiring!"

"WHAT'S backfiring? COME ON, ADENA! Barbara's in *trouble*! Bill *needs* us!" And now Mason was hankering for air or something while his voice damn near echoed through the streets, bouncing off of the glass of Starbucks and some mom-and-pop struggling bookstore. Both husband and wife were erratic in their thoughts and their actions, both of them in the middle of the street, pulling at each other—Adena pulling toward survival and a desperate quest to keep all she had left in the world, and Mason pulling toward what felt right in his heart, no matter what the loss, no matter what the consequences. He'd been here before with his brother, with his mom. And it felt the same. It felt like only *his* choices would make a difference in other people's lives. And *damned* if he was gonna make the wrong choices *this time*. This was a bout between forces that were stronger than the very people who embodied them. This was a supernatural fight between all that was right, all that was wrong, and everything in between.

# twenty-six

**N**ot since the great fire more than forty years earlier had this community seen so much yellow tape: POLICE: DO NOT CROSS. The bright yellow plastic was *everywhere*. The Main Street exit off I-80 was closed. *Closed!* Where cars (whether it was tourists, commercial traffic, or residents) had no choice but to move along to the next exit. The side streets that immediately surrounded the Days Inn were blocked with police, fire, and other such emergency vehicles. Even The Whale was back for its second appearance in as many days, serving as a mobile command post (exactly what it was designed for; not for hanging about, eating doughnuts, and watching the Sixers kick butt) and parked about five hundred feet from the hotel and its unfolding saga. In the meantime, while paramilitary gear hung off of auxiliary deputies, while unfitted helmets wobbled atop of one head or another, and as news reporters lobbied for position alongside authorities, inside the hotel was a dark, confused, and haunted world in its own right, since someone had shot up the hotel's main source of electricity. They sounded something like explosions to those unfamiliar with gunshots. And yet, it was enough to send everyone diving for cover in whatever spot they claimed in the building. The authorities were already outside with their vehicles lined up, calling out on megaphones for everyone to stay in their rooms, or:

"*Wherever you are. Please, stay put!*" the loud squawk announced.

And, although the hotel had few vacancies (thanks to welfare families and the truckers who stopped for that emergency stay-over), the majority of the hotel workers were those who were the most outspoken. Because, when it came down to it, they were the ones who were spending eight-hour shifts here. It was a second home for them, for however many years; not the same feeling as that of a family going through a "transition," or a trucker here to catch a few Zs.

"Is that the best they could do, considering that someone is blastin' away at the power generator, the phone system, and even taking pot shots out of the windows?"

"Is this some terrorist shit goin' on? Here in our pea-sized town of East Stroudsburg? You could hold your breath while driving down Main Street and before you turned blue you'd be in the next town! Damn! Why they have to pick my job?"

While authorities worked on negotiations, employees were congregated in the hotel kitchen and the hotel bar, and a number of employees were down in the laundry room. Not that any one of them couldn't make the attempt to flee, just that *who'd wanna make a run for it with bullets flying all over the place?*

**B**ERNARD TORRY! WE HAVE THE BUILDING SUR-ROUNDED! WE SUGGEST THAT YOU GIVE YOURSELF UP NOW, BEFORE THERE ARE ANY CASUALTIES. IT IS VERY IMPORTANT THAT YOU KNOW YOU WILL BE TREATED FAIRLY WHEN YOU THROW YOUR GUNS DOWN. THERE'S NO NEED TO TAKE THIS TO ANY LENGTH. WE'RE A SMALL TOWN, BUT WE DON'T WANT NO TROUBLE. . . ."

"What the F're you talkin' about, Parnell? *Gimme* that horn." The she-sheriff snatched the mic from her next in charge. She had just left the salon and—

"*Damned if I gotta get my nails ruined and hair mussed because of some lowlife with a itchy trigger finger.*" The sheriff turned her attention (and the megaphone) toward the room with the window blown out. "Hey, YOU in there. Ber-*naaaard.*" She went at him with the whole sarcastic, singsong approach; as though his name were a joke and that he might be accustomed to the teasing. "Bernard, if you don't bring your *punk* ass out here and let my hotel workers and residents go, *I'ma bust a cap in yer ass bigger than Katrina's butthole!*"

And was *that* really necessary? The mention of Katrina? Was she *trying* to tick this guy off? The way the sheriff announced it was mostly a challenge and nowhere close to a plea. Everyone, and especially those inside the hotel, had to be bracing themselves for what might come next. And she-sheriff went on to say, "I don't play that *hostage shit* in this town, boy. Now—"

And now the response made it so clear: The gunmen holed up in the second-floor room were *not* playing. Everyone's attention, including TV broadcast cameras, was focused on that one bedroom window where the dozen or so shots had been fired from during the past twenty minutes. However, *nobody* expected the response from the next room over, where a window shattered, and through which a body came flying, as if on cue.

The difference in volume, between the voice behind the megaphone and the voice without, was evident. However, now it was crystal clear who had the leverage, and whose voice had more of an impact.

"Now who's the *punk ass*, ya hillbilly dyke! Say some more stupid shit and I'ma send bodies *every* thirty seconds! We'll see whose butthole is bigger than Katrina's *then!*" Along with the gunman's voice came squeals and at least one scream that could be heard from this and that part of the hotel.

Somebody had better find a SWAT team, fast.

Inside room 212 was where all of the action was thought to have been. It's where Juggler had Barbara Clemons hostage and where TV cameras captured both of them in the window, her neck in his half nelson. However, the way Juggler was moving around the hotel, he had everybody fooled into thinking he had a crew that was maybe four to six deep. Still, it was only Juggler and Ace. Yes, Ace, who was, so far, the laid-back member of Juggler's crew.

Wielding his weapons, Juggler ordered residents and staff alike to stay in their respective rooms. And the person who asked the question, *Which respective room?* was the one who triggered that first blast inside the hotel. The rifle was pointed at the ceiling, but Juggler certainly made his point: *No silly-assed questions. Just stay out of the man's way, he's a lunatic!* And from there on Juggler had very little babysitting to do. His goal was simple, but it was also a secret.

"Tell you what, sheriff . . . you can get that Mason Fickle up here for a one on one with me. And, I mean, *one on one.*" Those were Juggler's latest words, right after the body flew through the window and splattered on the pavement. Thing is, the deputies and the sheriff were claiming that Mason had left the hospital and that there was no way to contact him.

Juggler wasn't trying to hear that. "Get that muthafucka up here, I don't care how ya do it. He needs to answer to me," Juggler growled. Meanwhile, either Juggler or Ace canvassed the hotel, terrorizing folks with their mere presence. Although, Ace was the softer of the two, allowing one or two to shoot down to the kitchen to get food for the others. There was even one who hadn't come back, and (he thought) probably snuck out somehow. But Ace knew

Juggler wasn't keeping that tight a count. And besides, Ace hoped Juggler didn't plan on keeping this going for too much longer. No sense in the two of them going up against the National Guard, or no dumb stuff like that. After all, Ace wasn't on a suicide mission.

J ust as Ace returned from the first floor, Juggler started shooting again.

"They think I don't see 'em gettin' closer to the hotel," said Juggler. "These toy cops ain't shit." And he blasted some more. "I'm puttin' sump'm on 'em now, then we gonna switch around to other rooms and start blastin' at random. I wanna make 'em think we got twenny ma-fuckas up here," Juggler swore. Ace merely shrugged and leaned in to one of the windows to assist in the war, blasting away at any and everything.

When the bullets took a break, Juggler said as he reloaded, "If this is the best they can do, we gonna win this and space this place, easy." But, just as he spoke, he caught a movement behind him, out in the hallway. He ducked down, cocked the rifle, and he fired right through the wall. The first shot evoked a hoarse scream. The second shot made a hole big enough to see a body slumping. And the third shot was a bull's-eye.

"So ya'll wanna play, huh? That's what ya wanna do? I gotcha." And Juggler reloaded again before grabbing a second weapon. Now, with both weapons pointed outward, Juggler swung out into the hallway, assuming that the now-dead policeman wasn't alone, and he started more senseless shooting, first down the east, then the west end of the hallway. He kicked the gun from the dead cop's possession and signaled for Ace to get it. Then he continued cautiously down the dark hallway. This was the reason he blew the generator in the first place, so that he wouldn't be seen as clear as day. And since he was one who loved the dark, this felt like he had the advantage over anyone that wanted to go to war with him.

Another ten or so minutes passed as Juggler played out his strategy, jumping from room to room, pushing his weight around so that his so-called hostages wouldn't try any hero shit. He was already deeper into this than he'd ever expected, so it was now time to go for it.

"This stairway, where does it lead to?" Juggler asked one of the scared housemaids. She stuttered when she answered. But instead of taking her word for it, Juggler pulled her from the corner of the room and said, "Show me."

Now he *really* had a hostage. And he made sure to stand behind her every step of the way, in case someone else came out from the shadows.

"Ace, hold me down!" Juggler shouted as he used the woman as his shield and carefully took the steps to the rear of the hotel. With any luck, this was the way down to where he'd left the Ram Charger, the truck that Sid once drove and that Juggler swiped after leaving him stranded in the woods.

*Maybe this'll be my getaway route,* Juggler figured. But, just as he thought of that, there was a rustling noise down at the bottom of the stairwell.

"Who's there? Betta answer before I drop another body," he warned. The woman with him winced and he tugged at her hair so that she'd be closer to him. "What's your name, boo?"

"Sh-haron."

"Okay, Sharon," Juggler whispered. "You're gonna put on a little show here. You're goin' for an Oscar. I mean, I wanna hear you beg for your life, 'cuz your life depends on it, you got that?" Juggler tugged harder at her hair. "Do you believe your life depends on your acting? Huh?"

"Y-yes. I believe you."

"That's real good. That's a real good answer," said Juggler, raising his voice again. "Hey, Bozo at the bottom of the stairs. I want you to know that you're responsible for Sharon's life right now. Sharon, you got kids?"

"Two," she replied with her trembling voice.

"What's their names, Sharon?"

"K-k-kimberly, and Jason," she answered quickly.

"Good. Kimberly is how old?"

"Five."

"Okay, down there . . . we're coming . . . and five-year-old Kimberly's welfare is on your shoulders! We'll see if you want that pretty lil' girl to have a mommy!" Juggler pulled extratight at Sharon's hair.

She squealed. "No. Please. Please don't hurt me, mista. I ain't done nothin' to you?" She wouldn't be able to see this, considering how dark it was, but Juggler made the strangest face, the response to her acting. Like he wanted to say, *You mind toning it down a bit?* But there were other concerns. Whoever was down below hadn't made his or her move. And Juggler, quite naturally, was getting worried.

"All right, now. I was afraid it was gonna come to this," said Juggler, still slowly descending the steps. "I'm gonna count to three . . . and then Sharon's body and her daughter's future will be on your soul until you see the roots of the earth. ONE." Juggler had the shotgun at an angle, with the business end of the weapon pressed against Sharon's temple. "TWO!" Juggler took another step, wanting to be as close as possible to his target. And, was this where he was supposed to say *two and a half*?

"*All right* already!" shouted a man's voice. And what came out from hiding was nothing more than a shadow. However, Juggler knew that voice anywhere.

"You muthafucka. Well, I'll be *damned*. Bingo! Sharon, this asshole just saved your no-actin' ass. Say hi to the great Mason Fickle."

# twenty-seven

Rewind:

When Mason and Adena showed up at the intersection of Main Street and Ferris Avenue, the roadblock was set up and nobody was permitted to pass. However, the deputy on duty was no match for Mason and Adena. The two conspired before they reached the intersection.

"Okay, but remember, Mason . . . whatever you do, don't flip his switch, okay? He's already desperate and out of his mind," cautioned Adena. "If you go up there and offer him a way out, an escape from the mess, I'm sure he'll be more than grateful. And you and I couldn't care less *what* happens after that. If they catch him? That's on him. But, play it cool. Follow the directions I gave you so you're not seen. And *remember,* Mason—" Adena kissed her husband. "Somebody loves you on this side. And it's me."

Adena hugged Mason and she went about her performance, likely one of the most important performances of her life.

"Ohmigod. Ohmigod. Deputy. *Deputy!* What a horrible Christmas! I woke up this morning and what did I see? I saw the TV with the hostages, and—*ohmigod!* What will I do? My *sister* is one of the employees at the hotel!"

"Ma'am, I'm sorry to hear that, but—"

Adena was already working her way around the yellow tape. She was on a mission.

"Ahhhhh? You're breaking the *law*, miss. Now step back behind the tape. I realize this is hard for—"

Adena was paying this guy *no* mind. All she needed to see was his attention on her and not Mason, who was crossing the line elsewhere way back, making progress to get to the hotel. And, even with deputies and various other emergency agencies scattered about, Mason was able to follow directions and to make headway. The first move was done. He was past the roadblock. Now he had to turn down the residential street, one that was positioned across from the hotel, but that led Mason in an opposite direction. Even he had no idea what this was about; however, Adena had explained it:

*If you know the area like I do, Mason, you'd know that I-80 is an overpass right where the Main Street exit is.*

*Okay. I know it.*

*Okay, well . . . right under the overpass is a little waterfall. Buuuut, it's not like a waterfall coming from a river, like Tarzan. It's from a tunnel. I saw some sewer workers out there a few weeks ago, they were working on a problem, or whatever. Anyway, I didn't think nothin' of it, but one of the workers I saw come up from the basement in the hotel. It's real grimy down there, maybe rats and stuff.*

*Whatever, Adena. Are you sayin' there's another way to the hotel, other than . . . ?*

*I'm sayin' you can go through a tunnel, Mason. And you'll find your way to the backyard, right behind the hotel.*

Mason had never heard of such a thing, and that showed on his face. But, what other options did he have? And, after all, Adena *did* work there. She had to know what she was talking about. So, with nothing to lose, they laid out their plan. And less than thirty minutes later, Mason was facing Juggler's shotgun, an incident that would've never come about if Adena had kept her mouth shut. Nonetheless, what was done was done.

As Sharon led the way through the basement of the hotel, Mason followed, and then Juggler. And they conversed along the way.

"What I don't understand is, why would you come and see me? I mean, not that I mind, since that's what I was planning *anyway*—one of my demands to the bigmouth sheriff. But, humor me, would you?"

"I just came to set things straight?"

"Pssssh . . . In *what way?*"

"I figured you're probably a little upset at me, and I felt I needed to help you get out of this mess."

"You, help me?"

"Exactly. I can take you right out of here, scott-free, Juggler. The same way I came in."

"Is that so? And I'm supposed to believe that and I'm supposed to follow you out the door so the SWAT team, wherever they are, can shoot me down like a sitting duck."

"It ain't like that, Juggler. Trust me when I tell you, I had to sneak in here to get to you. I can sneak out the same way. I didn't see a SWAT team outside, and I don't think anyone spotted me coming in. A lot of the action was out front," Mason said.

"I'll say it was," Juggler confirmed. "But, a-*duhh*; you think you're supposed to see the SWAT team? I'll tell you what . . . let's say you're right, and that I can walk out of here. Then what? What am I gonna do after I get away. I'm a goddamned fugitive, Mason. And, nothing you say is gonna change that."

Mason couldn't argue that. *Hadn't this fool killed a hostage already?* Therefore, he had nothing to lose. So Mason continued to play his hand.

"Listen, would I come back here if I couldn't help you? Now, think about it. I just got out of the hospital, Juggler. Use your head, man." Juggler was behind Mason while Sharon continued on through a tunnel in the basement. The constant drip, the cobwebs, and the dust in the stuffy, mildewed air was all that kept them company along the way.

"I am usin' my head. And that means that you two suddenly became my ridin' buddies."

No way in this dark passage that Juggler could see the expression across Mason's face, how he questioned this guy's audacity. And then he took a deep breath, bracing himself for what he was about to do. He began his own personal countdown. *Five, four three, two* . . .

And just a split second before Mason made his move, someone else made this. From out of the shadows, a thrust came at Mason as if to push him out of harm's way, and he grunted when he fell to the wet and icky basement floor. Thereafter, the skin-slapping punches began and the sounds of agony and pain that went with it. These were obviously punches being thrown, but Mason couldn't tell who was punching who. He could, however, see a skirt rushing away and understood that was Sharon making a quick getaway. *Good.* Still, he rose up from his fall and tried to make sense of things so that he could join in to capture Juggler before he became a fugitive. *The bigger body has to be Juggler.* And, when he saw that body was on the floor, Mason kicked with all of his might. There was a man-cry, and then nothing.

"*Shit!* Thanks, Mason. You really *were* on my side."

It was Juggler's voice Mason heard, and it was a sound that made him sick. *Who did I kick?* he wondered.

"Okay, let's keep it movin'." Juggler motioned. And there was soon some daylight to be relieved by, an open door in the near distance. It had to be late afternoon by now, and the two were careful—Mason especially—as they stepped into the light. Gunshots could be heard from somewhere in the distance. "Over there. Near the Dumpster," Juggler directed. And Mason knew that Juggler had to be watching the clock in his head, figuring he didn't have too much time before Sharon informed somebody about what was going on around back.

There was that Ram Charger near the Dumpster, and Mason recalled Sid at the hospital saying, *That fool took my truck, too!* However, this was obviously the getaway car that Juggler would vanish in. And he was apparently taking company along with him.

**W**ith the front end of the truck, Mason forced the Dumpster out of the way. It rolled and then spun before it toppled over and made a noisy, metal crash. Something that might be heard for a hundred yards. Part of the plan.

"Hold on to your horses, bubba."

And Mason put on his seat belt before gunning the accelerator. Not that Mason was any helluva obstacle-course driver, but to avoid the possibility of bullets he was surely doing his best work right now. Driving the Ram wasn't too much different than how he would drive the Yukon XL (that is, what *used* to be his Yukon XL). The truck swerved left, then right, before it hooked into the front of the hotel. Juggler was in the backseat, gripping a handle so that he wouldn't get tossed around. Meanwhile, he kept his body low just in case po-po wanted to shoot out the windows.

"*Hahaaaa!* We caught 'em by surprise! They don't even know who's in the truck! We could be hotel staff tryin' to make a run for it, for all they know. *Gun it*, nigga! Ha, *haaaaaaaa!*"

**Q**uiet as he kept it, Mason was scared . . . to . . . *death*. His heartbeat could rival any disco classic right now. But, it also fueled his every action, how he worked that steering wheel like a pro; just like he and Adena would fly up or down 402 to get to or from the house.

The roadblock now. And Mason immediately recognized the deputy from earlier. Adena was there talking to him, too! And even from a distance she was *helping*!

*Thank you, Lord!*

Mason could see as she pointed at the truck, most likely seeing him in the driver's seat, and maybe that prevented any potential attack. Still, Mason was sure that there was an army somewhere chasing behind him. Cutting left, the vehicle was directed so that it would avoid the police cruiser. But Mason lost control. The Ram suddenly felt foreign and heavier than the XL he was accustomed to. Maybe he was too hyper and his adrenaline was driving more than he was driving the truck. Nonetheless, the truck clipped the cruiser, veered right, and hit a curb before it somersaulted, flipping over twice, almost like a dolphin would, onto the grass in front of the Union National Bank. The madness had finally come to an end.

# conclusion

Adena had had her share of crying, wondering, and worrying for one day. Now, believe it or not, she was doing all of that, and laughing as well. The hospital joke was that these two should move in and rent a room at the hospital, as comfortable as they were becoming; Mason with the readmittance to that same hospital bed he'd left just hours earlier, and Adena either in the waiting room or by his side. Nobody considered that these two had nowhere else to live at the moment, nowhere they could call home. But, not only were they residents that nurses and doctors recognized as *famous for being freaky*, they were also somehow responsible for the hospital being so busy with new patients. Barbara Clemons was now a resident, although she was simply undergoing a check-up for possible trauma and so that there would be no complications with the pregnancy. Bill Clemons was the one to sneak up into the hotel basement, attacking Juggler like he did, and inevitably getting the kick in the head from Mason, of all people. *Ouch*. And, while Bill was expected to be okay in a matter of days, lucky to escape this nonsense with only a concussion, he still had no idea that one of his best friends was the one to do this; and to think that he only followed his maternal instincts, shooting up into that hotel to rescue his wife like some superhero.

Mason, in the meantime, was spared any serious damage, thanks to his seat belt and that the air bag deployed. However, it was Juggler who was tossed through the truck's windshield and banged up pretty good. It was determined that he had a torn diaphragm and some bleeding in the chest cavity. He was quickly admitted into surgery, handcuffed to the bed and all, where he was having his diaphragm repaired, and still, an operation was required on the chest cavity. What a mess.

Mason and Adena never changed the story Sid told the deputies. Not only that, the survivors of the fire, Bill and Barbara Clemons, and of course Sid himself, all chipped in to see Juggler become the scapegoat for everything and everybody. Therefore, anything Juggler said was determined to be a lie. In the meantime, somewhere in East Stroudsburg there was a group of girls ready to start up a video-vixen enterprise, something that all things digital would likely eat right up.

And then there was Loween. So isolated from any sense of family, she didn't have a crew of missionaries like Juggler had. And, she couldn't claim a lover like Adena could, with a load of money forthcoming from any insurance company. No, Loween didn't have that kind of hope to rely on, even in her final resting place. She didn't have any children who could tell her story and pass along her legacy. Loween, now a decomposed body with overgrown fingernails, toenails, and hair, wouldn't even receive the decent burial. Her body would be placed in the most inexpensive box and dropped in the most remote, unattractive plot. That is, until a couple of people stepped up to fix things.

"I'm sorry about your girl," Sid said from his wheelchair.

"I am, too. I'm sorry I never got to know her."

"Well, least you showed up. It's not like she had any family, 'cept for you and her Moms. Course, *she* ain't comin'."

There was no response.

"If it means anything to you, she was a nice girl. Real smart. I always admired her way about things; how her game was so tight. Just . . . she could never shake that asthma."

"It's hereditary. Almost every woman in my family line got it."

"It's crazy how that happens. You think you got whatever you need in life, and then some stuff like that comes out of nowhere and gives you that left hook."

Silence.

Sid said, "Well, I'ma leave you with your daughter. I'm glad you stepped up and helped out with the arrangements. They wanted to—well, that don't matter no more. Best of everything to you, homes. If you need anything while you up here, holla atcha boy."

The man who Loween (aka Cynthia) had recognized as "the donor" nodded his head as Sid worked his wheelchair into a pivot.


There was no poetic justice here, just a case of human error. From the cradle to the grave.

# THE HOTTEST BOOKS ON THE STREET
## ORDER NOW!

| Qty | Selection | |
|---|---|---|
| ___ | **Eve** • K'wan • 0-312-33310-2 | $14.95 |
| ___ | **Hood Rat*** • K'wan • 0-312-36008-8 | $14.95 |
| ___ | **Hoodlum** • K'wan • 0-312-33308-0 | $14.95 |
| ___ | **Street Dreams** • K'wan • 0-312-33306-4 | $14.95 |
| ___ | **Lady's Night** • Mark Anthony • 0-312-34078-8 | $14.95 |
| ___ | **The Take Down*** • Mark Anthony • 0-312-34079-6 | $14.95 |
| ___ | **The Bridge** • Solomon Jones • 0-312-30725-X | $13.95 |
| ___ | **Ride or Die** • Solomon Jones • 0-312-33989-5 | $13.95 |
| ___ | **Criminal Minded** • Tracy Brown • 0-312-33646-2 | $14.95 |
| ___ | **If I Ruled the World** • JOY • 0-312-32879-6 | $13.95 |
| ___ | **Nasty Girls** • Erick S. Gray • 0-312-34996-3 | $14.95 |
| ___ | **Extra Marital Affairs** • Relentless Aaron • 0-312-35935-7 | $14.95 |
| ___ | **Inside the Crips*** • Colton Simpson • 0 312-32930-X | $14.95 |

*Available November 2006

| | |
|---|---|
| TOTAL AMOUNT | $_____ |
| POSTAGE & HANDLING | $_____ |
| ($2.50 for the first unit, 50 cents for each additional) | |
| APPLICABLE TAXES* | $_____ |
| TOTAL PAYABLE | $_____ |

(CHECK OR MONEY ORDER ONLY—PLEASE DO
NOT SEND CASH OR CODs. PAYMENT IN U.S. FUNDS ONLY.)

## TO ORDER:

Complete this form and
send it, along with a **check
or money order,** for the total
above, payable to V. H.P.S.

## Mail to:
V.H.P.S.
Attn: Customer Service
P.O. Box 470
Gordonsville, Va 22942

Name:_____

Address:_____

City:_____ State:_____ Zip/Postal Code:_____

Account Number (if applicable):_____

Offer available in the fifty United States and the District of Columbia only. Please allow 4-6 weeks for
delivery. All orders are subject to availability. This offer is subject to change without notice. Please call
1-888-330-8477 for further information.

*California, District of Columbia, Illinois, Indiana, Massachusetts, New Jersey, Nevada, New York, North
Carolina, Tennessee, Texas, Virginia, Washington, and Wisconsin residents must add applicable sales tax.

 St. Martin's Griffin

CPSIA information can be obtained at www.ICGtesting.com
Printed in the USA
LVOW08s1933280116

472728LV00001B/75/P